A Body in 3B

A Murder at the Morrisey Mystery

Book One

Eryn Scott

KRISTOPHERSON
PRESS
Publishing

LOBBY

MANAGER'S APARTMENT

MAILROOM

MECHANICAL ROOM

THE MORRISEY

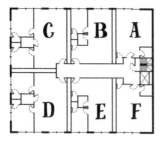

C B A

D E F

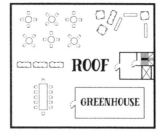

ROOF

GREENHOUSE

LIST OF APARTMENTS
AND RESIDENTS

ROOF	
5C - ALYSSA VERLICE	5F - BAILEY LUNA
5B - IRIS FINLEY	5E - QUENTIN MAPLES
5A - MEG DAWSON	5D - EDNA FELDNER
4C - W. UNDERWOOD	4F - PAUL KELLY
4B - LAURENCE TURNER	4E - WINNIE WISTERIA
4A - RONNY ARBURY	4D - GREG, OLLIE, LEIA PORTER
3C - KATE, OWEN, FINN, BRYCE O'BRIEN	3F - FATIMA AND URBANE JUNT
	3E - ANDREW SASIN
3B - MATHEW MILLER	3D - SHIRLEY AND BETHANY ROSENBLOOM
3A - JULIAN CREED	
2C - DANICA AND DUSTIN MCNAIRY	2F- HAYDEN AND TEAL NUTTERS
	2E - ARTURO CORTEZ
2B - DARIUS ROWLAND	2D - VALARIE, VICTORIA, NOEL, MIA YOUNG
2A - CASCADE GRYFFON	
LOBBY	
BUILDING MANAGER - NANCY LEWANDOWSKI	

ONE

The manager of the Morrisey apartment building gave the stack of papers she held two quick taps on the podium to straighten the edges. The sound of the paper hitting the surface cracked through the lobby like a whip, straightening the spines of my neighbors, who'd been slouching more and more as the meeting dragged on.

"Nancy didn't have a podium before, did she?" my best friend, Ripley, whispered.

I shook my head. The podium was definitely new.

But after five years away, I was more surprised by how much *hadn't* changed at the Morrisey than what had. I couldn't believe Nancy had convinced everyone to keep up these monthly building meetings, for one.

"That's it for our agenda items, everyone," Nancy Lewandowski said, index finger traveling down her list one more time. "Oh, actually, we have one last announcement. I forgot that Laurence isn't the only resident returning to us this month."

The small reading glasses balanced on the tip of Nancy's

nose wobbled precariously as her gaze swept through the rows of people uncomfortably hunched in decades-old plastic folding chairs.

Nancy's sharp eyes latched on to me. "Ah, there you are. I'd like to officially welcome Meg Dawson back to 5A." She clapped, glaring around the room as if she would write down the names of anyone who didn't give me a warm enough "welcome back."

To be honest, she probably would. That was our Nance: fierce, loyal, slightly terrifying, but part of my chosen family. Despite my less-than-ideal reason for returning to the Morrisey, I was happy to be back around these people.

Enthusiastic applause rose from the crowd, and a few of my neighbors turned to wave or grin in my direction. Despite having known most of these people all my life, heat still crept up my neck at having to be the center of attention. I ducked my head and raised a hand to return their greetings while I secretly counted down the seconds until their concentration would move off me once more.

"We're so happy to have our little Nutmeg back in the building." Nancy squeezed her shoulders up almost to her ears in her excitement.

"It's just Meg now, actually," I muttered.

"Louder," Ripley urged.

I shot my friend a glower that told her she should know better than to think I was going to voice a concern in a group setting.

Nance continued on. "We can't wait to see the artistic masterpieces you create up there on the fifth floor, honey." She fixed me with a maternal smile that would've normally erased any annoyance I'd felt at her use of my childhood nickname a moment ago.

But then she'd gone ahead and mentioned my art.

"Ruh-roh," Ripley whispered in her best Scooby-Doo voice, making me wish I could jab my elbow into her side.

Mostly because she was right. Art was a sore subject for me right now, one I should've known I'd have to confront sooner rather than later. Nancy's comment confirmed my suspicions that Aunt Penny had told the building's occupants a very different story about why I was returning to Seattle than what I had told her.

Her version had obviously been heavy on the "Meg just needs time to rediscover her love of painting" and light on the truth.

I didn't begrudge my aunt for remaining hopeful. Her version was undoubtedly much more pleasant. But it didn't change the fact that after graduating from Pratt, moving to Chicago to work in a prestigious gallery—where the only art I created was the pictures I drew on the to-go coffee cups I was constantly fetching for the "real" artists—and finally getting the chance of a lifetime to work in the New York gallery of my mentor, I'd realized I didn't have what it took to be an artist.

Nancy, unaware of the existential crisis her words had provoked, continued on, saying, "Oh, and speaking of Nutmeg and Penny, I know many of you have already signed up for the Penny message group, but here's your reminder to talk to me if you'd like to be added."

My stiff shoulders settled a few millimeters as Nancy moved on from talking about me to discussing my Aunt Penny, fulfilling her lifelong dream of living in Scotland.

"Fair warning." Nancy placed her elbows on the podium.

"Penny's pictures from the Highlands are enough to make you want to move to Scotland right along with her." Nancy let out one of her signature nasal cackles. But even that didn't so much as jiggle those precariously perched glasses of hers.

"How does she keep those things on there? Superglue?" Ripley wondered aloud.

I didn't know. Sheer willpower? Threats? Either way, I left Ripley hanging, not able to give a response as things finally ended.

Nancy flattened the agenda notes onto the podium with the force of a gavel and said, "Well, that's all I have for you today. Meeting adjourned."

The lobby of the Morrisey filled with chatter as people stood, broke off into side conversations, and began stacking the foldable chairs on a cart. Quite a few came over to welcome me back, but most simply waved from across the lobby. They knew me well enough to understand I wasn't particularly fond of—or good at—small talk.

"Whoa," Ripley said next to me as I folded my chair. Well, it was less of a word and more of a gasp. "When did Laurence get so hot?" She pointed to the other side of the room.

I kept my gaze down. "Laurie's always been hot," I whispered, using his childhood nickname, which was arguably better than mine.

Ripley placed a hand over her heart. "Megs, you should go talk to him. Ask him out, finally. You've been in love with the guy since—"

"I was six," I whispered, more to myself than her as I moved to the corner of the room so I'd be out of the way before turning around to look.

There he was. Laurence Turner. Laurie, to me.

The Rosenbloom sisters had cornered him, and despite the fact that the older women were probably making wildly inappropriate comments about how handsome he'd grown up to be, he listened to them with such focused attention, it was as if they were the only people he could see or hear. That was Laurie; he made people feel important. He made eye contact and nodded along with their stories, no matter how wild. The guy was a genuinely nice person.

He was also the reason I hadn't dated anyone long-term during my time on the East Coast. I'd tried. A few guys even made me forget about Laurie for a while. But eventually, they would all do something thoughtless or say something crass, and I would think *Laurie would never do that*.

Everyone else paled in comparison to my childhood crush.

As one of the few other children who used to live at the Morrisey, Laurie had been my companion growing up. Befitting anyone who'd carried a torch for the same person for most of their formative years, I'd found Laurie ridiculously attractive during all stages of his life—even the gangly teenage years when he had oily skin and braces. But Ripley was right: he was certifiably hot now.

He had on jeans that didn't look like they'd been picked up off a floor, and he wore leather shoes instead of sneakers. The sleeves of his gray T-shirt hugged arms that were much more muscular than they'd been the last time I'd seen him. The beginnings of a beard even shaded his jawline. He'd forgone his contacts in favor of black-rimmed glasses that made him look like a professor—the hot kind.

Ripley moved into my line of sight, blocking him from me. "Come on. You said yourself no one understands you like Laurie. He might be hot, but you're a knockout too." She gestured to me. "You've got that whole brilliant, shy, girl-next-door glamor going for you. Go over and ask him out, or at least say something sexy so he knows you're back and ready to mingle."

"Mingle?" I asked with a snort of laughter. I leaned back against the wall. "It's kinda hard to be sexy around a person you hung out with because the two of you bonded over a shared love of the Ninja Turtles. We became friends because neither of us liked to wear anything but sweatpants. I vividly remember a conversation we had about how jeans were too itchy and stiff. How can I bounce back from that?"

"I'd forgotten about the sweatpants phase you two went through." Ripley wrinkled her nose. "It doesn't matter. You're both gorgeous adults now, with no"—she paused, looking me up and down—"*fewer* weird hang-ups like that. Come on. Talk to him, at least." Ripley backed up like she was trying to lure me closer to the man.

But as she moved away from me, she inadvertently placed herself in the pathway of Mrs. Feldner, a woman who had been approximately a hundred years old back when I was a child, so she had to be breaking records at this point. Mrs. Feldner shuffled along, bent in half like she was walking with an invisible cane.

I winced, not having a chance to warn Ripley before the old woman walked straight into her.

Well, not *into*, but through.

Let me explain. Ripley was dead. I was the only one who could see or hear her. I'd been able to see ghosts my whole life, though Ripley was the only one who followed me around. She and I were practically inseparable and always had been.

So, I alone saw my ghostly friend's eyes widen with horror as Mrs. Feldner tottered through her spirit.

Ripley shivered and danced around like she might be able to physically shake off the encounter. "Oh, gross, gross, gross."

Rip had described the feeling of having a living person pass through her spirit as the same as sticking your hand into a bowl of peeled grapes and cold spaghetti, only ... with your whole body. It didn't sound pleasant, so her reaction wasn't a surprise.

Mrs. Feldner glanced back at me with a confused frown for a moment before she ambled on. She must've felt the oddly cold sensation that always followed coming in contact with a spirit. It was easy enough to explain away as a weird draft or a sudden shiver, so most people didn't think too hard when they experienced it. But I knew the truth.

"Sorry, I couldn't warn you," I whispered to Ripley, making sure no one else was within earshot.

After twenty-four years, I'd learned my lesson enough times to know I had to be careful talking to Ripley, or any other ghosts, in public. Doing so was how I'd earned the nickname NutMeg from my *oh-so-kind* elementary school peers after all. And even though my well-meaning Morrisey family had tried to help me "take back my power" by turning it into a cute, endearing nickname, it was yet another reminder of those hard lessons learned.

"Okay, I changed my mind about you talking to Laurie. Let's go back upstairs. The lobby's too crowded." Ripley shivered again.

My gaze returned to Laurie, still chatting with the Rosenbloom sisters. As much as I wanted to talk to him, I didn't want the first time we spoke after all these years to be in a crowded lobby full of people who'd known us since we were babies.

I turned to Ripley, whispering, "Of course it's too crowded. That's what I've been trying to tell you." Glancing toward the stairwell, I said, "I'll meet you upstairs."

Ripley winked and disappeared, instantly transporting herself up to our apartment on the fifth floor. Going our separate ways hadn't always been so easy for the two of us. There had been a time when Ripley could barely leave my side.

When I was younger, she couldn't get more than fifty feet away or she'd disappear and reappear right next to me. As I'd gotten older, her "tether" to me had gotten progressively longer. At twenty-four, Ripley could now be a couple of football fields away from me.

But that tether still brought her back if she went much farther than that.

We'd had bets about when, if ever, it would go away completely. Ripley had guessed my twentieth birthday would be the date since she'd died right before hers. That hadn't been it. I'd been sure my twenty-first birthday was going to be the ticket, but here we were, a few years beyond that and still tethered together. It was anyone's guess now.

Despite the many ghosts we'd consulted over the years, we'd yet to find a single soul who'd ever encountered a bond such as ours, let alone anyone who knew when or if it would sever. But it wasn't all restrictions. The tether gave Ripley a unique set of rules compared to every other spirit. Where other ghosts were limited to showing up only in the places they'd set foot when they were alive, Ripley could go anywhere as long as it was with me. Which was why she'd been able to join me on the East Coast.

Even though having my best friend constantly by my side seemed like a gift now, I couldn't help but think about the future. Someday I wanted to get married, start a family even, and it might not be as "cool" to have my ghost guardian next to me all the time. I knew Ripley longed for her freedom as well, though she'd never voice the desire.

Unable to transport myself in the blink of an eye like Ripley could, I was forced to walk if I wanted to reach the quiet serenity of my apartment, which I very much needed after that meeting. Weaving through the crowded lobby, I trained my eyes on the elevator for a split second, but there was already a line forming, and it wasn't my preferred mode of transportation anyway.

The old thing dipped when you stepped foot inside it, then it either took so long to start moving that you began to worry something was wrong, or it lurched into movement too soon and threw you off-balance. It also made sounds unlike any other elevator I'd ever ridden inside. The inspector Nancy brought in more often than she needed to swore it passed his list of safety codes, but I remained dubious.

Veering to the left, I shoved my way through the heavy stair-well fire door. I paused for a moment to revel in the cool air of the stairwell. Well, it was a little musty, but at least I was alone.

"I won't do it." The whisper sliced through the air, rico-cheting off the concrete walls from the stairwell above.

So ... not alone after all.

"Come on. I'm desperate. What do I need to do, double your coin?" a man asked, the question slithering out. The way he accentuated the word "coin" made a shiver rush down my back.

"I don't want your money," the whisperer answered.

I took a step toward the railing, hoping to catch a glimpse of who was having this tense conversation. It sounded like they were one, maybe two floors above me. I craned my neck forward as I peered up into the M. C. Escher-esque view of the stairs continuing up to the apartments.

My shin collided with the metal railing. "Ouch!" I called out, flinching at the sudden racket I was creating.

"Shhh," the slithery-sounding man said.

I backed away from the railing, locating the door that would return me to the lobby. *This might be a good time to take the elevator, actually,* I thought as my heartbeat pounded in my eardrums, and I rushed away from the mysterious fight I'd overheard.

Two

In my haste to get out of the stairwell and into the safety of the lobby, I immediately backed into someone.

"Whoa," the man said in surprise.

"Oh, I'm so sorry." I spun around, grabbing on to his arms to steady myself.

"Hey, Meg." Laurie blinked down at me, a big grin pulling across his perfect lips.

My hands dropped to my side and my neck grew warm. Words piled up in my throat worse than rush hour traffic heading out of the city every afternoon. I coughed, hoping to release some of them.

"Laurie. Hi," I managed to croak.

Well, I guess I wasn't going to get time to prepare before seeing Laurie after all. We certainly weren't going to have any privacy, either, I realized, as everyone standing in front of the elevator looked in our direction.

"It's great to see you." His brown eyes looked me up and down. It wasn't in a creepy, leering way. It was an appreciative, *I can't believe you're standing in front of me* kind of look. To back that up, he said, "Look at us, huh? Both back at the Morrisey."

I feigned a smile. *Yep. Look at us.* Though, I'd bet anything *his* reason for returning was less disappointing than mine.

Still slightly distracted by my encounter in the stairwell, I glanced behind me. But no one came through the door, creepy or otherwise, so I tried to let it go and focus on my friend. I did, however, gesture for Laurie to follow as I took a few steps to my right. I hoped it seemed like I was getting us out of the way of the stairwell door instead of moving to a place where we would have less of an audience.

When Laurie followed, I said, "So, you bought your parents' place. That's great."

Thank you, Aunt Penny, for keeping me in the loop about building gossip.

He nodded. "I thought about buying something in Redmond, closer to work, but I mostly work remotely, so I don't have to drive into the office too often. And prices are crazy."

Right. Penny had *also* told me Laurie was some big tech guy now.

"Plus," he said with a shrug, "it's the Morrisey."

I sighed happily. "And it hasn't changed a bit."

Doubts about moving my life back to the West Coast had been creeping around in the recesses of my mind over the past few weeks, like a dense Pacific Northwest fog. Beyond the obvious worries surrounding my career, I'd been apprehensive about whether my beloved Morrisey would feel the same after all these years. Had all my magical memories of the place been a product of the rose-colored glasses of childhood?

But standing here with Laurie, having been through my first building meeting, now that I was back, it all felt the same.

It wasn't just the building that felt locked in time either; the people were also a constant. That was what happened when people owned apartments in the heart of one of the pricier cities in the country. And they weren't letting go of those investments. Families often passed their apartments down, as was the case with Laurie and me. Most of the units had been paid off decades earlier, the only monthly payments needed being the housing fees due to Nancy and our electricity and utilities bills.

Basically, someone had to die for an apartment to open up at the Morrisey.

Nancy bustled into the hallway just then, looking past the dozen or so other residents milling about in conversation, her gaze settled on the two of us.

"Oh good. Kids, I need to see you for a moment." She flapped her hands toward herself, beckoning us over.

Laurie looked at me and hunched his shoulders in a *why not?* gesture. So, we followed Nancy around the corner to the seating area, where we'd held the meeting. The big table had already been moved back into its regular place. All that was left was Nancy's podium. She strutted over to it and snatched a clipboard from the top.

"I need your signatures to approve the purchase of our new firepit," she explained, tapping a pen on the page to show where we needed to give permission to release the funds.

Right. The new firepit. It had been the first item of business on her meeting agenda to collect signatures from "the stragglers" since our annual Fourth of July bash on the roof was coming up "this Tuesday, people."

Nancy handed the clipboard to me. "And don't worry

about the party," she said. "We decided at last month's meeting that you two don't need to bring anything since you're both in the process of moving in."

"Oh, thanks." I signed, then handed the clipboard over to Laurie, who followed suit.

When he held it toward Nancy, she held out her hands like stop signs. "Actually, I need one more signature, and I was wondering if you would go get that for me." She didn't even let us think about it before adding, "The only one left is Mr. Miller in 3B, so it makes sense that you would go, Laurence."

Even though Nancy delivered the statement with total seriousness, I couldn't help but flash a quick smirk at Laurie, whose body tensed at her comment.

"Sure," I said, with as straight a face as I could muster. "Who better to get the signature than the only person who's ever seen the reclusive Mr. Miller?"

The man was more than just antisocial. He'd moved in over a decade ago, and no one had so much as caught a glimpse of him the whole time. Well, except Laurie, when he was fifteen. Despite swearing he'd only seen the back of Mr. Miller's head for a split second, the residents were convinced he'd seen more.

"Perfect. Thank you, kids." Nancy pivoted on her heel and went over to move her podium out of the way. "Bring that back to my apartment when you're done."

Laurie shot me a withering look as he took off toward the stairs with the clipboard. "You shouldn't encourage them," he grumbled.

"I almost forgot about the infamous sighting," I teased as I followed him. We weaved through the people still milling about in the lobby corridor.

"It must be nice to forget. They won't let me." He stopped in front of the stairwell door, glancing back at me.

Giddy as I'd felt teasing Laurie moments before, I froze in place as he opened the door and stepped inside the stairwell. The memory of the angry, whispered voices I'd heard just minutes before made the hair on my arms stand on end.

"What's going on? Is there a mannequin in here or something?" Laurie asked, stopping with the door propped open when he noticed I hadn't followed.

A wide smile spread across my face, erasing the unease.

"I can't believe you remember my fear of mannequins." I shook my head and entered the stairwell, letting the door close behind us. My eyes were probably sparkling up at him, giving away my true feelings. If Ripley had been there, she would've made fun of me and told me to get it together.

Laurie scoffed. "Of course I remember. And with the way you came rushing out of here a few minutes ago, I thought there was an entire department store's worth."

Chewing on my lip for a moment, I said, "No creepy mannequins, but I did stumble on a pretty heated argument, and I didn't want to get involved."

"Between?" Laurie furrowed his brows together.

"That's the thing. I didn't recognize either of the guys. I can't pick out everyone's voices like we used to be able to." A memory flashed through my mind of us hiding behind the couches in the lobby and playing the game of *who could identify the most residents passing by without looking*. Mrs. Feldner was always the easiest because of her pungent perfume, but we'd had to rely on voices for the other residents.

Laurie pushed back his shoulders. "Well, there's only one

way to find out. Let's see if they're still here." He strode forward, craning his neck to look up the stairs.

Following behind him like the lovesick puppy I was, we climbed up the two flights, searching for any evidence of the men I'd heard. But as we pushed through the door to the third floor, we were still alone.

We stepped into the hallway, six doors situated throughout the space. As was the case with each floor, an ornate Art Deco chandelier hung from the middle of the ceiling, illuminating the hallway. The walls were painted a basic white so we could easily touch them up whenever there was a scuff or stain. A worn area rug from the Turkish carpet store down the street ran the length of the old wood floors to help soak up some of the wet footprints on rainy Seattle days—and trip you when you weren't paying close enough attention.

Stepping carefully over the patterned rug, we walked to the right, toward apartment 3B.

Laurie and I glanced at each other for a moment, prepping ourselves for the encounter. After Laurie's infamous sighting of the back of Mr. Miller's head all those years ago, we vowed to be ready to notice and describe him if we ever got the opportunity to set eyes on him again. In reality, it would probably be the same as every other time we'd come to get his signature on something: he'd grab the paper, sign it, and then slide it back under the door moments later.

Still, I readied myself as Laurie pressed the buzzer.

"Mr. Miller? It's Laurence Turner from the fourth floor. Nancy sent me to get a signature from you for a building purchase." Freeing the page from the clipboard since the metal at the top would prevent it from fitting, Laurie slid the paper under the door.

We watched, waiting for that exhilarating and unsettling moment when it would be snatched up by the reclusive man inside.

But that didn't happen. Laurie and I frowned at one another.

"Maybe his buzzer's broken," I suggested, knowing the temperamental things liked going in and out of service.

Accepting my theory, Laurie knocked three times, his knuckles rapping loudly on the wood. The force of his knocks caused the latch to *snick* open, and the door swung inward a few inches.

I gasped. Laurie coughed out in surprise.

Exchanging wide-eyed looks, we stared at the open door. Throughout our entire childhood, we'd never seen this door anything but tightly shut and locked. Seeing it ajar even a few inches felt unnerving, like the building was moving beneath my feet.

Proving we still shared the strong connection we had when we were kids, Laurie asked, "Remember that earthquake when we were really little?"

"Yeah," I breathed out the word, waiting for my balance to return. When it did, I called out his name, hoping he just hadn't heard us the first time. "Mr. Miller?" The wobbly feeling concentrated to the pit of my stomach.

What if he was in trouble? I reached out my hand, curling my fingers into an uncertain fist before convincing myself to stretch them out again and push open the door.

Laurie and I inhaled sharply as we got our first look inside the apartment. It wasn't as different as I was expecting. Like every other apartment in the building, the exterior window wall was brick and the oak floors were slightly warped from age. The apartment also featured the built-in wardrobes we all used as closets, and it shared an identical layout with the other one-bedroom units.

The tall curtains were drawn, only letting in a small amount of light through the gaps. That light, and what spilled in from the hallway, illuminated a desk with a computer on it sitting in the middle of the room. An office chair had been pushed back from the desk as if the owner had gotten up quickly. A single armchair was positioned in front of a television in the corner.

"It doesn't look like he's here," I whispered.

"Maybe he's in the bedroom or the bathroom," Laurie said, his deep voice tense.

I took a step forward, ready to investigate, but something just beyond the kitchen came into view. A sick feeling rolled through my gut.

"Whatisthat?" I gagged out the sentence, the words all jumbled together as I pointed.

Laurie peered into the apartment. "Oh." He stood up straighter, clearing his throat. "Just a creepy mannequin woman standing next to the kitchen. Totally normal."

Ghosts? No problem. I could handle them all day. Mannequins? Nope. The things freaked me out, as Laurie had pointed out moments before. When I was little, Penny could barely get me in a department store, and had to cover my eyes any time we walked by a mannequin. Now that I was an adult, I could *tolerate* them in stores. That was their natural habitat after all. I still made a point not to linger in clothing departments, but it was manageable because I expected them to be there. If they were somewhere I wasn't expecting, however, it was like a punch to the gut.

The weight of Laurie's hand settled on my shoulder, pulling

me out of my panicked state. I blinked, looking up into his brown eyes.

"You stay here." He held my gaze to show me it was okay. "I'll go check the rooms."

"Thanks," I squeaked out the word.

Laurie swallowed, his throat bobbing with the motion. "Right." He stepped forward, passing over the threshold. Stopping at the kitchen counter to his right, Laurie placed the clipboard he held next to a stack of mail and flipped through the letters. "He recently got a mail delivery, but without opening any of these, I can't tell what day they're from." He checked the front and back of each letter, then set them back down on the counter.

He peered into the bathroom. Finding it empty, Laurie called out for Mr. Miller as he walked toward the bedroom.

I leaned forward in anticipation, but stopped, making sure to keep the mannequin out of my line of sight. The fact that I could see Laurie as he inspected the apartment from where I stood, made me feel a little better. It felt less like I'd forced him to go in by himself and more like I was just supervising from the safety of the hallway. But I wouldn't be able to see him once he went into the bedroom. I gulped.

Laurie stopped at the closed door and knocked. "Mr. Miller?"

We waited. Listened. Hoped.

Nothing. Laurie opened the door and disappeared inside the room for a few moments. I held my breath, my heart in my throat until he returned, shaking his head.

No Mr. Miller.

The apartment was empty.

"Did he ever exist?" The question was mostly air as I exhaled the quiet words when Laurie rejoined me at the door.

Laurie swung the door partially closed, then open again, messing with the dead bolt above the doorknob. "Huh. This dead bolt is extra. You don't have one of these, do you?"

"Nope," I told him. "Mine just locks on the knob."

"Mine too." Laurie examined the doorjamb. "I wonder if Quentin installed this for him."

I didn't know why my neighbor up on the fifth floor would've put a lock in for Mr. Miller. Quentin worked on cars, if I remembered correctly. But maybe things had changed since I'd been gone.

Picking up the paper full of building signatures, I handed it back to Laurie with shaking fingers. "Nancy?" I asked.

Laurie dipped his chin once. "She'll know what to do. Oh, I forgot the clipboard." He stopped, and I waited in the hallway as he went back to grab it off the kitchen counter.

Leaving the door open, we went to find Nancy. We jogged down the stairs as if we were trying to stay ahead of reality, bursting out from the stairwell into the lobby corridor. At that point, most of the residents had finally made their way back to their apartments, so there were fewer obstacles as we rushed over to the manager's apartment. I poked at the buzzer while Laurie banged on the door.

It swung open, and Nancy stood before us, annoyance creasing her forehead. Her glasses still clung to the edge of her nose as her wild eyes took us in. "What is all this noise ab—"

Laurie waved the clipboard in the air. "We went to get Mr. Miller's signature, but he's not there."

An air of impatience moved over Nancy as if we'd told her we couldn't find the carton of milk she'd just placed in the refrigerator. She set a hand on her hip. "Now, kids." It was her warning tone, telling us this was not the time for shenanigans.

"And his door was open," I blurted, knowing that piece of information would get her attention.

Nancy's face froze, her lips parted in shock. "What did you say?"

I motioned to Laurie. "Laurie knocked on the door because we thought his buzzer wasn't working, and the door swung in. There's no one inside."

"You went in?" Nancy leaned forward. Any hint of scolding had disappeared from her tone, leaving behind only the basest sense of intrigue.

"We thought he might be hurt or in trouble, but he's just not there," Laurie explained.

"Well, you would know," Nancy said seriously, scratching at her chin contemplatively.

Her comment earned an exasperated sigh from Laurie.

But before he could remind her that it had only been the back of Mr. Miller's head that he'd seen all those years ago, Nancy snapped her fingers. "Let's go check this out together." She started off at a brisk march that even Long Legs Laurie had a tough time matching.

Nancy had been a baker for forty-six of her sixty-something years. She still woke up at four every morning and was in bed before nine. And even though it was sometimes hard to picture the no-nonsense building manager creating colorful, sweet confections, imagining her strutting through an industrial kitchen snapping other bakers into shape and calling out orders was never a stretch.

We'd heard Nance complain about her "no-good knees" enough when we were children that we didn't even expect her to use the stairs. She poked at the elevator button and then tapped her toe as she waited. The elevator groaned to a stop in front of us, the doors creaking open.

Nancy winced. The elevator had always been her least favorite part of the Morrisey, and she was constantly trying to improve the ancient thing. It was a testament to the urgency she felt about the Mr. Miller situation that she didn't stop to complain about or inspect the rickety mess. She simply snapped her fingers again, causing Laurie and me to hop into the elevator after her. The whole thing dipped a few inches as we did.

Just as the doors slid closed, Ripley appeared by my side. "Hey, what gives? I've been waiting in the apartment by myself for ages." Her ghostly shoulders slumped forward. That was until she noticed Laurie. "Oh." Her dark-red lips formed an O, and one of her perfectly plucked eyebrows hitched higher on her forehead. But then she saw Nancy, and the suggestive look turned into a scowl. "Oh." It was the same word but flattened by disappointment.

Having twenty-four years of experience with my ghostly gift, I knew better than to answer her while I was around other people. Instead, I said, "I hope Mr. Miller's okay."

Ripley's eyes went wide. "Wait. The guy who never leaves his apartment and who no one's ever seen?"

I touched my ear, the nonverbal sign for *yes* that Ripley and I had come up with years ago, so I could answer questions even if I couldn't speak. We'd tried using American Sign Language at first, but I'd caught enough confused stares from ASL proficient people, that we'd come up with our own signs.

"It's so weird that the door was open," I continued, my statements working to catch up Ripley while seeming like small talk to my living elevator companions.

"Oh, this I've gotta see." She vanished from the elevator.

Nancy wrung her hands together. "Yes, Meg. We all know what happened. You're making me anxious by repeating it. We're almost there."

When the elevator doors squeaked open a few moments later, Ripley stood in the hallway outside of apartment 3B. But when her eyes flashed over to meet mine, they held none of the sparkling excitement that should've accompanied getting a peek inside an apartment we'd always wondered about. Instead, they were clouded with concern.

At first, I thought she'd just noticed the mannequin in the corner. Then her expression darkened into the version I'd only ever seen her adopt when she talked about the night she died, about the fatal car crash she'd been part of, the one that had also taken the life of my mother. Worry made my chest feel tight.

"Megs, I think you should walk away from this," Ripley said, rushing forward, holding out her hands.

But Laurie and Nancy were striding toward the open door. When I hesitated, Laurie looked back.

"You coming?" he asked, his lips lifting into a half smile that made me feel like I was floating on air.

I walked forward, shooting Ripley an apologetic grimace. I *had* to follow. That conviction lessened as Nancy reached the open doorway first. Her hand flew to her mouth, she staggered backward, and she gasped. Finally, the small reading glasses perched on the edge of her nose fell, clattering to the floor in the hallway.

"I thought you said he wasn't here." Nancy's tone was harsh and accusatory.

Laurie rushed forward, then came to a sliding stop as he

peered into the open apartment. "Oh, gross." He bent over, placing his hands on his knees.

My legs felt weak at the sight. Laurie only ever reacted in that way when he saw blood. I stepped forward tentatively.

Sure enough, the door to apartment 3B was still wide open. And where, minutes before, there had been nothing, now a body lay in the entryway. The red stain on the man's white shirt was unmistakably blood. A lot of it.

THREE

"Is it Mr. Miller?" I asked, checking with Nancy.

She was bent over, grabbing her glasses off the floor. "How should I know?" she asked, motioning to Laurie. "He's the only one here who's ever seen the guy."

Laurie had only just managed to stand up straight when he noticed our attention on him. "Huh?" he asked. His dark skin shone with sweat.

"Is that Mr. Miller?" Nancy asked, leaning against the opposite wall.

"I saw the back of his head, *once*, when I was fifteen," Laurie snapped. He never raised his voice, but it seemed like everything had finally gotten to him.

"Aren't any of you going to call the cops?" Ripley shouted, snapping me out of my dazed thoughts.

"Oh, right. Nine-one-one." I pulled out my phone and called, staring at the man lying on the floor in apartment 3B.

Ripley turned to me. "Did you go inside?"

I tugged on my ear, knowing what she was thinking. Ripley

was not only limited to where I was but also where I had been, because I'd never set foot inside before, she'd been unable to poke around inside the reclusive man's apartment—as much as we wished she could over the years. And even though I hadn't gotten more than a few paces inside, stepping foot over the threshold, as I'd done, was enough to grant Ripley access to enter as well.

But as Ripley reached the same threshold, she staggered back as if she'd walked into an invisible wall.

"What the—?" She tried a few more times but was thwarted by the same barrier.

My focus split as the dispatcher picked up and began asking questions. I breathed my first sigh of relief when he said the police would be there within minutes.

While that was fast, they still couldn't beat the Morrisey's residents. It wasn't ten seconds after I hung up with 9-1-1 that we heard frantic whispering coming from the door of apartment 3D.

The Rosenbloom sisters.

Nancy and I locked eyes, doing our best not to grimace as the door swung open at the end of the hallway.

"Shirl. Bethie. There's nothing to see out here." Nancy spread her arms out wide and walked toward the elderly sisters as if they were wild horses she was trying to corral. "Why don't you just stay inside your apartment." It wasn't a question.

With the Rosenbloom sisters being taken care of by the indomitable Nance, I turned to Laurie. Approaching him carefully, I reached out and placed a hand on his arm. "You doing okay?"

Laurie blinked down at me, smoothing a hand over his face

as he came out of whatever trance he'd been stuck inside. "Yeah, I'm okay. Sorry, I've just—"

"Never been good around blood," I answered for him. My lips tugged up on one side as I let my hand drop away from him. "I remember."

Wetting his lips, Laurie let out a thin laugh.

"Okay-y," Ripley emphasized the last syllable, dragging it out as she waggled her eyebrows in my direction. "I see *you*, flirting around a crime scene."

I shot a scowl in her direction and pretended to adjust the heel of my shoe, a sign I'd come up with just for myself that meant I was annoyed with her.

"Fine." She raised her hands in the air. "I'll leave since I can't get inside anyway. But don't you think for one second I don't know what the shoe thing means." She pointed an accusatory finger at me as she vanished, probably to go pout in our apartment.

Ripley may have left, but my problems were far from over. Shirl and Bethie's yammering had alerted the O'Briens next door. The married couple added to the chaos by asking loud, alarming questions about what was going on. Nancy tried her best to keep all four of them calm.

Turning my attention back to Laurie, I said, "This is wild, right? We were just here, and the place was empty."

Laurie squeezed his eyes shut for a second, then opened them. "I'm seriously questioning my grasp on reality. It *was* empty." He pointed to the kitchen counter where he'd set the clipboard. "Hey, the pile of mail is gone."

It was. I gulped. "And based on the bloodstain on the front of his shirt, I'd say he didn't die from natural causes." I crept forward toward the door, peeking inside once more. It wasn't that I wanted to see the mannequin again, but I needed to check that it was still there ... and that it wasn't suddenly holding a knife.

"Are we sure he's dead?" Laurie asked, the question tiptoeing out of him.

Confirming that the mannequin was in the same position, and was unarmed, I cut the air with my hand. "No, he's gone. Trust me."

Lifeless bodies had a dullness to them I'd learned to recognize over the years. They looked like the matte version of a painting when the rest of the people walking around were coated in resin. Souls had a shine to them that wasn't truly noticeable until it was gone.

Experience told me that even if Mr. Miller's spirit stuck around, it wouldn't settle for at least a few weeks, possibly even months. Not everyone who was killed had unfinished business, and some people who died naturally still had things to take care of before they moved on. But while I wasn't sure if we would see Mr. Miller's spirit at all, I could be sure the man was dead.

I flinched at the confident way I'd said, "Trust me." The last time this had happened—me standing over a still squirrel on the playground and flatly saying, "It's dead," when my classmates had convinced themselves it was just sleeping—hadn't gone over so well. In their defense, I'd talked to "myself" a lot before I got wise and learned that not everyone saw the things I did. NutMeg was probably a nice nickname compared to what they could've called me.

But of course, I didn't need to worry about Laurie making fun of me. He saw the world through a lens of kindness I strove to understand, if not emulate. "Did you deal a lot with dead bodies during your time on the East Coast?" he asked, interest lurking behind his still-disturbed brown eyes.

Swallowing, I let out a strangled laugh. "Not a lot, but New York and Chicago see their fair share of this kind of thing."

"Still ... sometimes I wish I'd left Seattle, at least for a little bit." Laurie scratched the back of his neck. "It's so cool that you've worked at those big-time galleries."

Really not wanting to talk about art, I fell back on an old standard and redirected the conversation toward him. "Talk about big-time. You literally work at your dream job, Laurie," I said, exasperated.

The elevator dinged open at the far end of the hallway. I prepared myself for the police, but a rush of Morrisey residents spilled out of the rickety box on steel strings.

Half the residents from the second floor and a smattering of ones who'd still been hanging around the lobby after the meeting rushed forward, chattering and craning their necks as they closed in on apartment 3B. The new crowd was concerning for many reasons, not least of which was that the old elevator was only rated for seven people.

Nancy, who'd just convinced the Rosenbloom sisters and the O'Briens to go back into their apartments—yet she hadn't convinced them to close their doors yet—shot Laurie and me a desperate look. Reading her loud and clear, we stepped forward, our hands outstretched as if we were about to herd our own wild animals.

"You all need to stay back," Laurie's deep voice stopped them in their tracks. And even though most of them had known Laurie since he was born, he'd grown up to be tall and imposing.

I even gawked up at him for a split second, surprised by this new, commanding version of him. Having just seen the scared-of-blood version, this assertive Laurie was yet another facet of the man I measured all others against.

The gaggle of gawkers stopped in their tracks, though a few still craned their necks, trying to see around us.

"The cops are coming, and you're going to be in the way." Laurie stepped toward the crowd, causing them to shuffle backward a few steps. "Unless you know anything about Mr. Miller in 3B, or who might want him dead, we need you to stay off this floor."

I winced at Laurie's statement, unsurprised by the shower of exclamations and questions that came pouring out of the group after his use of the word "dead." He may be tall, commanding, and intimidating, but he hadn't lived in the building for years either, and he'd obviously forgotten that less information was more when it came to the residents of the Morrisey. He glanced at me in dread as he realized his mistake.

"The recluse?" Darius asked.

"How do you know it's him? No one's ever seen him," Art called out, then added, "Aside from Laurence, of course."

The group muttered a consensus, and Laurie's large shoulders slumped forward like he wanted to sit down.

Rushing to help him, I used my most powerful tone and said, "If you don't know anything, then you need to leave." I gestured back toward the elevator.

A dozen eyes blinked back at me. Even Laurie turned to stare. As someone who rarely spoke louder than a whisper in large groups, they took notice when I said something forceful. And I hadn't even stopped to consider whether I was worried about speaking up. I would do anything if it could help Laurie.

Muttering in disappointment, the residents wandered back

where they'd come from. The ding of someone pressing the elevator call button sounded in the silence, and they stared at us forlornly over their shoulders. When the elevator arrived, they piled in again, but Arturo's pudgy finger pressed down on the door-open button, and they waited there for a moment.

"Fine, you can stay there." I clenched my teeth in frustration. "Just make sure you're not in the way."

The stairwell door flew open, making me jump. Out poured medical teams and police. In the center of the chaos was a woman in a smart gray suit. Her black hair was so shiny, I almost felt the need for sunglasses.

Zeroing in on us, she strode forward. While many of the other officers seemed out of breath from climbing the stairs, her heart rate didn't appear even slightly elevated. Laurie pointed to the open door behind us, and the EMTs and crime scene techs filed inside.

"I'm Detective Anthony. Apologies for the time it took us to get here. We were in the area but made the mistake of waiting for the elevator. I think it might be broken. You really should get a sign for it."

I cut my eyes over to the end of the hallway where Art gingerly removed his finger from the button that had been holding it open. The doors squeaked closed.

"Were you the two who called this in?" Detective Anthony asked.

"Yes," Laurie said. "We knocked at his door to get a signature. The door was open. I looked around inside, but there was no one there. Minutes later, the body was here when we came back with our building manager." Laurie hitched a thumb over his shoulder to where Nance was pulling on the Rosenblooms' doorknob while she used her other hand, and the heel of her right foot, to push them inside.

The detective's sharp gaze flicked from Nancy over to the body visible through the open door. "I'm assuming the deceased is the resident who lives there?"

"Here we go," I muttered sarcastically.

Detective Anthony frowned, her attention jumping between Laurie and me.

"The thing is..." Laurie sucked a long breath through his clenched teeth.

Since I'd already broken my quiet streak once in the last few minutes, I decided I could do it again. "None of us know what he looks like. He never left his apartment."

Instead of treating that as the shocking statement it should've been, Detective Anthony tapped her pen against her lips. "Which makes the open door even more concerning."

Nancy, having finally contained the Rosenblooms, raced over. "If you need to identify the man, you should flip him over and see if Laurence will recognize him from behind."

Laurie squeezed his eyes shut for a second out of embarrassment.

The detective, who hadn't been fazed in the least by learning the man was a recluse, blinked unbelievingly at Nancy.

I put a hand on Nancy's arm. "Nance, I don't think Laurie having seen the back of the man that lives in 3B, ten years ago, is going to help the investigation."

Nancy squinted. "Oh, right. How silly of me."

Turning my attention back to Detective Anthony, I said, "Sorry, we're not sure who he was or what he looked like. None of us can be sure if that's Mr. Miller."

"Don't worry about it. We can use dental records or fingerprints if he's in the system." The detective brushed it off as if she encountered this kind of thing every day.

Nancy, who didn't, paced in front of us. "Oh, sure. We won't worry about that." She let out an unhinged cackle. "But we probably *should* be really worried that somewhere in the Morrisey, there's a murderer."

FOUR

Nancy grabbed on to my hand, squeezing tightly as she wobbled from side to side after her outburst.

"A murderer in the building?" I repeated as the hallway tilted and warped around me.

Or maybe that was the effect of the space suddenly becoming crowded with people. The Rosenblooms and O'Briens were back, joined now by the group from the elevator, who must've never disembarked in the lobby. More residents spilled out of the stairwell and crowded the perimeter Detective Anthony's crime scene team had created around Mr. Miller's apartment.

Among the people I recognized, there were also those I'd never seen before in my life. A man with blond eyebrows stood next to a woman wearing jeans with flowers embroidered up each leg. Another woman held a bouquet like she'd been delivering it to a resident, while a man in a hat stood near the edge of the crowd, holding on to what looked to be a bottle of liquor with a red bow. Julian Creed, who lived in 3A, gaped at the scene with a pale expression that made me worried about the state of his stomach. Ripley was also back, apparently unable to stay away. She stood in the corner, probably so no one would accidentally walk through her.

Laurie's hand landed on my shoulder, pulling my attention back to him and the detective. "Meg, do you think this has anything to do with the fight you overheard?"

"Oh." I blinked. "I'd almost forgotten about that." I studied the ceiling as I thought through the oddly threatening conversation I'd walked in on. Lowering my gaze, I found Detective Anthony staring at me, her pen poised over a notebook. "I can't say. Two men were arguing in the stairwell after our meeting. I didn't see their faces or recognize their voices, though."

The detective's pen dropped to the side in defeat, and she lowered the pad of paper.

"There was definitely a stack of mail on the kitchen counter that isn't there anymore," Laurie said. "Would it help if I went through the apartment with you and pointed out anything else that might be different?" he asked, being the very considerate person I knew and, *cough*, loved.

Detective Anthony nodded. "That's a great idea." She motioned for him to follow her inside, ducking under the police tape, and holding it up for Laurie before realizing how tall he was and dropping it so he could step over instead.

Rubbing my hands up and down my arms, I observed the detective as she beamed up at Laurie. They stopped in the entryway to apartment 3B and scrutinized the scene. She reached out and touched his arm, getting his attention as she asked a question.

Ripley sidled up to me. "Meg, let's watch those looks you're throwing around. We've already had one murder today."

I cut my glare over to her. "What are you talking about?" I whispered so none of the building gawkers would hear.

"You look like you're going to follow her home and poison her dinner." Ripley shot me a sidelong glance.

Instead of replying to Ripley, I turned to face the crowd that was also watching Laurie with the detective, and said, "Don't worry, everyone. Laurie's just filling the detective in on what he knows. He's the one who saw the guy after all. That's all that's going on here."

"Meg," Ripley said. My name was a low warning. "Why don't we go upstairs? You don't need to stick around, do you?"

I scratched my chin, our special sign for no. I actually wasn't sure if I could leave, but they knew where to find me. Plus, now that I'd made that declaration to the group, their eyes were all trained on me as if I might have more information. Deciding Ripley might be right, I angled myself toward the stairwell and pulled open the door.

For the second time that day, I reveled in the silence and solace of the space. Well, after I made sure there were no arguing men. Hearing none, I started up to the fifth floor.

Ripley followed, walking alongside me as I climbed the stairs. Now that she wasn't as tethered to me, she rarely traveled with me if we were going somewhere close by, choosing to vanish and reappear wherever I was headed. But it seemed that my brief outburst back there made her think I needed a companion for the trip.

I studied our feet as we climbed, not ready to talk just yet. It was such an odd juxtaposition that my ballet flats would make more noise than Ripley's big, clompy Doc Martens. But as large and imposing as her favorite boots were, they made no sound as they climbed step after step alongside me.

Ripley had spent a lot of time being grateful that ghosts showed up in their most authentic clothing instead of wearing the exact outfit they'd died in. Whereas she'd always appeared to me wearing boots, black tights, cutoff jean shorts, an oversized Soundgarden T-shirt, and a red-and-black flannel shirt, the night she'd died, she'd been wearing an "evil black minidress that kept riding up." A fashion choice she was glad she didn't have to *live* with for the rest of her afterlife.

Though my best friend kept darting worried glances at me as we climbed the two flights of stairs up to the fifth floor, she remained quiet. Her silence spoke more to her understanding of the Morrisey than anything else. Sound in the stairwell carried —something the creepy man from earlier obviously hadn't realized. And even if we *thought* we were alone, Ripley and I had been in enough scrapes throughout the years where someone had heard me talking to "myself" to know we should keep quiet until we got to the apartment.

But as I pushed through the fire door, and walked onto the fifth floor, I realized we wouldn't be heading inside to talk about Laurie and the pretty detective just yet. A man paced in front of my apartment door as if he was waiting for me. He was tall, had long curly brown hair, and I would've assumed he was at the wrong door if he hadn't also been transparent.

These were the kinds of spirits I appreciated the most. They were immediately identifiable as ghosts. Spirits like Ripley appeared and sounded just like a living person to me. It was why I'd learned to observe and watch before speaking. When I was younger, and getting used to my ability, I'd started talking to too many ghosts in crowded rooms before realizing I was the only one seeing them.

Ripley stopped and said, "Whoa." The word was more

breath than syllable, just like when she'd noticed Laurie for the first time down in the lobby. Her glazed-over gaze traveled right past me, through me in a way that made me feel like maybe *I* were the transparent spirit.

"He looks like—do you see who he looks like, Megs?" Her eyes widened as she snapped her ghostly fingers at me.

"Erm..." I checked once more but wasn't immediately hit with the identity of his doppelgänger like Ripley seemed to be.

She shot me a scowl as intense as her charcoal eyeliner. "My one true love," she said.

"Oh." I knew this now. "Chris Cornell?"

Ripley had died in 1999, when she was almost twenty. She'd been immersed in the Seattle grunge scene at the time and hadn't ever moved beyond it. As much as she was in love with Pearl Jam, Nirvana, and Stone Temple Pilots—to name just a few, Soundgarden, and lead singer Chris Cornell, had been her favorite. His death in 2017 had been the hardest day I'd seen her have in the twenty-four years I'd known her.

I surveyed the ghost with the music legend in mind. Squinting one eye, I said, "I guess I can see it. But didn't he have a goatee?" I used my thumb and index finger to draw a triangle around my mouth, signifying the facial hair that was missing.

Ripley rolled her eyes. "Young Chris had no facial hair. He was all long luxurious locks with a grunge soul." She ogled the ghost like he was food instead of a person. Well, I suppose he was neither.

He wasn't particularly observant either. Ripley and I had been stage-whispering at the end of the hallway for minutes now, and he'd yet to even acknowledge our presence.

"You should go talk to him." I spun around, curled my

fingers, and backed up, beckoning her toward him like she'd done earlier to me with Laurie.

Our reactions to such a challenge showed our differences. Whereas I'd cowered and made excuses, Ripley pushed back her shoulders and lifted her chin.

"I'm gonna do it," she said. The girlish excitement evident in her statement did nothing to take away from her cool, confident vibe. She strode forward.

I followed behind, keeping my distance so I wouldn't interfere.

Finally, as Ripley approached, the spirit looked up. His hazel eyes brightened and his lips curved into a handsome smile fit for the cover of *Rolling Stone* magazine. It didn't hurt that Ripley was right. Between his long rocker locks and the Nirvana T-shirt he was wearing, he really did look like a musician.

"Are you waiting for me?" Ripley asked with all the confidence I'd never had. "Because I think I've been waiting for you my whole afterlife."

The ghost's eyebrows rose. Instead of returning Ripley's line with something equally flirty, the man's expression dropped and he frowned. Concern etched itself further into his features.

"Actually, I'm not sure why I'm here." He scratched at his forehead. As his hand dropped back down by his side, he glanced at it and froze. "Why am I..." He didn't finish the question, instead just rotated his hand palm up to palm down as he marveled at his transparency.

"Abort." I rushed forward. "He's a newb," I whispered to Ripley.

We'd experienced enough spirits to know how disoriented newly dead ghosts could be. It took some spirits longer than others to come to terms with the fact that their bodies were gone, even longer for some to accept that they were stuck here on earth for one reason or another. I didn't blame them; it had to be terrible to realize your life on earth was over. Which was why I tried to approach each new spirit I met with as much empathy and kindness as I could.

As was the case with everything else, Ripley was even better at it than I was. She held out a hand and took a step forward. "It's okay. I know I don't look like it, but I'm also a spirit." She wafted her hand through the wall to prove it to him. Then Ripley jabbed a thumb over her shoulder, toward me. "This one's still alive, but she's cool. She can see you too. We can help you figure out what you're still doing here. Let's start with your name."

I was proud of her for not tacking on a pickup line such as, "And end with your number," like I'd definitely heard her drop on hot ghosts before.

It turned out to be a good thing she hadn't, however, because her first request gave the ghost enough trouble. He ran his fingers through his long curly hair—it really *was* gorgeous—and began pacing again.

"Is it weird that I don't know?" His voice was strained.

Ripley and I exchanged a worried look.

"You don't remember your name?" I asked.

The ghost's now-wild eyes flashed up to meet mine. "I don't remember anything."

While he continued to pace, Ripley stepped back to stand next to me. "A spirit with amnesia is a new one," she whispered.

I closed my eyes for a beat before peeling them open once more. It had been a long day between the meeting, the murder, and now this. All I wanted was to go inside my apartment and regroup. But it seemed like that was as likely as Laurie seeing me as anything more than a friend.

"Never a dull day at the Morrisey, is there?" I sighed and resigned myself to the fact that I would need to help this poor, lost soul.

FIVE

Twiddling my fingers as if it might help my brain generate ideas of what to do next, I froze as the rhythmic squeaking of the elevator grew closer. Someone was coming up to the fifth floor.

I pointed toward my apartment. "We should go inside, right?"

"Megs," Ripley said my name like a sigh. "Who's the newb around here?"

Right. If this guy hadn't been in my apartment while he was alive, he wouldn't be able to enter now that he was a spirit.

I unlocked my door. "Well, you two can stay out here for a moment, but I've got to disappear or else I'm going to get caught in the web of small talk."

"Sure. Or, even worse, whoever's in there could catch you talking to yourself in the hallway," Ripley teased.

"Mine's worse," I said with a shiver as I pushed open my door and rushed inside.

There was not much I hated more than small talk. My choice to quit painting had only intensified my worries about getting into the boring, casual conversations. I could easily foresee my neighbors tacking on questions like, "What are you painting right now?" or "What's your plan now that you're back in Seattle?"—effectively weaponizing whatever mundane topic we'd started with.

I'd just closed the door and pressed my eye up to the peephole when the elevator doors screeched open. Bailey Luna and Quentin Maples stepped out. Both were terrible small talkers; Bailey was always going on about her most recent terrible date, while Quentin genuinely seemed to like discussing the weather.

They parted ways, walking past Ripley and the new ghost to their respective apartments across the hall from mine. I waited until I heard their doors latch closed moments later.

Opening my door as quietly as I could, I regarded the two ghosts. They, however, were just staring into each other's eyes as they swapped compliments.

Ripley: "I like your T-shirt."

Ghost: "I like yours even more."

Ripley: "Those are great boots."

Ghost: "I mean, yours are pretty cool too."

I cleared my throat, and they both jumped, gazes snapping over to me.

"Now that we're in the clear, do you want to try walking in here, just in case?" I asked the new ghost. When Ripley let out an exaggerated exhale, I said, "We don't know the kind of company Penny kept while we were away. She could've had young gentlemen callers."

My Aunt Penny may have been in her fifties, but in a lot of ways, she acted more youthful than I ever had. The woman wrote steamy romance novels about Scottish lords and ladies, hence her move to Scotland. She was fed up with doing research about the scenery online and wanted to be immersed in the landscape. She'd also never settled down with anyone, so it wasn't out of the question that she might've had some twentysomething boy toy.

Ripley dipped her chin. "Touché. Your aunt's still got it."

"Aunt?" Chris Cornell's ghostly doppelgänger asked, acting disgusted.

"You wish you were so lucky," Ripley said, turning on him. The defensiveness drained from her as she got lost in his brown eyes once more. "Hot aunts are a thing, okay?"

He shrugged.

"Why don't you just try, so we can get this over with?" I said in lieu of an exasperated sigh.

The ghost stepped forward, but just as he hit the threshold, he vanished. Seeing it happen reminded me that vanishing was the normal thing that happened when a ghost couldn't enter a space. With everything else going on, I hadn't clocked how weird it had been that Ripley had bounced back from 3B as if there had been a force field. There was something going on there. But my attention turned back to the mystery ghost as he appeared three feet back, where we'd first found him pacing in the hallway.

"So that's a no." I chewed on my lip. "But the answer to that question brings up so many more. Why do you keep showing up here in the hallway, right outside my apartment, if you can't go inside?"

Most ghosts I'd met reported reappearing at the place they had the strongest connection with anytime they vanish while attempting to venture outside the realm of where they'd visited when they'd been alive. There was no way this guy's strongest connection was with the hallway outside my door … was there? I'd never seen him before in my life.

One thing was for sure, I couldn't stand here with my door open, chatting with thin air, for much longer before my neighbors heard something. We needed to move this conversation somewhere other than the hallway. I glanced at the ceiling above my head to think.

Like many of the older buildings in Pioneer Square, the Morrisey apartments boasted fifteen-foot ceilings, though the hallways were closer to the norm of eight to ten. It not only made our apartments feel bigger, it gave us the ability to create lofted spaces, which added an even more usable area. It was why Penny hadn't needed to move when my mom had passed away, and I joined her in her studio apartment. She made a bed for me up in the loft where she used to write, moving her writing desk to the corner by the window or going to a local coffee shop to write when I was old enough to be by myself.

But looking at the ceiling made me think about what was on the other side.

"Well, why don't we test whether Chris Cornell Two can join us on the roof?" I suggested.

"Chris Cornell? Awe, man. I loved that guy. He was my idol … I think?" The ghost scratched at his chin as he squinted one eye.

"No kidding?" I asked dryly.

Ripley just grinned at him, blinking dreamily like everything he said were lyrics from her favorite song.

"Okay, since we don't know your name, and you approve of looking like Chris Cornell—" I started.

He puffed out his chest and interrupted me, saying, "You can call me Spencer."

"Spencer?" I scoffed before I could stop myself. "Why? What does that have to do with Chris Cornell?"

The ghost grunted. "I dunno. It's the first name that came to my mind."

"Spencer." Ripley tested out the name as she let her head tilt to one side, then the other. "I like it."

"Okay, well, Ripley and Spencer, I'll meet you up on the roof." I moved toward the stairwell after pulling my apartment door closed behind me and pocketing my key.

Ripley vanished first, followed closely by Spencer. I walked the remaining flight up the stairs, pushing open the heavy door that led from the small vestibule, which held the elevator and stairwell entry, onto the roof. I kicked a large rock to prop the door open. Technically, our keys to the front door were also supposed to open the roof door, but the lock up here had gotten fiddly and rarely opened, no matter how much you jiggled it. We all found it safer to prop the thing open.

It was my first time being up on the roof since returning. I stepped forward, noting the similarities and differences. Other than a few new chairs, everything appeared to be the same.

The roof's contents were a mishmash of potted plants that residents couldn't keep alive in their apartments, random outdoor furniture we'd collected over the years, and Hayden Nutter's greenhouse, which he allowed us to peruse in exchange for getting to take up so much roof space. A four-foot brick wall ran the perimeter, allowing for a little privacy, if you didn't count the high-rises surrounding Pioneer Square, such as the Columbia Tower, Smith Tower, and the half dozen fancy condo buildings that had been built over the last two decades.

A cool breeze wafted over me, feeling amazing since the temperatures were in the high eighties. A small sliver of sadness buried itself into my heart at the memory of coming up here with Penny on summer days like this. The sounds of the city seemed so far away compared to the clicking of Penny's laptop keys as she drafted her latest novel. While she wrote, I would paint. I'd been so joyful, so hopeful back then.

Pushing that thought out of my mind, I immediately caught sight of multiple ghosts on the roof. Two of them were Ripley and Spencer, standing off to my right. The third was Rooftop Rachel, but she was always up there.

We didn't actually know if her name was Rachel, but Ripley swore she looked like a Rachel, and it fit alliteratively with rooftop since she never left. Along with never leaving, Rachel also never spoke. She just floated above the edge of the building, staring out toward the water. Her white nightgown and gaunt expression made us think she was from the early nineteen hundreds, but again, we couldn't be sure since we'd never heard her speak.

Seeing Rachel again after so many years still gave me an eerie chill down my back, much like the first time I'd encountered her on the rooftop as a kid. I gave an unreturned wave to Rachel and skirted toward the sitting area, checking around each of the largest planters to make sure we were alone. An early summer evening like this would've normally pulled at least a few of the residents up onto the roof, but it seemed they'd all gotten stalled on the third floor.

I wasn't complaining. It gave me the perfect opportunity to talk to Spencer. But it also brought up more questions, like how could he come up on the roof? Only residents came up here.

Maybe he was renting apartment 3E, I realized with a start. Penny *had* mentioned that Andrew had been subletting it out to short-term renters and vacationers since he'd moved in with his girlfriend last year. I'd have to ask someone else if that were the case, though. Spencer obviously wouldn't remember.

It seemed I was the only one feeling trepidation about where Spencer had come from, though, because as I joined in on Ripley and Spencer's conversation, it sounded more enthusiastic than anything else.

"I totally agree," Ripley exclaimed as I stopped in front of them. Her eyes shone with interest as she studied Spencer. Turning to me, she said, "Meg, this guy is definitely from the nineties, like me. He loves Soundgarden more than Audioslave and actually knows who Mother Love Bone is. Not a lot of people from 2023 can say the same."

My gaze flicked to Spencer, who nodded excitedly at the prospect of figuring out more about himself. The hope in his expression made it hard to disagree, but I couldn't help it. "I mean, *I* know about Mother Love Bone and like Soundgarden better than Audioslave." I settled into one of the chairs. From that vantage point, I could monitor the door, making sure no one else came up here while I was chatting with ghosts. "And I wasn't born until 1999." I finished my point.

"Yeah, but that's because you have me." Ripley wafted a dismissive hand as if my words were annoying mosquitoes.

She wasn't wrong. I'd been the odd girl in fifth grade who was listening to the Smashing Pumpkins on repeat, while the rest of my classmates were obsessed with Katy Perry or Maroon 5, and it was all because of Ripley's musical influence. However, this seemed like an important consideration, so I pushed back.

"I'm just saying, we can't confirm that he died back in the nineties purely from his musical tastes. We both assumed he was a newb downstairs. If he's not new, that means he's either been wandering around as a ghost with amnesia for over twenty years or something recently happened to his spirit that made him lose his memory and show up at my door. Why don't you ask him some questions only someone from the nineties would know the answer to?" I placed a hand on my hip.

Ripley huffed. "Fine."

Her momentary frustration with me dissipated as she became more excited about coming up with the questions than she was about being upset. I knew that would get her. Ripley loved the nineties and was constantly telling me how much better it was than the two thousands. She was the perfect person to handle this task.

"Okay," she said, her eyes shining. "Spencer, first question. What is a Tamagotchi?"

Spencer frowned for a moment, but then his lips parted, and he said, "An electronic pet you had to feed and take care of or else it died." At that statement, he cringed. "I have a terrible feeling I may have killed a few."

Ripley cackled. "We all did. Don't worry about it. Pass. Okay, second question." Her mouth curved into a conspiratorial smirk as she asked, "Please accurately recreate the sound dial-up internet used to make while connecting."

While I'd known what a Tamagotchi was because of Ripley, I had no idea how to answer her second question. She was good. Ripley had described the fact that they used to need a phone line to connect to the internet, but I didn't know there had been a sound that was connected to the action.

Spencer was gaining confidence. He lifted his chin before making beeping noises, like someone dialing a phone number. He followed that by making a succession of screeches at different pitches and then immediately added a *ba-ding ba-ding* sound. After that was just static.

Snorting out a laugh, I said, "Okay, that has to be wr—"

"Correct!" Ripley declared.

"What?" My mouth hung open.

But Ripley was on a roll. She wasn't waiting for me to catch up. "Final question." She narrowed her eyes at Spencer.

Potentially finding his place in the recent timeline must've given him even more confidence because he crossed his arms and widened his feet in a *bring it on* stance.

"Spencer, what was the best tool to rewind a cassette tape when its filmy guts spilled out by accident?" Ripley tapped her finger against her lip while she waited for the answer.

"I mean, that question doesn't even make sense," I muttered to myself.

Ripley glared in my direction, letting me know she didn't appreciate my commentary.

Apparently, Spencer thought it made sense. He smirked as he said, "A pen. A pencil will also work."

"Ding, ding, ding!" Ripley jumped a few times in celebration. Then she turned toward me, flourishing her arms like he was some sort of royalty. "I present to you, a person who lived during the greatest decade in recent history. The nineties." She said the last part in a haughty accent as she bowed.

"Okay, I believe you." I chuckled. "But now that we know he was from the nineties, that limits our options. You and I didn't arrive at the building until 1999, and we obviously don't recognize the guy, which tells me he wasn't around during the eighteen years I was here growing up. So where was he during that time? Why is he only just showing up at my door today? Aunt Penny moved into the place in 1993, so she might know who he is, but it's"—I checked my watch—"midnight her time, so we can't exactly call her."

Ripley chewed on her lip. "What about someone else? Half the building has been here for decades."

"Yeah, but half the building is about as reliable as reading a copy of *The Onion*," I said, mentioning the tongue-in-cheek periodical.

"What about Nancy?" Ripley suggested. "Didn't she move in during the nineties? Maybe she knows?"

She had and, based on the stories I'd heard her tell over the years, her memory was just as reliable as her internal clock, which still got her up at the same time every morning.

"Good idea," I said.

"Knowing Nance, she's probably still hanging around the police. We'll meet you down there," Ripley told me before gesturing for Spencer to follow her.

The ghosts vanished, leaving me by myself on the roof. Heading back toward the door, I kicked the rock out of the way, called a goodbye to Rachel, and wound down the stairwell. But as I jogged down the second flight, the door on the fourth floor opened, almost swinging right into me.

"Oh! Sorry, Meg." Laurie flinched as the door closed and he saw me. "Did I hit you?"

"No, I'm okay. Plus, I ran into you earlier, so it's your turn." I smiled, but any sense of joy at seeing him left me as it became clear something was wrong.

There was a tightness to his normally loose posture, his features were bunched in discomfort, and he gripped something in his right hand.

"What's going on?" I asked. "You were racing out of there like there's a fire."

Finally meeting my gaze with his flighty eyes, Laurie said, "I'm a little freaked-out, to be honest. I just got back to my place after talking to the police, and I found this slipped under my door."

He shoved a piece of paper toward me. It held a scribbled warning in all caps.

STAY OUT OF THIS UNLESS YOU WANT TO END UP LIKE MILLER.

Six

The stairwell always amplified sounds, but in the seconds that followed my reading that note, it felt as if I were in an echo chamber. My heartbeats and breaths felt deafening as they rang in my ears.

My fear was mirrored clearly in Laurie's concerned face. He reluctantly took back the paper as I handed it over.

"Are you going to show that to the police?" I asked, connecting the note with how he'd burst into the stairwell moments before.

Laurie nodded resolutely.

"Even though that might be considered *not* staying out of this?" I swallowed the terrible taste that cropped up in my throat.

Inhaling, Laurie scratched at his jawline. "I guess, but what's the alternative? This handwriting could be a clue the cops need to solve the case." He tapped the piece of paper.

"Why are they singling you out?" I wondered aloud. "I was right there with you."

"I can't figure that out either." Laurie frowned.

I shifted my weight uncomfortably as an idea came to mind. "Oh no. I might know why." When Laurie's eyes met mine, I explained, "When I was leaving, I may have mentioned that you were the right person for Detective Anthony to speak to since you'd seen *the guy*."

Laurie shook his head. "Anyone from the building would've known you were referring to Mr. Miller and my sighting of him ten years ago."

"That's right." I snapped my fingers. "Which means the killer isn't from the Morrisey."

"Good thinking," Laurie said. "And when you said that, the killer probably thought you were saying I'd seen them."

"Him," I said, holding up a finger. "At least we know it's probably a guy. I said *the guy*, remember?"

Grimacing, Laurie didn't seem as excited about that distinction as I was.

"That means the killer was there, on the third floor, watching everything going on with the investigation." A shiver crawled up my spine.

Laurie's expression darkened. "I need to let Detective Anthony know about this right away."

"I was going that way," I said, placing a hand on his arm. "Do you want company?"

"I'd love it." His lips pulled into a side smile.

Hearing Laurie say the word love in any capacity used to make teenage me swoon with longing. Now that we were adults, I could hold it together a little better, but my face still flushed with heat. I started moving to keep him from noticing. We headed down the stairwell to the third floor, where there was still a large presence of onlookers being held back by police tape.

Ripley and Spencer were already there, frowning at the stairwell. When I emerged with Laurie, Ripley's expression relaxed and she jabbed an elbow toward Spencer. I knew my best friend well enough to guess that whatever she was whispering to Spencer had to do with me having a huge crush on Laurie instead of her being relieved that I hadn't run into trouble in the stairwell.

Ignoring Ripley, I nodded with encouragement toward Laurie as he ventured over toward Detective Anthony. He kept the threatening note hidden in his palm as he approached the detective, leaning in close as he whispered to her, not wanting to be overheard by anyone nearby. I scanned the crowd, searching for anyone who might be guilty of taking Mr. Miller's life and threatening Laurie.

Knowing that we were looking for a man now, I inspected the crowd for the strange men I'd noticed earlier. The man with the blond eyebrows was still there, chatting with Julian now instead of the woman with the flower jeans, who'd left. But he didn't pay any attention to Laurie as he spoke with the detective. In fact, he turned toward Julian to challenge him in what seemed like a heated discussion about some local sports team. The man who'd been carrying the bottle of liquor with the bow attached was gone. But a red bow sat on the floor next to the garbage chute to my left. Had he tossed the bottle of amber liquid? Or had the bow simply dropped off as he fled the scene?

The whole thing left an uneasy feeling in my stomach. But it was nothing compared to the gut punch I experienced as Detective Anthony placed her hand on Laurie's arm, much like

I had just done in the stairwell—though her gesture was backed by a heck of a lot more confidence and gravitas than mine had been.

I forced myself to look away, searching the crowd for Nancy. Surprisingly enough, the nosy building manager was nowhere to be seen. Maybe I'd been wrong about the number of changes that had taken place at the Morrisey in my absence. Had Nancy learned to mind her own business?

Ripley must've noticed Nancy's absence at the same time I did because she jerked her head toward the stairs. If she wasn't here, it was a good bet she was downstairs in her apartment.

I turned on my heel to point myself toward the stairwell as Ripley and Spencer disappeared. Winding down the staircase two more floors, I came out into the lobby corridor.

Nancy answered the door moments after I pressed the buzzer. The familiar aroma of rising bread poured out of Nancy's apartment. She still made her own bread almost every day, often giving away slices to residents in the lobby as they walked by. My stomach grumbled at the smell.

"Oh, dear. Grown up, yet still our sensitive little Nutmeg," she said in a maternal way that told me my appearance on her doorstep was not a surprise. "Do you need to talk about what happened today?"

It was always interesting to me the things that people attached to my personality along with my quietness, as if they must go hand in hand. I didn't count myself as even remotely sensitive. I'd seen, heard, and experienced a lot more terrible things in my lifetime so far than many people would their entire lives. Sure, I hated small talk, and I had become more reserved in group settings because of my propensity to stay silent until I could ascertain who was alive or dead, but I wouldn't describe myself as a shy person in general.

Around people I knew and felt comfortable with, I wasn't quiet at all. The fact that most of those people were either related to me or dead didn't necessarily help my argument.

"Actually, I have a question for you." I messed with the hem of my T-shirt. "Not related to poor Mr. Miller or the investigation going on upstairs."

Eyebrows hitching higher with intrigue, Nancy waved me in. Ripley followed, but when Spencer tried stepping forward, he vanished again, just as he had when trying to enter my apartment. Ripley shot me a frown, but she didn't go after him. Just like last time, he'd probably reappeared in the hallway on the fifth floor of the Morrisey.

Together, we walked inside. Nancy's apartment was decked out in her favorite two colors, pink and green. She'd painted every wall but the brick ones a Pepto Bismol pink. Her couch was covered in a vibrant forest-green velvet. Her bed, visible through the open bedroom door, tucked in the back corner, was neatly made with a pink-and-green floral quilt. A Matisse painting featuring goldfish and plants sitting on a table tied it all together.

Nancy maintained that the bright colors helped her combat the seasonal depression that came with the gloomy winters in the Pacific Northwest. Penny and I had a different theory. We'd visited the bakery she used to own over near the Seattle Center a few times before she'd closed. The colors inside were the same pink and green, chosen by her previous business partner who passed away from breast cancer only a few years after they opened Seattle Center Sweet Treats.

Whatever the reason, Nancy was free to decorate in whatever way made her happiest.

"What can I help you with?" Nancy asked, motioning for me to have a seat on the green couch. "Can I get you something to eat? Toast? A scone?"

My stomach grumbled louder in response. "I'd love a scone. Thank you, Nance."

She beamed. Nancy always seemed at her happiest when she was running building meetings and when she was feeding people. "Start talking. I can hear you."

"Is Andrew still renting out his apartment?" I asked, getting my first hunch out of the way.

"Yes," Nancy called from the kitchen, and even though I couldn't see her face, there was exhaustion in her tone. "Those short-term renters are going to be the death of me."

Intrigued, I asked, "Have you seen the one who's here right now?"

Ripley frowned at me, obviously unsure where I was going with this line of questioning.

"I did see him," she said. "Middle-aged guy, maybe Penny's age, I'd say. Brown hair."

"Short or long?" I asked.

Nancy chuckled. "I've never heard of tall people referred to as long before."

I shook my head. "No, his hair. Is it short or long?"

Bustling out of the kitchen, Nancy said, "Oh, short."

Well. That answered my first question. Spencer was not the person renting 3E. Which meant he really might've lived here in the nineties. I focused on that line of questioning as Nancy approached me with the scone.

"I was wondering if you knew of a resident who might've been here in the nineties. He was about my age with long, curly brown hair." I used my hand to mime the flowing, side-parted locks Spencer continually shifted from one side to the other. "He kinda looked like a guy in a grunge band."

"Like *the* guy in *the* grunge band," Ripley muttered.

I ignored her, knowing that would be the only information Nancy would need. The woman might've lived in Seattle during the grunge era, but in addition to green and pink, I also knew she loved Whitney Houston with a passion that made her sure that if Whitney didn't sing it, it wasn't worth listening to. Chris Cornell and Whitney hadn't exactly run in the same musical circles.

Nancy handed me the scone. "I'm sorry, hon. That doesn't ring any bells."

She'd cut the scone in half and spread a little jam on it before placing it back together like a sandwich and wrapping it in a paper towel.

"But, you know, I didn't move in until midway through the nineties as it was." Nance shrugged. "Have you asked Penny?"

I took a bite of the scone, shaking my head while I chewed. "Not yet," I said once I'd swallowed. "It's still the middle of the night over there."

"Oh, you're right. I keep forgetting." Nancy snapped her fingers. "You could always check with Opal."

"Opal?" Ripley asked, sitting up straighter.

I took another bite of the scone, hoping my expression would communicate the same question.

"She was the building manager before me. She got too old for the manager position, and there weren't any open units here at the time, so she moved to an assisted-living complex over in West Seattle." Nancy flared her nostrils as if the thought of anyone living anywhere other than our building was so terrible. "She might remember. I can get you the name of the place where she moved."

Swallowing, I said, "Perfect. Thank you." I popped the rest of the scone in my mouth.

"Why do you ask?" Nancy peered at me through her glasses.

I took longer than I strictly needed to chew and swallow the final bite. "Oh, I was just moving some stuff under the sink in the kitchen and found an old newspaper clipping with an obituary for a guy with long hair. The name had ripped off," I said, not sure how convincing the lie was. "I just wondered if there was a story behind why it was here."

Nancy clicked her tongue. "Now, Nutmeg, you know better."

I winced, sure I was about to get scolded for lying.

"You shouldn't be messing around under that sink. Did you learn nothing from the time Penny tried to 'fix' it?" Nancy waggled a finger in my direction.

The kitchen sink in our apartment had leaked my whole life. Penny and I simply got used to it, dumping the water that collected in the bowl we placed under the pipes each week so it wouldn't overflow. But there had been one fateful day that Penny had almost caused a flood in our apartment when she'd gotten on a fix-it kick and tried her hand at stopping the infamous leak.

Exhaling, I told Nancy, "I won't mess with it. I promise. Thank you for the scone. It was delicious." I waved and started for the door, Ripley following on my heels.

It sounded like we were taking a trip to West Seattle.

Spencer was back, waiting for us in the lobby. He studied strands of his hair as if he were checking for split ends. His eyes brightened as they landed on Ripley.

"Did she know me?" He stepped forward.

Ripley and I shook our heads in tandem. I gestured to the seating area around the corner. Normally, Art and Darius would've been camped out there, but they must've still been upstairs as well, so we had the fireplace room at the front of the lobby to ourselves.

"She pointed us in the direction of someone who might, though," Ripley explained.

"We have to go to West Seattle. Do you think you'll be able to follow?" I asked.

Spencer kicked at the fireplace hearth only to have his foot travel right through it. Embarrassment burned behind his expression as his gaze shifted anywhere but on us. "Probably not."

"Maybe you should stay here," Ripley said, her tone full of compassion. "You can tell us what's been happening with the investigation when we get back."

My lips parted, and I sucked in a breath. "Or, Spencer, would you mind keeping an eye on apartment 4B? My friend lives there, and he got a threatening note. I want to make sure he's okay."

"Wait. Threat?" Ripley spat out the question. "Is that what the two of you were talking about?" Unease tightened her posture.

I nodded. "I'll fill you in on our trip. We should get going."

That appeased Ripley, for the moment.

Happy to have a job, Spencer saluted me. "I'll watch his door like a hawk, Meg. Don't worry."

As nice as it was to have eyes on Laurie's apartment, worry remained the overriding emotion swirling around inside of me. I had a feeling that wouldn't go away until this killer was caught and justice was served.

SEVEN

The bus I caught a block down from the Morrisey swayed as it wended its way through the Historic South Downtown neighborhood. As was the case with every bus in the city, it had a disturbingly enigmatic smell that fluctuated between bad soup and old laundry, and there were at least three people staring at me far too intently.

Ripley joined me, which spoke to exactly how eager she was to hear about the threat Laurie had found. Sitting on buses was her least favorite pastime, especially when they were crowded with commuters and she had to dodge people left and right. I held my phone in my lap and tucked ear buds into my ears, then filled her in on the note.

The wheeze of the air brakes became a backdrop to our conversation as the bus stopped and started a million times, or so it seemed. Ripley voiced many of my same concerns and theories as I stared out the window, gazing over the port as we made our way over the West Seattle Bridge to our destination.

Opal Halifax resided in an assisted-living building in the smaller, but still bustling, community of West Seattle. Her building was shaped like a cylinder and painted so it looked kind of like the filtered end of a cigarette. Somehow, I doubted it had been the designer's intent, unlike the infamous Experience Music Project building, now called the Museum of Pop Culture, built in the shadow of the Space Needle and created to look like a deconstructed guitar. This seemed more like a case of an unfortunate choice of exterior paint colors.

"Oh, man. There used to be the coolest bar right across the street." Ripley crossed her arms and pouted when she saw the place she'd been talking about was now a Zeke's Pizza.

"Sorry," I said. It was my standard answer anytime Ripley pointed out places she used to hang out or party when she was younger. There were a few clubs still open, but most of her favorite places had closed down in the decades since she'd passed away.

"It's fine," she said with a huff. "It's not like I can taste their whiskey sours anymore."

Rolling my eyes at her, I said, "You weren't even old enough to drink."

"Tell that to Natalie Smith, the woman on my fake ID." Ripley winked as we walked inside the apartment building.

Unlike other assisted-living places I'd visited, where there was both a section of housing for independent living and then a wing for residents who needed more intensive medical care, the West Seattle Assisted Living Apartments seemed to be a true-blue assisted-living complex. There was a man running the front desk and a few nurses on staff, but it seemed like the residents were still fairly independent.

My observations were further reinforced when I walked up to the man behind the computer, asked for Opal Halifax, and he said, "She's in 3B. You can go right up and talk to her. All our residents are mobile and can operate on their own. We're here just in case." He fixed me with a friendly smile before peering back at his computer screen.

Ripley had floated behind him, studying his computer as if she worried he might not give us the information, and she would have to look it up over his shoulder. I thanked him for his help and stood in front of the elevator. Ripley joined me as I waited.

Once I stepped inside the elevator, and checked to make sure there wasn't a security camera, I turned to my friend. "Do you think it's weird that Opal lives in the same unit as the dead guy in our building?"

Ripley frowned. "Not as weird as what that guy was searching for on his computer."

I wrinkled my nose, not wanting to know.

"Beanie Babies," Ripley shared anyway, surprising me with how innocent the truth actually was. "Those things haven't been profitable for decades." Her eyes narrowed. "Unless ... he knows something we don't."

Laughing, I said, "We are not getting into Beanie Baby collecting."

Though she described herself as "totally grunge, through and through," Ripley also admitted to having been sucked into the frenetic collecting of the stuffed animals during the nineties. She'd acted like an enormous weight had been lifted from her shoulders the day she'd told me the truth, and we'd spent that evening looking up the rare versions she'd collected.

The elevator opened onto the third floor, giving me a physical exit from the Beanie Baby conversation, thank goodness. The beige carpet of the hallway we stepped into had been stained over time, yet another difference between the Morrisey and the West Seattle Assisted Living Apartments. To my right, a very different apartment 3B stood in front of me. This time, without Laurie by my side, I was the one who knocked.

An older woman answered the door. She had long, gray hair that was braided down her back, oversized blue glasses, and she wore black leggings and a black long-sleeve shirt.

"Hello?" she asked, confusion filling her shaky tone. It wasn't just her voice, she was also physically wobbling quite a lot, hanging on to the door in a futile attempt to keep herself still.

"Hi, Mrs. Halifax. I'm Meg Dawson. I live at the Morrisey. Are you the same Opal who was the building manager before Nancy Lewandowski?"

Her expression brightened. "I am." It was almost as if she'd grown a few inches, that was how much the woman straightened at the mention. Some of her unsteadiness even disappeared. "Ah, I cannot tell you how much I miss the Morrisey. This silly building has no charm at all except if you count looking like the butt of a cigarette," she said in her raspy voice. "Which I don't."

I barked out a laugh.

"Okay, I like her," Ripley said.

"Come in. Come in." She waved a gnarled hand at me and beckoned me to enter.

I eyed a pull cord hanging against the wall in the hallway. There was another in the kitchen and by a chair in the small living room. That must be how residents called the front desk for help. Opal caught me inspecting them.

"Pieces of garbage, if you ask me." Opal swatted one into the wall as she tottered past me. "I wish I could've stayed at the Morrisey. No pull cords or night crew, but the people there take care of each other and are more interesting than the snoozers who rent here."

I stifled a smile, and Ripley said, "Opal is my new favorite." She watched the old woman with fascination.

"So what brings you here today, dear?" Opal asked. Her milky-blue eyes lit up. "Are you here to tell me there's an apartment available?"

My heart sank. "Oh, I'm sorry. I'm not ... er ... there isn't."

Ripley coughed. "Well, technically..."

She was right. Now that Mr. Miller was dead, there would be a vacancy. But without knowing the contents of Mr. Miller's will or who the place would go to now that he was gone, I didn't want to get the woman's hopes up for nothing.

Opal's tiny shoulders dropped. "That's all right. What apartment did you say you were in?" She forced a grin as if she were trying to be nice, but talking about it was just making her remember what she was missing, all over again.

"Five-A," I said reluctantly, not wanting to rub it in her face, but also not wanting to be rude by refusing to answer.

Her face pulled into a thoughtful smile. "Penny's place. She moved in during my last few years there." Opal glanced around the room as if there might be someone there who would overhear. "I read all her books, you know." I didn't need any more proof than the blush that crept into the woman's cheeks.

Aunt Penny's books were steamy, some scenes even making Ripley—my bar for all things wild and free—giggle with embarrassment.

"She's my aunt," I said proudly.

Opal seemed to be lost in thoughts of Penny's books. Her gaze wandered over my shoulder and out the window.

"Wonder what scene she's thinking about there," Ripley said with a suggestive eyebrow waggle.

"Um." Wringing my hands in my lap as I tried to think of what to say, I finally settled on, "Opal, the reason I came to see you today is because I'm looking for information about a man in his twenties who may have died in the building during the nineties. Nancy said she didn't get there until the mid-nineties, but that you might remember."

Of course, I wasn't sure if Spencer had actually died at the Morrisey, but I was following a hunch. It was the only thing that might explain why he kept showing up there.

Opal snapped out of her trance and turned back to me. "A death in the Morrisey?" she asked no one, a contemplative tone to her rhetorical question. "You say he was in his twenties?"

"Around there." I opened my palms and then closed them, wishing I had a picture of Spencer to show Opal.

"Tell her he's super hot. That might jog her memory," Ripley added, unhelpfully.

I was about to tug at the heel of my shoe when her comment made me realize I actually did have a picture I could show Opal. Holding up a finger, I pulled out my phone and searched for a picture of a young Chris Cornell, back when he had long hair and no goatee.

Turning the phone toward Opal, I said, "This is him. Does he look familiar?"

Opal studied the picture from a few different angles, her expression vacillating between intrigue, recognition, and surprise, but finally settling on unamused. "Young lady, don't think for one moment that I don't know the lead singer of Soundgarden when I see him. What are you playing at, saying he died in the Morrisey during the nineties?"

I rarely broke my rule of not looking straight at Ripley when I was in the company of living people, finding it too hard to explain if they caught me and asked what I was staring at. But the surprise that washed over me in that instance made me throw that rule right out the curved windows of the cylindrical building. I blinked wide-eyed at Ripley as she did the same back.

"If I didn't love her before, I do now." Ripley swooned in admiration.

Brushing off the comment, I said, "I don't have a picture of the guy, but he does look a lot like a young Chris Cornell. I didn't realize you would recognize him."

Opal glared at me. "Girlfriend, who do you think contributed to the food fight Nirvana started in the Re-Bar the night of their *Nevermind* album release?" She jabbed a thumb at her chest. "I may be old, but what really kicked me out of the Morrisey was the stroke I had a few years later. Kicked me on my butt, and I couldn't be the manager anymore. But that can't stop me from having a grunge soul."

Ripley settled her chin on her palms, leaning forward. "Teach me everything. Please be my grandma."

"But now that you mention it"—Opal tapped her lips with a curled finger—"I do remember a young man who looked a little like he could've been in one of the grunge bands. It would've been about thirty years ago." She held up a shaky finger. "He didn't live at the Morrisey, but he did die there." Her eyes adopted that faraway stare once again.

This time, however, there was no color rushing to her cheeks. Her face paled and she swallowed.

Her wobbly voice leveled out as she began the tale. "It was a rainy fall night. You know, one of those evenings where it feels like it's midnight, but it's only seven?"

I nodded. I knew them well. During the fall and winter, the early sunset often made it feel like it was way later. The effect was even more pronounced when it had been rainy and gloomy the entire day.

"Well, I caught sight of a young man hanging on to the oak tree outside of my apartment," Opal explained.

The windows in that first-floor apartment were right next to the sidewalk, which was why Nancy had installed blinds that opened at the top instead of the bottom so she could let in light while still maintaining some of her privacy from the constant foot traffic around the building.

"At first, I thought he might've just had a little too much to drink, or might possibly be on some kind of drug I didn't want to deal with. But then he swayed into the light from the street-lamp, and I saw the back of his head was matted with blood. I called an ambulance and brought him inside the lobby and let him sit by the fire." Opal's blue eyes crackled with the memory. "He was disoriented, but the last thing he could remember was going to the bathroom in a nearby bar. He was missing his wallet and couldn't remember who he was." Opal flinched. "He didn't make it. Died right there in the Morrisey's lobby before the ambulance even arrived."

Ripley swore under her breath as she sat back.

"I'm so sorry," I said. "That sounds like it was an awful thing to go through."

Opal pulled her face into another fake smile. "I like to think I gave him a warm, safe place to go."

Unable to jump up and leave Opal after such an intense story, I stayed and chatted for a while, filling her in on all the gossip around the Morrisey—well, almost all. I didn't mention Mr. Miller's untimely death. I also promised to come back and visit her again, which wasn't a difficult commitment to make. Ripley wasn't alone in her admiration. Opal Halifax was an amazing person I wanted to get to know better.

Close to an hour after we arrived, Ripley and I left the cigarette-butt building in awe. It was fully nighttime, and the city was covered in darkness.

"Could Spencer really be the same guy from Opal's story?" I asked as we stood, waiting for the bus.

Ripley shrugged. "It all matches up. He got hit on the head. Must've been mugged. That's why he didn't have any ID on him and couldn't remember who he was."

I wanted to feel as sure as Ripley sounded. But if that were the case, where had Spencer's spirit been for the last three decades, and why was he drawn to me?

EIGHT

Ripley may have ridden the bus with me to West Seattle, but she was too excited to talk to Spencer about what we'd learned from Opal. She ditched me once we got into the SoDo neighborhood after we'd passed by the sports stadiums.

I used my key and wandered into the Morrisey a while later, the questions that lingered about Spencer's death feeling like bags I was lugging over each shoulder.

"Having a good evening, Nutmeg?" an old man sitting in a chair in the lobby asked as I walked inside.

I grinned as big as I could muster after such a long day. "Trying to, Darius."

The man sitting next to him added, "Terrible business about that Mr. Miller." He tsked and shook his head.

"It really is, Art." I waved.

Arturo and Darius liked to call themselves the Conversationalists. They spent most of their days plunked right there in those two chairs, brought down from their own apartments so they wouldn't take up any of the other seating, and people watched while talking to the residents as they came and went.

Because our building was so old, we didn't have any high-tech way to let visitors enter beyond coming downstairs and letting them in ourselves. Art and Darius often acted as doormen, letting in visitors and directing them where to go if they looked lost. Everyone appreciated the service.

Unlike stereotypical old men, they were absolute night owls, sleeping in late and staying up even later, so it wasn't a surprise to see them occupying their regular spots in the lobby even though it was past nine.

"Good to have you back, darlin'," a third old man said, but instead of sitting in one of the chairs or the sofa, he floated.

I shot a discreet wink at the ghost in response.

George considered himself the third member of the Conversationalists—unknown to the other two members, of course. He was content to float next to them, adding to the banter where he could. He'd been a doorman for the building back in the seventies. And even though he'd died of natural causes, he really had loved his job. He'd often said that he could spend the rest of his days opening the front doors of the Morrisey and greeting its residents, so when he'd passed away and showed up in the foyer of the building he loved, he wasn't surprised one bit.

"Well, have a good night," I said as I made my way to the stairs.

"Meggie," George's voice followed me.

I glanced back just as he pointed to the elevator. I sent a final longing look at the stairs but realized if he wanted me to take the elevator, he had something to tell me. The ghosts in the building knew all about the echoey stairwell and how it wasn't safe for me to hold conversations there.

The elevator doors opened with a noise like a pterodactyl screech. I stepped inside, cringing as the thing dipped with my weight. The doors squealed closed, feeling more like a trap than a safety measure.

"What's up?" I asked, mentally counting the seventeen seconds I knew it would take for the elevator to start moving since it didn't immediately jolt into an ascent.

"I heard about the threatening note Laurence got," George said solemnly.

"You did?" I asked, wondering how much of the building knew. Had they also heard it was my fault he'd gotten it in the first place?

George held up a hand to stop me from worrying. "I overheard him talking to that detective, so I don't think anyone else is aware. But I think I know who did it."

"Who left him the note, or who killed Mr. Miller," I asked, then realized ... "or both?"

He shot me a knowing look. "A man came in just before the building meeting today. He was upset, and he was asking around about Mr. Miller. Instead of calling him Mathew, he referred to him as Mathias." George wrinkled his forehead.

"How'd he get inside?" I asked, before remembering the Conversationalists. "Never mind," I added. "Did you find out why he was searching for Mathew—or Mathias?"

"I think he might've been a psychic," George said.

Blinking, I asked, "The guy looking for Mr. Miller?"

"No. Mr. Miller himself," George corrected. "The man asked Art and Darius if a Mathias the Medium lived here. They said no, but we did have a Mathew Miller in 3B. I followed him.

He started toward the third floor, grumbling about how 'he'd pay for what he did.'"

"Did he knock on Mr. Miller's door? What happened after that?" I asked.

"Well..." George glanced down at his worn boots. "I got distracted." The ghost rubbed at the back of his neck. "Danica and Dustin McNairy walked by with a bag from Uwajimaya, and I wanted to see what they were making for dinner. Ever since Danica found out she's pregnant, they've been making some adventurous meals."

I couldn't fault George. I loved the local Asian market as much as the next Seattleite. Plus, there was no way George could've known the man was going to kill Mr. Miller. As someone who felt a lot of guilt surrounding the threat Laurie had received, I didn't want George to worry that he could've stopped Mr. Miller's death.

"And the McNairys don't come to building meetings, so you must've been with them the whole time," I said, thinking out loud.

The couple had moved in while I was on the East Coast, but Penny filled me in on "their deal," especially since the married couple didn't seem to want to socialize with the rest of the building. It had been a bit of a slap to the other residents' proverbial faces since the Morrisey was like a tight-knit family. The residents had dubbed them the "Wary McNairys," based on their antisocial behavior.

"They made congee and had a ton of different toppings." His eyes sparkled with excitement before he remembered he was supposed to be upset. "But, back to the man ... From what I saw and heard, he wanted Mr. Miller dead. He also seemed desperate enough to threaten Laurence. I would've done more investigating, but I've haven't been able to get past the doorway to that apartment since Miller moved in."

"You'd been inside before that?" I asked, checking with the ghostly travel rule. "During your life?"

George dipped his chin. "Mr. Darling used to live there. He needed my help bringing his groceries up as he got older."

"Ripley couldn't go inside either," I mused, more to myself than to him. "Do you remember what the guy looked like?"

George's eyebrows rose. "Pretty average, except he had really blond eyebrows."

Blond-eyebrows guy. He had to be our killer. He'd been there when I'd made that offhand comment about Laurie and had been watching the police work.

The elevator stopped, lurching disconcertingly and sitting there for a few seconds before it opened the doors onto my floor.

"Thank you, George," I said with a salute. "I'll check into it."

When I stepped out onto the fifth floor, I found Ripley and Spencer waiting for me. They were chatting and laughing. It was good to see Ripley having fun with another ghost. There had been a few throughout the years, but because she was tied to me, she couldn't always keep up with what they were doing or where they went.

Ripley lifted her chin in greeting. "George still trying to convince you to try his chili recipe?" She addressed Spencer. "Our Megs makes some of the best chili around. Because of it, people are always pressuring her to try out their famous recipes to see if she thinks they're better than hers. They never are."

It was a bold statement coming from someone who couldn't taste or smell, but I appreciated Ripley's support.

"Actually, it wasn't the chili thing this time," I said, pulling out my phone so if any of my neighbors peered through their peepholes into the hallway, they would think I was on the phone instead of talking to myself. "He was telling me that Mr. Miller in 3B might've been a psychic called Mathias the Medium." I scratched at my neck in confusion.

Ripley and Spencer made up for my lackluster reaction to the unfamiliar name, both sucking in surprised breaths.

"Mathias the Medium?" Spencer asked. "He's, like, a huge deal."

"His commercials were everywhere in the nineties," Ripley explained. "I haven't seen them in a while, so I assumed he'd stopped working. I bet that's why I couldn't go in his apartment," she said, snapping her fingers. "He must've smudged the place or done something else to keep spirits out."

Sitting in the hallway, my back pressed against my door, I propped my phone against my ear. "That would make sense. George couldn't get inside either."

Ripley clicked her tongue. "Imagine that. Another medium in this building the whole time."

I waved my hand back and forth like a head shaking no. "Uh-uh. You know I don't like that word. I see spirits. I don't get messages about people's futures like Mathias did."

"Megs has a bit of a complex about her gift," Ripley told Spencer. "I keep telling her she could totally capitalize on it, but..." She lifted her shoulders and then let them drop.

"There is a difference." I glared at Ripley. "I can't summon spirits, and I definitely can't see the future."

"Not that you've tried," Ripley muttered.

I kicked at the corner of the hallway rug, ignoring her comment. "Anyway, that's not the most interesting thing

77

George told me. He mentioned there was a guy who came into the building earlier today, searching for Mathias the Medium. Art and Darius told him there was no one living here by that name but that he could go in and look."

Ripley pinched the bridge of her nose. "Why do we even lock the doors? We're just inviting murderers inside the building."

Softening, since I knew Ripley worried about me and my safety, I said, "Well, Art and Darius may have let him in, but George followed him. He said the guy kept muttering about how he'd 'make him pay.'"

Spencer's eyebrows jumped. "That sounds ominous."

"Agreed." Ripley frowned. "But how does someone get *that* mad at a man who never left his apartment?"

"Maybe Mathias gave the guy a reading he didn't like," Spencer offered. "My friend Burt's girlfriend left him after she went to see a psychic, and the person told her she was destined to be with a guy who had a lion tattoo. Burt didn't have any tattoos, so she left him. He was pretty broken up about it for a long time."

Ripley and I stared at Spencer.

"What?" he asked. "That's a true story."

I laughed. "We're not doubting that."

"We're surprised that you remembered something about your life," Ripley explained. "That's great, Spencer."

She looked like she wanted to give him a hug but couldn't. The brief interaction probably would've escaped most people's attention, but it made my heart hurt.

"Oh, man. You're right." Spencer swiped his hair to the other side as if his brain might work better if he shifted the weight. "But that's all I've got. I still can't remember my name."

"That's okay." I smiled encouragingly. "The fact that you remembered anything is huge. Maybe things will start coming back to you bit by bit. We're here to help."

There was a noise behind Alyssa's door in 5C. I stood, dusting off the backside of my jeans. "I should probably go inside," I said into my phone. "See you later?" I asked Ripley.

She nodded and stayed with Spencer as I slipped inside. Shutting the door behind me, I leaned back and closed my eyes for just a moment, letting myself sit in the sadness over the loss of Ripley's life and how she wouldn't ever be able to hug another person no matter how much she wanted to.

Moving through the grief for what could've been, I opened my eyes and took in my apartment. After visiting a couple of other apartments inside the Morrisey during my adventures that day, it felt good to be back home. It was late, but after everything that had happened, my mind spun, and I felt wide awake.

If this had been last year, I probably would've pulled out my paints and started a new project. But, unlike the rest of my belongings, which I'd packed up this month as I'd gotten ready to move from New York back to Seattle, I didn't plan on unpacking my art supplies. And even though I felt the loss of art in my gut like a physical hole, my old mentor's words rang in my ears:

"I know it's hard to hear, but I'm saving you a lifetime of hardship. It's better to learn this lesson now instead of after struggling for years, or decades, and making zero headway."

Tucker Harrison hadn't been the first one to tell me I didn't have what it took. Most people who create for a living have scores of anecdotes about folks who said they weren't good enough and would never make it. So, no, Tucker wasn't the first to tell me my art would never sell, but he was the one I'd listened to. The man had not only been my mentor during art school, but he was one of the predominant voices in the New York art scene. If he didn't think I had what it took, I would be silly not to listen. And while I knew quitting art as a career didn't mean I couldn't paint at all, every time I even thought about unpacking my supplies, I felt sick to my stomach all over again.

Making myself a mug of tea, I grabbed a journal Penny had gotten me for my birthday last month and journaled about the day. I hoped that getting some thoughts out of my mind might help me sleep. Sitting at the desk where Penny used to write, I scribbled as I sipped. Before I knew it, I had pages and pages of journaled thoughts about what had transpired today. It wasn't only a recap of the murder and subsequent investigation happening in the building, though. Writing about my interactions with Laurie morphed into thinking aloud about how hard it was to convince the people who loved me that taking a step back from my art was a smart move. They were too close to me and couldn't be objective like Tucker had been.

A gasp sounded behind me. I jumped, tossing my pen up in surprise. It landed with a plunk into my tea.

"Sorry," Ripley said, cringing in apology as I fished the pen out of my, thankfully, mostly empty cup. "I know we have a rule about sneaking."

I clenched my teeth. We did. A very hard-and-fast rule that had helped us remain friends for twenty-four years.

"But I got so excited to see you at the desk, and I thought…" She shot a disappointed glance at the journal. "Oh."

She thought I'd been painting.

Tapping the page in front of me, I said, "Just getting some thoughts down about what happened today." I closed the journal, not wanting her to see what I'd written about my art. I knew I could—and usually did—tell Ripley anything. But somehow admitting my insecurities about my art aloud felt too vulnerable, like taking a treasured item out of its protective box.

"Right. The murder." Ripley twiddled her thumbs. "I've been thinking about that."

I waited for her to elaborate.

"You should try to solve the murder in 3B, Megs." Her eyes sparkled with excitement.

"What? Why?" I leaned back.

Ripley paced through the living room. "Think about it. The killer not only took away our feeling of safety in the Morrisey, which was a jerk thing to do, but they threatened Laurie, who you love. If you solve the case before Detective Perfect, Laurie will fall in love with you for saving his life."

I let out a dry laugh. That was quite the leap. "Rip, I'm not a detective."

Ripley kept pushing. "Detective Anthony might have access to databases, department resources, and maddeningly shiny hair, but we can do things she can't. You can talk to ghosts who might know things living people don't. George is a great example. Darius and Art let the angry guy in the building, so they might've told that to the detective, but they also didn't know he was angry. Only George knew that because he followed him, and only George could do that because he's invisible to everyone but you."

Pursing my lips, I had to admit the woman had a point. "I'm not going to try to outdo someone else for Laurie's interest." I crossed my arms.

"You don't have to," Ripley explained. "Your motivation can be that someone threatened the man you love—"

I tensed.

"Your friend," Ripley amended. "Your friend is in danger, and if your ghostly abilities can help you figure out who wants to hurt him, you can keep him and the building full of people you love, safe." She smirked, knowing I was already convinced.

Laurie likely wouldn't even be in this predicament if I hadn't gotten jealous of him and the detective and blurted out all that nonsense to the waiting crowd. If I could help right the wrong I'd created, I should.

Exhaling, I said, "Okay. I'll try to figure out who killed Mr. Miller and who threatened Laurie, for the greater good."

Ripley bounced up and down with excitement. And even though a fair bit of exhilaration surged through me in that moment, I reminded myself that this wasn't a game. Whoever I was trying to find had killed before, and based on the note they'd left for Laurie, they'd be willing to kill again to keep their secret.

NINE

Ripley followed me into the kitchen as I dumped the remains of my tea. I didn't want to drink it anymore now that it had the added taste of my pen.

"Okay," she said. "Should we talk about who our suspects are?"

I chuckled. "Someone's eager."

"Someone's being cavalier about Laurence being threatened." She shot me a scowl.

"You're right." I coughed, mirroring her serious expression. "Well, we should start with this man George told me about. I'll see if I can get any more information out of him, but it sounds like the man was upset by something Mathias the Medium predicted would happen."

"And if there's one person wacko enough to get mad about something like that, there have to be more." Ripley held up a finger.

I frowned. "What I can't figure out is how he found out Mathias lived here at the Morrisey. I mean, even *we* didn't know."

Ripley nodded. "True. Maybe we could check online and see if there's any trail leading someone here."

"Sure," I said with confidence I didn't have in my ability to follow internet trails.

"And I can ask the other building ghosts if they noticed anything odd," Ripley said. "George can't be the only one who saw something."

"I mean, I doubt Rachel saw anything from the roof."

"Not that she'd tell us anyway," Ripley said flatly.

"And the basement ghosts are a no-go." I cut the air with my palm.

Ripley widened her eyes. "Yeah, they're even creepier than Rachel. Maybe the Squares will know something."

The Pioneer Square gang, or the Squares as we called them, were a ragtag group of ghosts who primarily hung out in Pioneer Square Park, a small urban park in the heart of the neighborhood. They were a mixture of spirits from all different time periods and walks of life.

"True. They could've seen something outside that we didn't." I pulled out my laptop. "I suppose I should start digging into Mathias the Medium, so I can figure out who he was and why someone wanted him dead."

"Okay. Good luck. I'll go chat with the Squares. Don't wait up." Ripley winked.

I DEFINITELY DIDN'T WAIT UP. It turned out that the tea and journaling had done their job quieting my mind because I woke up early the next morning with my chin resting on my chest and my computer still sitting in my lap. Ripley wasn't back yet, so I made some coffee and started over in my internet search.

An hour later, when Ripley appeared in the apartment, announcing herself like she was the husband in a '50s' sitcom, I'd searched through Mathias the Medium's website and social media channels.

"Morning." She floated by and perched on the windowsill.

"You're in a good mood." I cocked an eyebrow at her. "Did the Squares know something that might help us?"

Ripley cut the air with her hand. "Oh, no. They knew nothing. Apparently, that pigeon that attacks people's hair is back, so that's been consuming most of their time."

I patted my head and made a note to walk quickly through the park the next time I went out.

"Spencer and I spent the night walking around Pioneer Square." She flushed. "It was magical."

Biting back a smile so I wouldn't embarrass her, I said, "Well, I'm happy for you. Sounds like a perfect date."

"What about you? Did you fare any better?" Ripley asked, her eyes narrowing into slits as she took in my appearance. "Or did you immediately fall asleep once I left?"

"The latter," I told her. "I looked up his website and social media accounts just now, but I don't see any comments there that would suggest someone was angry with him."

"He probably has someone who monitors them and takes down anything ugly." Ripley studied the ceiling.

"I also couldn't find any way to trace Mr. Miller to the Morrisey," I huffed. "But that's not saying much. I'm definitely better with canvases than I am computers."

I didn't catch my slip right away, but Ripley did. Her mouth twitched at my mention of art.

Moving right past the comment, so she wouldn't read too much into it, I added, "And you're no help since you had that weird dial-up internet." I tapped my fingers on the keys of my laptop as I thought.

"Meg," Ripley said. When I reluctantly turned toward her, she said, "We need to talk." Her tone was as flat as my hair after sleeping on the couch.

Pretending I hadn't said anything about art hadn't worked after all.

I sat back with a groan. "Do we have to?"

"I'm worried about you." She moved next to me.

Grabbing the closest pillow, I picked at the corner. "I need some time to figure things out. It's a big deal to make a new plan when the one you've had your whole life doesn't pan out."

"I wish I'd broken more than that man's easel," Ripley grumbled as her dark eyebrows lowered over her heavily shadowed eyes.

I flinched as she mentioned Tucker. Ripley hadn't been around during my infamous conversation with him about my future in art, thank goodness. She hadn't reacted much better when I'd explained why I was so upset after work that day. She'd transported herself straight to the gallery and had knocked over a few of his paintings, broken his prized easel, and spilled a bunch of paint all over his studio.

In my experience, spirits could send pulses of energy into the physical world. It was highly unreliable and tied to their emotions, making things like picking up a coffee mug almost impossible while knocking things over was easy, especially if a spirit was angry.

The police had paid me a visit the next day since Tucker figured it had been me trying to get revenge for what he'd said.

Luckily, a friend had invited me out to dinner, so I'd had both surveillance footage and credit card proof that I'd been blocks away during the damage, and he hadn't been able to press charges. Still, he was sure I'd had something to do with the mess, so he'd fired me soon after.

Which was another reason Penny's call about the open apartment had come at such a great time. Owning the Morrisey apartment meant my monthly costs were low. As long as I paid my building dues, akin to HOA payments in a neighborhood, I could stay as long as I needed.

"Rip, I'm figuring things out," I reiterated, trying to get through to her by saying the same thing slower and more forcefully.

"Are you?" She exhaled a wry laugh. "Because it looks like you're just sitting in your old apartment playing detective to distract yourself from the enormous decision you made—off one opinion, by the way—to quit the thing you love most in this world."

"Hey!" I snapped. "The detective thing was your idea. And you *know* my favorite thing in the world is animals wearing clothing."

Ripley ignored my comment about animals. "You're right. Maybe I was wrong to suggest it." She stood and walked away from me a for few steps before pivoting and adding, "I guess I thought being back home might kick you out of this faster. But it's clearly way worse than I imagined. So I think it's time for me to get tough with you."

Folding my arms in front of myself, I said, "Oh, really?"

She mirrored the action, narrowing her eyes. "Really. I don't want you to do major damage to your life that you can't undo, kid."

"Kid?" I frowned. "I'm older than you now, and you're not my mom." It was ironic that I was arguing like a child to get my point across about how mature I was.

That comment made Ripley's expression burn with anger. "You're right. I'm not. I'm the reason she's dead, which means it's my job to make sure you don't mess up your life." Her anger smoldered throughout the sentence, but it dropped away at the end. She sat on the couch again, her gaze dropping to her black boots.

My heart broke. "Ripley," I whispered. "We've been over this. You didn't kill my mom."

Sure, Ripley had died in the same car accident that had killed my mother, but she hadn't been driving. Mom had been nine months pregnant with me, and they'd been able to save me with an emergency C-section. I'd been the only survivor of the crash.

I'd spent a long time wondering why Mom's spirit hadn't been the one tethered to mine, why it was Ripley who'd stayed behind instead. I mean, I didn't think there was a greater example of "unfinished business" than a newborn child.

But after showing her picture to as many spirits in the area as I could, visiting Mom's old house and the site of the crash, and begging the universe to let me talk to her even for a moment, I'd come to accept that my mom's spirit must've moved on.

A big tear dripped down Ripley's cheek. "The universe obviously thinks I did. It's why I'm tied to you. I took your mom, so I have to watch over you to make sure you grow up to be the best person you can be. And if you throw away your dream of being an artist, I've failed you."

If she'd had a body, the tears falling from her heavily made-up eyes would've created mascara streaks like nobody's business. As it was, they just disappeared after dropping from her chin, leaving her black eyeliner in place.

I scooted closer. "Ripley, there's no way you could fail me. I'm not sure why the universe picked you for me, but I'm so glad it did."

She reluctantly glanced at me.

Knowing she needed more, I added, "And even if you weren't there, Axel might've still crashed into my mom."

She curled her lip. "True, Axel was the *worst*. I can't believe I went out with him."

Even though he'd been driving like an idiot, speeding and swerving all over the road, and Ripley had tried to get him to slow down, she still blamed herself for getting in that car.

"See?" I said. "Yet another thing I've learned from you. I've never dated an Axel because I know the true dangers of falling for boys whose hair looks like it's wet when it isn't," I said with the utmost seriousness.

Ripley laughed. "He used *so* much gel." She swiped at the tears that were no longer running down her cheeks. "Sorry I got all strict with you," she said, with a big exhale.

"That's okay," I told her. "I know it's because you care."

There were things in my life that I never had to question. The reason I saw ghosts always made sense to me. I'd been born of death. It was no wonder I could communicate with the dead. Ripley had always been by my side, always had my best interest at heart. I knew that deep in my soul. But I also knew that she, Penny, and my Morrisey family were my biggest cheerleaders. They saw the good in everything I did. Which meant there was no way they could be objective about my art like Tucker had been.

Regardless, this wasn't a problem we were going to solve right now.

"Hey, what do you say we wander our way up to Pike Place and get there when they're setting up so we can get one of the first bouquets?" I stood, grabbing my purse and ducking under the strap so it sat across my body. I snatched my keys from the bowl by the door and tucked them into my palm. My gaze flitted to the counter where a vase sat empty.

Aunt Penny had always kept fresh flowers in the apartment. She'd hit it big with her books rather early in my life, so we could spend money on the large, ornate bouquets they sold at the market. I'd gotten used to it as a staple of my life in Seattle.

Changing the subject like this usually elicited exasperation from my best friend. Today, however, Ripley's expression fell, and she sighed. "Okay, Megs. Let's go to the market."

"Wait." I turned my head to the side to get a different view of her, wondering if I was seeing this all correctly. "You're not going to continue to lecture me?"

Ripley chuckled. "Thanks for the vote of confidence."

"Well ... the last few times we've talked about this, it hadn't been this easy to get you off the topic." I opened my palms. The keys sat in my right hand like a peace offering I didn't need in a fight that wasn't happening.

"Yeah, but all those other conversations didn't make a difference, so why would this one?" Ripley placed her hands on her hips. "I've decided that maybe I need to come to terms with your new plan. So, whenever you're ready to talk about what you want to do with your life, I'll be here to listen." She pressed her lips into a thin line.

Because Ripley was so blunt by nature, if she stepped back and showed her more sensitive side, I knew it was usually something she was worried about. To be honest, it was something I was worried about too. But it was a beautiful summer day in the city. Why not enjoy some fresh air?

I smiled as we left. One minor crisis averted, for now.

"See? Getting out is going to be good for us." I told her as we joined the other early weekend risers on the sunny streets of Seattle. Earbuds in place, I held my phone in front of me so I could talk freely. "And even though it's a bit of a hike to the market, it's better than taking the bus where there are weird smells and awkward conversations."

Just as I spoke, a cloud of the mysterious steam that comes out of city vents billowed into my face as I sidestepped to avoid a guy who stopped in the middle of the sidewalk to retie his shoe.

Coughing, I grimaced. "I may have to take back the part about smells."

"Still better than New York and Chicago, in my opinion," Ripley muttered.

"That's because Seattle is part of your soul." I eyed her, noticing she'd let go of the concerned expression she'd been sporting back in the apartment. My attention caught on the glittering Puget Sound as we passed by a street that led down to the water. "It's part of both our souls," I amended with a smile.

"You've got that right." She beamed back at me.

Sometimes our relationship was odd. She'd helped raise me, but she was also my best friend. Over the years, some of her protectiveness had dropped away. But even if I didn't always see it, conversations like the one we'd had back at the apartment reminded me it was still there.

I didn't know how our dynamic would change over the upcoming years or decades, but I was glad she was by my side.

I was feeling more optimistic by the time we reached the entrance to Pike Place Market. Starting at the big bronze piggy bank under the iconic sign, and next to the place where they threw the fish, Ripley and I entered, getting lost in the throng of people. Apparently, we weren't the only ones who'd had the idea to get there right when the place opened.

The market was an interesting mix of covered and open air, growing more enclosed the farther you ventured back. The primary thoroughfare was full of the heavy hitters and neon signs. After the fish market, there were cheese mongers, butchers, deli stands, and the flower market, of course. But if you took a turn down one of the side aisles or ventured to the other pavilions, folding tables replaced the bigger, more permanent stalls, and the signs became more hand-drawn, the wares less flashy but no less valuable.

The place was packed. It was summer, after all, and the city drew quite a lot of tourism. Despite being in a crowded market, I felt a level of anonymity that was almost the same as being alone. Talking to Ripley wasn't a big deal in the sizable crowd because no one around me knew who I was or wasn't talking to.

We picked out a bouquet wrapped in brown paper and paid. We were on our way home when a small table set up down a side aisle in the market caught my attention: Psychic Readings. The sign made me pause.

Ripley, who'd been caught off guard by my sudden stop, raced through me.

She groaned as she let a shudder wiggle its way through her body. "Megs, what were you thinking?" she hissed.

I cringed at the icy shiver that washed through me. "I'm sorry," I hissed back. "I don't like that any more than you do." I pointed the bouquet over to the psychic's stand. "I got distracted by her."

Ripley's eyes widened from the accusatory, annoyed slits they'd been narrowed into. "Oh."

"Do you think..." I chewed on my lip.

She held up her hands. "It's worth a shot."

We walked forward, hoping the psychic was the real deal. Maybe she could help us figure out who'd offed Mathias the Medium and why.

TEN

The single folding table set up in the bustling market was covered with a purple scarf. A few crystals sat next to a stack of business cards. On the other end of the table, a sign told us our psychic's name was Heather, and she could do a yes-or-no reading for five dollars, palm readings for fifteen dollars, psychic readings for twenty, and an aura cleanse for thirty-five. She was flanked by booths on either side: one selling hats and the other with a person who seemed to exclusively sell ceramic dog magnets.

I stopped a few feet away, not sure if this was a good idea. Heather didn't sound like a particularly metaphysical name, but I appreciated her candor. I was a Megan who could talk to ghosts, so I knew a name wasn't a predictor of psychic ability. Mathias the Medium had turned out to be the very plain Mathew Miller, so at least Heather was being honest.

I stepped forward, ready to give her a chance.

Nothing else except the table she sat behind seemed particularly psychic. Heather was probably in her twenties, around my age. She wore jeans and a black North Face fleece. It may have been summer, but it was chilly in the shade this close to the water.

We stopped at Heather's table, and my gaze flicked between her and Ripley, wondering if she could see my ghostly friend. Ripley wore an equally eager look.

But Heather stared straight at me. "Good morning. How can I help you?"

It was the greeting I would expect to get if I walked into a local Starbucks, not stepping up to a psychic's table. I wasn't sure what I was anticipating—a vague warning about my future or a gasp in surprise as I passed by—but Heather's chipper greeting wasn't it.

I shoved my hands in my pockets so I wouldn't be tempted to fidget. "Hi, Heather. I ... well, there's a situation. It's complicated, really, and I—"

"You want to ask me about another psychic," she said, her expression deadpan.

Silence stretched out between us for a few seconds as I caught my bearings.

"Uh, yeah." I blinked. "How'd you—?" I cut myself off midsentence. Right. Psychic. The man next door at the hat booth shot me an incredulous glare, like I must be stupid.

Heather laughed. "I read energy and follow intuition." She pointed to her sign. It wasn't in a *duh, that's what it says on the sign* kind of gesture, but more like a segue into *and here are the services I offer*.

Moving closer to her table as a group of shoppers passed by and jostled me forward, I said, "Well, yes. I was wondering if you knew of the psychic Mathias the Medium."

Ripley snorted. "What, like all the psychics in Seattle get together every year for a Christmas party?"

"Actually, I didn't go to the Christmas party last year." Heather studied me for a moment before giggling. "Kidding! There's no Christmas party." She waved a hand. "We do have annual get-togethers and conferences, but Mathias hasn't gone to those since before I joined the local society."

I didn't know whether it was safe to look at Ripley, but I couldn't seem to take my eyes off Heather. She was still staring straight at me, her gaze not shifting to Ripley once. If she read energy, maybe she was reading both our energies; she just thought it was coming from me.

"Okay," I said, trying to catch up. "But you've heard of Mathias?"

"He's super famous. Of course I have," Heather said. "But he pulled back, decided not to interact with people anymore. Which makes his death even more sad."

"You heard about that?" I leaned forward, palms on the table.

She pointed at me. "I just did."

I sucked in a surprised breath.

"This girl must be super fun to have as a friend," Ripley said sarcastically.

I wanted to elbow her, but I couldn't argue. It was disconcerting to feel like someone was reading your thoughts.

"I'm not reading your thoughts." Heather folded her arms on the table.

"Not a great way to convince me of that." I narrowed my eyes. "Since that's what I *just* thought."

Heather chuckled again. "You have honest energy. I'm getting a clear sense of the topics on your mind. Well, except you have a shrewd inner voice, which is pretty fun. I'd say that worldly inner commentary keeps you balanced. You almost seem to talk yourself in or out of things, depending on what's in your heart."

She thought Ripley was my inner voice. Ripley sent me a knowing look that I'm sure had everything to do with what we'd just been discussing back at the apartment that morning. Not wanting to get into that again, I focused on what she'd said about Mathias.

"So ... Mathias *pulled back*?" I asked. "Does that mean locked himself up in an apartment and never came out?" A group of women crowded around the dog-magnet table, causing me to take a step to the side when one of their large purses jabbed into my ribs.

Heather, who seemed used to the chaotic nature of doing business in the crowded market, simply said, "It's pretty common with folks who have psychic abilities. A lot of times, being around other people is too much. There are techniques that help you shut off or dull your abilities when you don't want to use them, but some people aren't able to turn off their gifts, and being around other people's thoughts and energies becomes too much." Heather's lips pressed into a grim line. "From what I've heard, it all became too much, and he locked himself up."

Remembering back to the fact that neither George nor Ripley could enter the apartment, even though the ghostly rules I was used to meant they should've had no problem, I asked, "Do you think that included spirits too?"

Heather nodded somberly. "I'm sure physical locks on his doors were not the only protections he took to keep living and nonliving souls out of there."

The extra dead bolt in his apartment came to mind. "And you have no idea who killed Mathias?" I asked, peering at her as if she might be keeping the information inside her powerful mind.

"Nope. All I know is that you didn't do it," she said.

Instead of feeling better that she knew I wasn't a murderer, having her read me like that felt disconcerting.

As if sensing I needed more, Heather added, "But I can tell that you're looking for someone who was upset about a reading Mathias may have given them. That's a good place to dig."

"I tried that, but I couldn't find anything on Mathias's website or social media platforms that might point to an angry customer," I explained.

Heather tapped her fingertips against her table. "Did you check Yelp?"

Ripley and I laughed in tandem.

Heather's expression remained serious.

"Oh, that wasn't a joke." I frowned.

"No, a surprising number of people only leave reviews on Yelp." She nodded as if willing me to believe her. "And bad reviews can't be erased there like they can off a website you manage."

I pursed my lips. "Okay, Yelp it is, then. Thank you, Heather." I fished out some cash from my wallet, referring to her sign. We'd kind of done a psychic reading, just a little more intense, so I plopped thirty dollars on her table.

She ducked her head in thanks. "Anytime. Oh, and Meg..."

Pausing in my retreat, I doubled back.

"I have a sense that you're really trying hard to talk yourself out of something." She frowned. "I think you should take another look at why."

I stepped back toward her. "Wait. What?"

"I can't say more." She waved a hand at me. "It's something you need to figure out for yourself."

I staggered away, lost in my thoughts. How could she be so sure I would figure it out? I walked out of the market and took a right turn down a tunneled alleyway that dropped below Pike Place. To my left, tourists posed in front of the infamous gum wall. To my right, Ripley jogged to keep up.

"That was wild," Ripley said as I came to a stop as Post Alley spit us out into the daylight, finally alone. "I have to say, I feel a little offended that I didn't even register as a person to her."

"We're pretty in sync after decades of being around one another. You raised me along with Aunt Penny, so I bet our energies feel very similar." A smile crept over my lips as I started to feel normal again. "Except you're the more shrewd, worldly one of us."

Ripley pretended to buff her nails on her flannel shirt. "That's right. Okay, now I feel better."

"Do you think she's right about Yelp?" I asked, pulling out my phone and opening a browser.

Ripley scoffed. "Wait. That's your takeaway from all of that?"

I moved my gaze from my phone to Ripley's incredulous face. "It shouldn't be?" I asked warily.

She threw her hands up in the air. "The bit about you talking yourself out of something you shouldn't. That's not more interesting to you? Now I don't want to take credit for helping raise you."

Chuckling, I said, "Well, of course that's interesting, but it was also vague as all get-out, and I'm not sure what she was referring to."

"It's obviously your career in art," Ripley said.

I knitted my brows. "It could be that, or it could be about getting involved in this case, or even talking to Laurie, or about getting my hair cut. I didn't tell you, but I was thinking of making a big change." I held my hand up level with my chin. "My point is, we don't know. Plus, my curiosity is getting the better of me about all this Yelp stuff." I typed in Mathias the Medium and then darted a questioning glance at Ripley before I pressed enter.

She crossed her arms and huffed. "Fine. As long as you promise to revisit the other part of her advice."

Holding my pinky in the air, I said, "Pinky promise."

Ripley did the same, touching her ghostly finger to mine, the only effect of which was a chill that surrounded my nail for a moment. Because we couldn't hook pinkies, it was the compromise we'd come up with over the years.

I pressed enter and found a long list of reviews for the telephone psychic known as Mathias the Medium.

"Whoa," I exhaled the word. "Heather wasn't kidding. Yelp is definitely the place people go to leave reviews, especially angry people who want to complain about psychics." I scrolled through the evaluations, landing on my first one star. "This one says he's a fake. The next one complains he killed their cat. Oh, this one's in all caps."

A shiver rushed down my spine. The threatening note tucked under Laurie's door had been in all caps as well.

"Read that one." Ripley moved behind me so she could peer over my shoulder.

"Do not trust this man." I read in my most intense voice without yelling. I didn't want to attract too much attention. "He is a real psychic, but he uses his powers for evil. He read my mind, figured out my bank password, and drained all my accounts. I repeat. Do not trust this psychic. He will steal all your money. It was posted by a man named Evan Grady."

"And Evan lives in Seattle," Ripley said, pointing to the reviewer information.

We locked eyes.

"Maybe he wanted revenge on Mathias. Found out where he lived. And got it." I gulped. "But how did he convince Mathias to leave his apartment?"

Ripley rubbed her hands together. "There's only one way to find out. We need to meet up with Evan."

ELEVEN

A group of tourists moved toward where I stood just outside of the Post Alley tunnel. They'd obviously taken their fair share of pictures in front of the gum wall because they kept checking their phones and passing them around as they squealed and cackled at the photos.

I peered at my phone screen, too, but for a much different reason. I clicked on Evan's name and Yelp profile. "Maybe we should go back to the Morrisey, so I can do this next part on the laptop," I said, squinting at the small screen. "Internet research is hard to do on a phone."

Ripley placed a hand on her hip. "Back in my day, there were only, like, five sites on the internet. We had to do our information finding in person."

"Yes, it was very hard for you back in the Stone Age." I shot her a fake sympathetic pout, hoping to appease her.

She stuck out her tongue and led the way back to the Morrisey. Once we were home, I pulled my laptop over to the couch Penny had left behind for me because "it just fits so well there"—and definitely not because she didn't want to transport all her furniture across the Atlantic Ocean, or that she hated the lumpy futon I'd had in my place back in New York.

"Okay, Evan. Where can we find you?" I hunched over as I peered at the screen and clicked on his profile.

Luckily, Evan seemed to be one of those people who logged everything they loved and hated on the site. I nodded, impressed, as I scrolled through his ratings list.

"Hey," I cried out. "How can he hate on the hot-dog guy that sells Seattle dogs in front of the stadiums, like that? Sure, cream cheese on a hot dog is an acquired taste, but the fact that he didn't like it isn't Joe's fault."

Ripley clicked her tongue in disappointment. "If you get that angry about hot dogs, you can't be a stable person. He's our murderer. Solved it."

I giggled. "I'm not sure Detective Anthony would agree with that investigative proof." Clicking on another review, I said, "Oh, well, he *really* likes this place. Flatstick Pub. It's just a few blocks away."

Ripley read his review. "And he goes every Sunday because they have trivia." Her eyes went wide. "It's Sunday *today*. Oh, they also sell tacos." She shot me a mischievous grin. "Feeling like tacos for dinner?"

"Always. And if it means we can learn a little more about Evan, even better." I paused. "How will we find him? I don't know what he looks like."

Snapping my fingers, I clicked off Yelp and went on to Flatstick Pub's social media account. I combed through their reviews and found one written by an Evan Grady. Clicking on his account, I found a picture of a man in his thirties with very distinctive light eyebrows that matched his swooping blond hair.

My eyes lost focus on the screen for a moment. "I *do* remember seeing him that day. When we gathered around the police tape, he was in the crowd on the third floor. He was talking to Julian. It's very likely that he's also the same guy George followed inside who'd asked for Mathias the Medium."

Ripley sat back on the couch. "See? Done. Solved. We did it. Now we just have to get him to confess over tacos and trivia tonight at this Flatstick Pub place."

"Oh," I said, "there's indoor mini golf."

Ripley stopped short. "What?"

"Flatstick Pub, that's what it stands for. It's an indoor mini golf place with beer and tacos." My eyes widened for effect.

"Okay, I have to agree with Evan. That does sound like the 'best place ever invented,'" Ripley said, following her statement by suddenly sitting forward and clasping her hands together.

I took the motion to mean that she wanted to leave now, so I said, "Trivia doesn't begin until seven thirty, so if we're hoping to run into him, we'll have to wait. Sorry."

"No, that's not it. I mean, yes, I wish we could go now, too, but Megs, I just got the perfect idea." Her face lit up. "You can't go to Flatstick by yourself. Not only would that be sad—"

"Thanks." I shot her a sidelong glance.

"But it would also look suspicious." She turned to me. "If you brought a date, someone who has just as much interest in solving this case as you do, that would probably seem more natural." Ripley waggled her eyebrows.

My stomach fluttered with nerves, because I knew exactly who she was referring to. Despite my apprehension, the thought of Laurie and me playing mini golf made a smile spread across my face.

"I don't know..." I dipped my head to one side. "Doesn't that sound like a date?"

"Would that be so bad?" she asked.

I widened my eyes. "Yes," I answered honestly.

"What are you scared of?"

I held up a finger. "Um, that he only sees me as a friend, and I'll embarrass myself by asking him out. Also, that if everything blows up, I won't just lose a relationship but a close friendship, and that he won't think I'm good enough."

"Like Tucker Harrison?" Ripley asked dryly.

Lips parting in surprise that she would bring that up, I couldn't fight her. She was right. "Touché." Holding up my hands, I admitted, "You're right. Maybe Tucker's feedback messed me up in more ways than I was willing to admit at first. But you heard psychic Heather. It's my mess to clean up. I need to figure it out."

"I can respect that." Ripley nodded.

"And I can admit that having Laurie come with me to the pub sounds fun," I conceded.

"See?" Ripley cocked an eyebrow at me. "I have good ideas."

Rolling my eyes, I asked, "Do I look okay to go talk to him now?" I stood and smoothed my hands down the front of my shorts.

Looking me over like I imagined my mom might've if she'd lived, Ripley smiled. "You look perfect."

"You have to say that. You love me." I tugged at the hem of the shirt.

Ripley stood. "Yes, and if he's smart, so does Laurence. If he doesn't love you just how you are, he's not worth a second more of your time." She lifted her chin.

"Thank you. Okay, that's settled, so I'm just going to go ask out the boy I've loved my whole life. No big deal." I waved a hand.

Ripley chuckled. "You've got this, Megatron." She used to call me that when I was little, trying to convince me I had superpowers like the Transformers, whom I'd loved almost as much as the Ninja Turtles.

Pulling in a deep breath, I grabbed my keys and walked out the door. Dizziness swirled in with the nerves as I wound probably too quickly down the stairs to the fourth floor. I stopped in front of 4B and pressed the buzzer before I could talk myself out of it.

Ripley appeared by my side just as three deep barks sounded from the other side of the door. We glanced at each other, intrigued. The door opened, and there was Laurie, bent over so he could hold on to the collar of a large brown-and-white spotted dog who strained forward, his nails scratching at the wood floors.

"Hey, Meg," Laurie said, puffing out his cheeks with the effort of pulling the dog back. "Sorry about this beast. He's really friendly, but he's young and is still learning his manners. Sit, Leo." He looked down at the dog, who plopped his bottom on the floor, still panting and smiling up at me. "Good warning barks, Leo," he said to the dog.

Leo barked three more times.

Laurie groaned. "We're still working on that command. It's supposed to just be three barks when he hears the buzzer, but I've inadvertently taught him to do it anytime I say warning barks too."

Three more barks spilled out of Leo.

I laughed. "He's very cute." My gaze flicked between the dog and Laurie. "Can I pet him?"

Laurie puffed out his cheeks. "If you don't mind dog slobber or fur."

I sank to my knees. "I don't mind when they come in a package as cute as this." Calling him to me, I opened my arms. "Hi, Leo."

With one last glance up at his dad, Leo bounded forward, slamming into me with all probably eighty pounds of his glorious self. I cackled as I felt blindly for his collar in the tornado of movement. Fingers clasping around the leather collar, I held tight, and used the same firm tone Laurie had. "Leo, sit." His bottom immediately sank to the floor, but energy buzzed through the dog. "That's the most not-still sit I've ever seen." Now that he was more contained, I stroked his head and scratched behind his ears. "He's a very sweet guy."

When I looked up, Laurie was watching me and Leo, his face tight as if he might break into tears. My expression must've turned worried, because Laurie stepped forward and said, "Oh, sorry. I'm just so happy you like him. Many people treat him differently because he's part pit bull, but I should've known you wouldn't do that."

"He's a doll," I said with a lightness in my chest. "Plus, you know me and dogs."

Aunt Penny had always had at least three dogs when I was growing up. The place she'd bought in Scotland had seventeen acres, so even though she only had five canine companions the last time I talked to her, I expected it would rise exponentially by our next conversation.

Laurie nodded. "I still remember that one Penny had ... was her name Bread?" he asked, screwing up his face in question.

"Toast," I answered, giggling as I remembered the sweet black Lab. "She was the best." I squinted one eye. "Speaking of names, is he named after..." I couldn't seem to say it.

"Leonardo." Laurie smirked. "The greatest Ninja Turtle."

Holding up a finger, I made a tsking sound. "Untrue. Michelangelo was the greatest."

"Agree to disagree." Laurie motioned for me to come inside. "Come in. Have a seat. You haven't seen the place for a while." I followed Leo and Laurie inside.

Unlike the very floral-heavy décor his mother had preferred, Laurie's style was all dark woods, grays, and sleek lines. I liked it. While I lived in a studio apartment, Laurie and his parents had a one-bedroom unit. Comparatively, it had always seemed huge. But I knew he'd also used the loft space as a bedroom, just as I had in our studio, so the square footage probably wasn't too much more.

Ripley moved into the space, looking around with the same amount of wonder and awe I felt but was too worried to convey. Instead, I sat on the couch when Laurie gestured to it. Leo jumped up, plopping his top half in my lap. I wrapped an arm around him, hugging the sweet guy to me as he let the weight of his big head settle in my arms.

"No pictures of girlfriends," Ripley sang out happily as she studied each photograph and frame in the place.

Laurie settled into the chair next to the couch, giving me a reason not to pay attention to Ripley. "Leo's another reason I bought this place from Mom and Dad instead of looking elsewhere," he told me.

"That pit bull thing is still going on?" I ran my fingers up the slope of Leo's nose, smoothing the fur between his eyes. He melted even more.

A muscle jumped in Laurie's jaw as he nodded. "It's getting better, but a lot of places still won't rent to you or let you buy a unit if you have a pittie."

"You know that's why Penny landed here in the first place, right?" I said, forgetting if I'd already told him this story.

He shook his head. "No way."

I smiled, glad I hadn't bored him with a story he'd already heard. "Yeah, at the time, she had two rescues, one of which was a pit bull. Most places turned her away immediately. But then she found the Morrisey. 'It was meant to be,' she always said."

Laurie rubbed at his stubbly chin. "The stigma is getting better, but there are still owners who abuse them and use them for the wrong reasons. And there are still people who cross the street when they see us together."

The thought of anyone being scared of either Laurie or Leo made me want to laugh. Unfortunately, I knew the dog wasn't the only part of the equation in that story. Laurie had been treated differently because of his skin color his whole life and had some upsetting anecdotes to prove that even though we'd grown up in the same building, we'd had very different experiences once we stepped outside the safety of our beloved Morrisey.

Instead of gushing about how lovely Laurie was, which could've turned weird fast, I turned my attention toward the dog. "You can't help it that you have big teeth, can you, Leo?" I peeled back his lips and made it look like he was smiling. He licked my face, making me giggle.

It could probably be argued that I was almost too comfortable around dogs. But that was what happened when your only siblings growing up were ghosts and canines. Dogs felt like family to me, just as much as Ripley or the other Morrisey residents.

Leo settled his head in my lap, heaving out an enormous sigh. "Am I remembering right that your parents bought a place on Queen Anne?"

Laurie's eyes lit up. "Yes, and it's Mom's dream house. She said they were lucky to find it at such a good price. It needs some work, but it's beautiful."

"I'd love to see it, and them, sometime soon," I said, feeling comfortable inviting myself over. Martin and Lynae Turner were two of the nicest people I'd ever met. They'd invited me and Penny over many times and had even let us crash a big family party they'd planned on the roof once, which remained the best party I'd ever been to in my life.

"They'd love that," Laurie said.

Ripley, who I'd forgotten was there, made a throat-clearing noise. "Focus, Dawson. Focus."

I blinked. What had I come here for again? Being around Laurie was an intoxicating mix of comfort, hope, and happiness that made me lose all sense of time.

"Oh, right. I came here for a reason," I said. "I was wondering if you had any plans for tonight."

The edges of Laurie's eyes crinkled as he smiled. "Uh, I think I'm free. Why?"

Mustering all my strength, I said, "I learned about this place called Flatstick Pub. I thought I might check it out."

His eyebrows lifted. "Oh, yeah. I've been there a few times. It's really fun."

"It sounded like it. Plus, tacos," I added awkwardly. "And tonight, they've got trivia, not that we'd have to play. We could just watch while we play mini golf. But if you've already been, maybe it's not something you want to do." I grimaced, wondering why I was talking him out of it.

"Oh, no. You're not getting out of it that easily." Laurie patted his flat stomach. "You mentioned tacos and beer. Now you have to take me."

Pressing my lips together so I wouldn't grin like the Cheshire Cat, I nodded. "Okay," I said way too loudly, startling Leo, who jumped off my lap. "Sorry, buddy."

I reached forward and grabbed at the air after him. He went to sit in a dog bed next to Laurie's fancy desk setup. A groan sounded to my right. I didn't need to look at Ripley to know she was probably letting her head roll back out of exhaustion.

Without a dog in my lap, I stood. "Well, I'll pick you up at six, then?"

Laurie nodded. "I'll be ready."

TWELVE

I made it to the stairwell before I let out the squeal of excitement I'd been holding in ever since hearing Laurie's answer to my invitation out that night. It broke my rules about making noise in the stairwell, but I didn't care.

Ripley jumped and danced along with me.

There were so many moments when I wished I could hug my friend, and that was one to add to the list.

She urged me up the stairs. "Okay, stop stalling. We have to get you ready for your date."

I glowered at her. "It's not a date. It's just Laurie and me going out for tacos and beer, and maybe some mini golf."

"*Sure,*" Ripley teased. "Well, I'm going to hang with Spencer on the roof for a bit, then, since a person who isn't going on a date won't need any advice on what to wear."

"Spencer," I said, slapping my palm against my face. "With all the psychic and Laurie stuff, I forgot to ask if you told him about what Opal said."

She let her head drop to one side. "Meh, he was sad. It didn't trigger any memories like I hoped it would. I told him we'd look into newspapers to see if they ever figured out his name."

We definitely could search for that. But there was a wobbly feeling in my gut that told me things still weren't adding up. Like, if Opal's story had been the truth, and it really seemed like it had been, the man only made it into the lobby before he died. How was Spencer able to walk through the hallways and up on the roof? But I didn't want to burden Ripley with those worries just yet.

We parted ways. Once back in the apartment, I picked out a cute summer dress to wear and wound my hair into sock curlers like Ripley had taught me when I was a teenager. That taken care of, I went back on Yelp and read through the one-star reviews once more, even studying the twos and threes, just in case, to make sure we'd found the right guy. Evan remained the only one from Seattle who'd left a review. This had to be right.

"I'm back," Ripley said, announcing herself—as per our agreement—as she wafted into the apartment a while later. "Um, are you looking at the time?" Ripley asked, glancing from me to the clock on the wall.

It was five minutes to six.

Eyes wide, I said, "Omigosh, I completely lost track of time." Panic coursed through me. "What do I do?"

Ripley pushed back her shoulders and took a deep breath.

I followed her example.

"Okay, first, take out the socks." She motioned to my hair.

My fingers grabbed at the tangled and tied mess on my head. "Ouch, ouch, ouch." I peeled them out of my hair, fluffing it out as I dragged my fingers through the curls.

Ripley beamed up at me. "Perfect, as always. Okay, now, get into that outfit."

Doing as she said, I ripped off my clothes and threw on the dress I'd picked out earlier.

"Your face is beautiful, and you don't have time for makeup anyway, but I would run some deodorant over those pits." She waved a hand in front of her nose.

While she couldn't smell, she had a point. I swiped my deodorant under each arm before standing for inspection. I'd read a phrase once that had said, "The best mirror is a friend's eye." Well, I had the best mirror around.

"Perfect," Ripley said, fanning her fingers out as she evaluated my appearance. "Now, don't forget your ID, your phone, or your keys."

I stopped. "You're not coming with?"

Ripley glanced away. "Megs..."

"Of course you aren't." I laughed uncomfortably. "That would be weird." I messed with a long curl. "I just ... I mean, you've always stayed close by on my other dates, and I thought with us looking into the guy who might be a murderer and—"

Ripley fixed me with a serious stare. "I thought you said this wasn't a date."

"Right. Yes. I stand by that," I blurted.

She smiled encouragingly. "I stayed close by on those other dates because I didn't trust those guys. This is Laurie. You're in great, hot hands." She gave me a crisp nod. "As for the potential murderer, see my last statement."

She was right. I was safe with Laurie. It seemed that even though Ripley was the one who couldn't stray too far from me, I had my own invisible tether to her that I needed to work on loosening.

"Okay, don't wait up." I blew a kiss in her direction as I repeated the line she'd used on me last night.

"Literally can't sleep," she called after me. I could hear the grin in her tone.

Laurie answered the door after my first knock. I glanced at his feet, expecting another happy greeting from Leo, but only Laurie's fancy leather loafers waited in the threshold. He'd also changed, now wearing dark-gray khaki shorts and a black polo. He must've put contacts in because his glasses were gone.

"No Leo?" I asked, pushing out my bottom lip.

"He's in his crate. He's still not super trustworthy when I leave. I tried it last month, and he chewed holes in a bunch of my socks." Laurie stepped toward me and pulled the door shut behind him. "But don't worry, because of my work schedule, I never leave him for very long. He also loves his crate. Hangs out in it even when I don't close him in there."

I nodded. "Penny always crate-trained her dogs too. Don't you remember when she had so many that she stacked the little ones on top of the bigger crates?"

"Oh, right." Laurie laughed. "I *do* remember that. It was like puppy Tetris."

We started downstairs. My mind was abuzz with excitement, making me a poor conversationalist. Laurie picked up the slack. Unfortunately, he chose the one topic I didn't want to discuss.

"You know, I searched for you while you were gone," he said. The statement made me shoot him a questioning glance. "I wanted to see what brilliant pieces of art you were creating now that you were a fancy East Coast artist. But I couldn't find any of your art online. Is there a reason for that?" he asked.

"That's a long story," I said, coming to a stop at the landing on the second floor.

"Luckily, we have time." Laurie's handsome mouth tipped

up in the corner as he waited for me to continue down the stairs.

I wouldn't have opened up to just anyone about my art, but Laurie was so easy to talk to. Still, shame and uncertainty surrounded my decision, so I chose the easier parts of the story to tell. "Well, during school there were too many assignments to worry about posting anything online. Plus, they were mostly briefs I had to follow for my professors."

Though all my classmates had started websites in school, I'd held off, wanting to make sure I was only showing my best work. My stomach clenched in discomfort as I realized my issues with confidence surrounding my art might've started before Tucker's advice.

Laurie listened as we pushed our way through the stairwell door and headed through the lobby.

Moving past that realization, I said, "And then, my first job out of school was at this incredible gallery."

"Right. The one in Chicago. It looked amazing." He smiled.

I loved that he had researched the gallery. "It really was. But I wasn't doing any art myself. I was busy organizing shows and doing all the legwork for those. Then a space opened at a gallery in New York, with my mentor from school. It felt like fate. I guess, in a way, it was. That job showed me I'm not cut out for the art world." I waved at the Conversationalists as we walked by their normal hangout spot, glad for the chance to glance away from Laurie while I'd said the hardest sentence in my whole story.

I reached for the front door of the building. But Laurie's big hand reached forward, flattening onto the glass and preventing me from opening it.

"What?" The question cut out of him like it was physically painful.

I couldn't look him in the eye. Instead, I kicked at the entryway mat with the toe of my sandal. "I decided I'm not going to be an artist."

The silence that followed, however, pulled my gaze up out of curiosity.

"Meg." Laurie grimaced. "I'm so sorry. What happened at that gallery in New York?"

Swallowing the terrible taste in my mouth that cropped up every time I thought about that, I said, "Exactly what's supposed to happen to people during the year or so following college. We might find out we have what it takes to survive in our chosen field." I held a hand toward him. "Like you. Or we find out we need to pivot and make a different plan." I jabbed a thumb at myself. "Like I'm doing now."

A muscle in Laurie's jaw tightened as he pulled the front door open. "So that's why you're back?" he asked as we made our way through Pioneer Square Park. "You're starting over from scratch?" Laurie's usual soft tone was still there, but it held a harder edge to it than I was used to.

Smiling up at him with all the nonchalant charm I didn't possess, I told him, "That's the plan. So, tell me how you got into Microsoft?" I asked, changing the subject.

Laurie shrugged, taking a moment to calibrate to the new topic. "It's not much of a story. I went to the U, as you know," he said, referring to the University of Washington. "And once I got out of there, I interned at Microsoft, and here I am." He flashed me a handsome grin as we worked our way through a back alley that would take us to the pub.

"That's the most modest story ever." I shot him a smirk over my shoulder.

In my distraction, I stepped off the sidewalk, not realizing there was about a foot drop-off from that section of the curb due to the old, warped streets. Laurie's eyes went wide, and he lunged forward, catching me before I fell on my face in the middle of the road.

His arms wrapped around me protectively as he pulled me back up onto the sidewalk and waited for a car to pass by.

"Thank you," I breathed out the words. "I've forgotten how manic the sidewalks are around here."

Laurie chuckled. "No problem. I've got you." As he said that, he let go and motioned for me to follow him across the street, holding on to my hand until I was on the pavement.

Internally, my heart was aflutter at the contact. My mind, ever the rational one, had to come in and remind me that Laurie was always this nice and friendly. He would've saved anyone who was about to fall into the road. This behavior was nothing new. Just because he was sweeter than any other guy I'd ever met didn't mean he saw me as anything more than a friend.

Picking up our conversation once more, I said, "As for your work, I can't help but extrapolate that very sparse story. Don't worry. I can see it all. Laurie coming in and revolutionizing everything they used to do and impressing everyone until Bill Gates tries to hand over the keys to Microsoft."

Laurie let out his signature laugh that always made me feel weightless, surrounded by his joy.

"I mean, Bill's not there as much anymore, and there are a lot more keypads than physical keys, but sure." He beamed, stepping aside so a group of rowdy men could pass by us. His hand slipped onto my lower back as he pulled me toward him and out of the way of the group.

I held back the shiver of excitement I wanted to let out, loving walking through the Seattle streets with Laurie.

"Here it is," he said, gesturing toward a sign in the next block, and making me wish this place was at least a dozen blocks away.

Between the uneven streets, and the crowds of people we had to dodge, I longed for a farther walk and the possibility of getting close again. But we had tacos to eat, mini golf to play, and a potential killer to catch.

The entrance to Flatstick took us down a long staircase. After a bouncer checked our IDs, we entered a hot, crowded space where music blared and bumped through hidden speakers. I smiled up at Laurie, who lifted his eyebrows in an *isn't this great?* way.

We got into line for beers, and after ordering our drinks and food, we followed signs for the mini golf station. Even though we wanted to eat first, we paid for our round and got our balls and clubs, setting up at a small standing table near the action. Throughout the space were mini golf holes. They were smaller, but they still had traps and miniature obstacles. The last hole featured a scale model of the Space Needle.

Excited, we watched others go through as we sipped at our beers and ate our tacos once they came out. Wiping my mouth after devouring my meal, I smacked my hands together, dusting them off.

"Okay, Turner. You ready to get mini-dominated?" I gave him my best intimidating stare.

His eyes danced as he teased, "Not if I mini-beat you first."

The next half hour felt like that part of every romantic

comedy when there's a montage of all the fun the two love interests are having, all set to great music. But around hole eleven, the soundtrack screeched to a stop, and my vision blurred a little. A man with blond eyebrows stood around a table with a large group of guys.

Evan Grady.

I'd forgotten that we were really here to do some digging about the murder of Mr. Miller in 3B and whoever had left that note for Laurie.

"That guy owe you money or something?" Laurie whispered, focusing on the same man I was.

Startled, I jumped. For the umpteenth time that evening, heat rushed to my neck. I'd been caught. "I ... uh, he..." I pointed noncommittally in a few different directions, as if it might distract Laurie from Evan.

Laurie fixed me with a glare. "Megs." He said my name as a warning, just like Ripley did any time she was tired of my shenanigans.

My shoulders slumped forward. "I think he might be the guy who killed Mr. Miller and who left you that note."

Laurie's expression darkened, and he leaned down. "What? How? This—"

I grabbed on to Laurie's arm. I wanted to let him finish, but there was no time for that because Evan was storming toward us, anger seeping from every pore on his body.

THIRTEEN

Evan came to a stop about three feet closer to us than I felt comfortable with. But given the red tinge to his pale skin, and the way his eyes darted angrily between me and Laurie, proximity was part of his point.

"Excuse me, but that's mine." He motioned to a green golf ball at Laurie's feet. "My friends think they're hilarious and chucked it across the room," he added, sending a withering glower over his shoulder at his friends who were shoving each other and jeering back at their table.

All the fear that had built up during the time it took for him to stomp over to us left me in an instant. Laurie bent to retrieve Evan's golf ball, handing it over warily. Evan grabbed the ball and jogged back to his friends, grabbing one of them around the neck and rubbing the golf ball on the top of his skull in retribution.

But if I thought I was out of trouble, I was mistaken.

Laurie turned to me, his mouth pressed into an unamused line. "What was that all about?"

Wincing, I said, "Um, did I not mention that I've been doing a little investigating into that case yesterday?"

"You failed to mention that." Laurie crossed his arms.

"Well, I am, and I *may* have discovered that Mr. Miller was a prominent phone psychic, and Evan over there accused him of stealing his banking information and cleaning out his accounts. That, added to the fact that I saw Evan in the building yesterday, makes me fairly sure he's the one who killed Mr. Miller and left you that note." I blurted out the whole story, hardly taking a breath in between words.

The couple behind us finished the previous hole, so Laurie pulled me aside and let them play through.

"So you invited me here tonight to help you look into this guy?" Laurie asked, his shoulders dropping a bit.

Had that been from sadness or relief?

"And to have a fun night out," I added. "But, yeah, I thought you might want to help, especially given that you have a vested interest in finding out who hurt Mr. Miller before they hurt you."

Laurie's throat bobbed as he swallowed. "I mean, yes, I definitely want to help find the creep that did that, if I can, but it sounds like I have some catching up to do." He placed his hands on the tall table next to us as if to ground himself. "So, Mr. Miller was a phone psychic? This is so confusing."

"Tell me about it," I scoffed. "But I don't want to go to Detective Anthony with anything less than a confession from this guy. Mostly because, without that, it all sounds pretty ridiculous."

Laurie let out a reluctant chuckle and then glared at me as if he were mad at me for making him laugh when he was supposed to be cross with me. "How'd you find out Mr. Miller was a psychic?"

I chewed on my lip. It wasn't as if I enjoyed lying to Laurie. But there were just things I couldn't share with him, like my abiding love for him and also my ability to talk to ghosts. I mean, even Aunt Penny didn't know the truth about the spirits. She'd explained away my propensity to chat with thin air as a child as my way of coping with the loss of my mother. Penny had called Ripley my invisible friend and I'd never corrected her. I'd thought about telling both Penny and Laurie the truth about my gift over the years, but I always stopped myself at the last minute, unable to take the possibility that they would look at me differently or think I was losing my mind.

Which meant I couldn't tell Laurie how I'd found out that Mr. Miller was actually Mathias the Medium. George had given me that information. But thinking of the unofficial third member of the Conversationalists gave me an idea.

"Evan came into the building on Saturday asking for a Mathias the Medium. Art and Darius told him there was no one by that name, but they said he could look around," I explained.

Luckily, Laurie seemed to be focused on the lack of security in our building, just as Ripley had been, instead of focusing on where I'd heard the information.

He scratched at his temple. "We've really got to do something about how many people they let through that front door."

"Yeah. Anyway, Evan came in looking for Mathias, and then Mr. Miller turns up dead. Not a coincidence, if you ask me." I went on to explain the Yelp review that led me here, and how Evan had accused Mathias of cleaning out his bank account.

Laurie tapped his mini golf club against the toe of his shoe as he thought. "That *does* sound like he wanted revenge. Which means we need to figure out how to get Evan to confess." The determination in Laurie's expression made me a little worried and in awe all at the same time.

Ripley had been right. Involving Laurie in all this had been a good idea. She was going to love hearing that.

Rubbing his hands together, Laurie faced me and leaned in close. "Okay, we have the upper hand here because we know more about him than he knows about us."

"Sure," I said, positive I would agree to whatever Laurie said when he was this near to me.

"Do you think you can follow my lead?" He caught my eyes with his.

I swallowed and nodded.

Laurie jerked his head to the right. For the second time in so many days, I followed behind him. I just hoped, this time, we wouldn't be stumbling on any more bodies.

LAURIE DID a weird serpentine around the pub. I wasn't sure if he was walking in such a surreptitious pattern for a reason or just because the place was packed. It was closing in on seven thirty, when the trivia was set to begin. Teams had established their home base tables, and a woman was setting up audio equipment in the corner.

We still held our mini golf clubs in one hand, clutching our individual golf ball in the other. That was, until Laurie stopped, plucked the ball from my hand and tossed it a few yards away.

"What?" The question burst out of me before I had a chance to stop it.

Laurie shot me a *go with it* look. Oh. That must've been part of his plan.

The ball bounced around the feet of the same group of guys, now seated in a big booth. The closest guy to us was Evan Grady. I stifled a grin as I trotted after Laurie.

"I'm so sorry. It looks like it's our turn." He let out a good-natured chuckle and waited while the guys in Evan's group kicked the thing around, trying to stop it as it rolled around under their table. While his friends were occupied, Laurie pointed at Evan. "Hey, I think I recognize you."

Evan, who'd been focused on filling out his team's trivia answer card, flicked his eyes up at Laurie in annoyance. "Yeah, I just saw you over there." He gestured to where we'd been standing with the small golf pencil he'd been writing with.

Laurie shook his head. "No, from yesterday. You were at our building." He widened his eyes. "The crime scene."

At that, Evan focused on Laurie, only breaking his stare to look at me for a moment.

"Did the cops talk to you yet?" Laurie asked conversationally. "They questioned us multiple times. Made me feel like I was the killer. I didn't want to get my story wrong."

Evan faked a laugh. His pale skin glowed pink, and his eyes shifted from us to his group. They'd just retrieved my golf ball. Evan snatched it out of his friend's hand and said, "I'll be right back, guys." He slid out of his seat, pushing us away at the same time. "What are you talking about?" Evan hissed once we were a few yards away from his friends. He shoved the golf ball in our direction.

Laurie whispered, "Sorry about that back there, man. I didn't know how to get you away from your friends so I could warn you." He held up the golf ball as evidence that it had been his plan all along.

"Warn me about what?" Evan took a step back, but he realized he was blocking the hallway to the bathroom, so he had to move closer to us once more.

"The cops," Laurie repeated, glancing at me.

"We recognized you from the scene yesterday, when you came to get your golf ball," I said. Outwardly, I worked on remaining calm. Inside, I was buzzing with energy, hoping I didn't mess it up. "And we thought we'd warn you that everyone who was at the scene is getting questioned, so you should get your story straight."

Evan blinked and coughed.

Laurie placed a hand on his shoulder. "Look, man, we all hated the guy, so no hard feelings if you took him out."

"Yeah, he told my friend that the man she was destined to be with had a tattoo, so she broke up with her boyfriend of seven years because he didn't have any tattoos and didn't want to get any." I borrowed Spencer's story and channeled Ripley's energy for my character. "Now she's miserable, and I was supposed to be the maid of honor at their wedding."

"What did he do to you?" Laurie asked.

Evan's gaze moved between the two of us. He seemed in shock. Then he finally croaked out, "How do you know he did something to me?"

"The guys at the door," I lied innocently. "They said you were really mad and were looking for Mathias. Don't worry. You're not the first angry customer to come looking for him. We're used to it."

"Though, if you killed him, that *would* be a first. And last." Laurie sobered. "Sorry, I know that's dark. It's just that the guy stole my bank account number and password. He cleared out my savings." He narrowed his eyes, repeating what I'd told him about Evan's Yelp review.

"He stole your money too?" Evan blurted. He ran his fingers through his hair, his blond eyebrows furrowing together. "Man, I can't get anyone to believe me, but maybe now that you had the same thing happen, we can—" He cut himself off midsentence.

My pulse doubled instantly, sure he'd caught onto us and was about to run.

But then he said, "It's useless now that he's dead. We won't get any of our money back now."

Laurie paused, taking a moment to recalibrate. "So, you weren't the one to kill him?"

Evan shook his head.

"Then why were you there yesterday?" I asked, annoyance slipping into my tone.

If Evan noticed, it didn't bother him. "I thought I could reason with him in person. I was sick of dealing with his assistant."

My ears perked up at that. "Assistant?"

"I'd been emailing with the assistant for weeks about my money, but I finally got the guy on the phone," Evan explained. "Talking didn't help. After that conversation went nowhere, I got desperate and posted on a pretty shady forum, asking if anyone knew Mathias's address. It only took two hours before I had an answer, and I only got that once I paid for it. And it turned out I wasn't the only one who wanted the information. Someone else commented on my post, saying he'd pay to learn the address too."

"Who?" I asked.

Evan looked at me in disgust, like I was too naïve to be a part of this conversation. Laurie glanced over, narrowing one eye at me in a way that told me it wasn't something we could find out.

Right. If people were on a dodgy forum, they probably weren't using their real names.

"PPP1979 was the other guy. If you ask me, the person who ended up giving us Mathias's address was the assistant I'd been talking to." Evan leaned in close. "He just wanted me to pay for it."

"Why would he do that?" Laurie asked.

Evan snorted. "Hated Mathias. When I finally got him on the phone, he told me to drop it. He said his boss was a jerk, and he wouldn't budge, so I should stop wasting my breath."

"He said Mathias was a jerk?" I cocked my head.

"That's not all he said," Evan scoffed. "The guy ranted about how Mathias basically ruined his life."

"And you're sure it wasn't just Mathias pretending to be his own assistant?" Laurie asked.

"Not unless he was really good at changing his voice. Mathias had a deep voice during our call, but Kenny's was much higher. He sounded younger too." Evan shrugged.

I drummed my fingers on my leg. "Kenny. Did you get his last name?"

Evan pulled out his phone. "It was at the bottom of the first email response he sent me." He scrolled through for a moment before saying, "Kenny Knapp."

"Thank you." Laurie gripped the mini golf club and tensed like he was ready to leave.

"I don't think it's worth it, if you ask me," Evan said. "I didn't get anywhere talking to Kenny. I doubt you will."

Laurie lifted his chin in response and said goodbye. We wandered down to the mini golf equipment counter and returned our clubs and balls. Even though we hadn't finished our round, there was an unspoken agreement between us that we needed to leave.

Evan might not have been our killer, but he'd given us two more possible suspects: Kenny, the assistant who hated his boss, and the mystery person on the forum who'd also paid to find out where Mathias lived.

FOURTEEN

After being inside the bright, loud pub for so long, the nighttime air felt luxurious, and the normally crowded city felt practically deserted.

It was because of that relief I didn't notice Laurie wasn't next to me as I crossed the street. Stopping next to the Waterfall Garden, I turned to find him. He'd paused in the middle of the sidewalk, the light of his phone illuminating his handsome features in the setting sunlight.

"Is everything okay?" I checked the road before jogging back over to the other side of the street.

Expression softening, Laurie said, "Oh, sorry. I have a coworker that was talking about some site where he found a virtual assistant. There's some kind of database. I was just texting to see if he could send me the link."

Snapping my fingers, I said, "Ah, because since Mathias was a recluse, Kenny must've been a virtual assistant and he might be listed there."

Laurie nodded.

"A jaded assistant getting revenge on his jerk boss sounds like a good motive for murder," I said, then immediately wanted to take it back. "Sorry, that's a really callous way to talk about someone we've lived around for years getting killed."

Laurie playfully ran his shoulder into mine. "It's okay. I know what you meant. It's hard to see him as a real person, though. He's been such a myth our whole lives."

I turned to leave, but Laurie reached out and took my hand. I stopped, glancing back at him.

"What's going on?" I asked, my voice barely a squeak. Was it just me, or did Laurie seem like he wanted to kiss m—

"Meg, I tried not to say anything in there because I didn't want to ruin the fun but..." His shoulders slumped forward as he rubbed at his arm, unable to meet my eyes.

Okaaay, so not a kiss.

His flighty gaze finally locked on to mine. "I just can't believe you're quitting art. What are you going to do instead?"

"Not you too." I groaned.

He scratched at his nose, hiding a smile. "I'm guessing Penny isn't taking the decision well?"

Coughing, I said, "Yeah, she's not thrilled." The truth was, Penny was the least of my worries. I was much more affected by the ghost chirping in my ear all day, every day.

"I can't imagine Meg Dawson not being a famous artist." He ran his knuckles along his stubbly jawline. "You're so talented, and I just want to know what happened in New York that made you decide that wasn't the truth."

Letting out a long exhale, I told him, "Laurie, it's so kind of everyone in my life to root for me so fiercely, but none of you can be objective about my art. You, Penny, everyone at the

Morrisey, you're all too close to me. What happened is that I heard the truth from real professionals in the field."

We started walking again, moving in silence for a few moments as we paid attention to where we were stepping on the jarring Seattle sidewalks.

"I think maybe it's more about you giving up." Laurie finally broke the silence just as the Morrisey came into view, all warm, yellow light spilling out, reflecting off the gold pieces edging the lobby windows.

"I don't see it like that." I stretched my arms out as I admired our building. "It's a fresh start."

Laurie's phone beeped, and he unlocked the screen. "My coworker just sent me a reply. I've got the website." His eyes shone with excitement.

"Do you want some company while you search for Kenny? I mean, you can obviously do that on your own, or maybe you need to get to bed." I glanced at my watch, noticing it was only eight. Embarrassment crawled over me. Laurie was a twenty-five-year-old guy. He didn't go to bed at eight on a Sunday night. What was I thinking?

He held the front door open for me. "I'd love company."

I smiled as I walked inside, reveling in the familiar scent of the Morrisey lobby. Over the years, I'd come up with the perfect way to describe it. It was 50 percent antique store, 20 percent library, 10 percent bakery—from Nancy, 15 percent floor wax, and the final five was rosemary.

Everyone agreed that the lobby smelled like rosemary, yet no one knew why. Well, Ronny Arbury told a very unconvincing story about a Thanksgiving dinner gone wrong back in the eighties, but no one took him seriously. That was what happened when your favorite hobby was improv acting, and all your neighbors knew it.

Waving to the Conversationalists, Laurie and I headed toward the stairwell. At the bottom of the stairs, however, Laurie turned to look at me and raised an eyebrow. I knew exactly what that meant. A race.

I slid my left foot back to give myself a better starting position.

"Go!" Laurie called.

We shot up the stairs, taking two at a time and pulling ourselves up with the railings along the side.

"This isn't fair," I said with a cackle. "Your legs are twice as long as mine now."

The truth was it had never really been fair. In all our races over the years, I'd only ever beaten him twice. Both those times had been before he'd hit his big growth spurt in middle school.

He let out a maniacal laugh and vaulted up to the next platform. "It's been part of my plan all along."

Two flights later, we stood, panting at the door to the fourth floor. I rested my hands on my knees as I buckled forward to wheeze. Laurie's large palm claimed the fourth-floor door. His chest heaved up and down.

"Man, that was easier when we were teenagers." He winced.

Needing all my breath for my burning lungs, I didn't even attempt words. I simply nodded and staggered forward, toward the door. Laurie pulled it open for me, and we slipped into the fourth-floor hallway.

We took a brief break from the investigation as we let Leo out of his crate and took him out to do his business. Minutes later, however, Leo and I were seated on the couch again, and Laurie clicked away at his large computer.

I surveyed the room while I waited. Propped against the arm of the couch, a blue and silver metal baseball bat caught my eye.

"Omigosh, is this the one we used to play with on the roof?" I grabbed the bat and examined it as Leo picked his head up off my lap and surveyed it along with me.

Laurie let out an embarrassed laugh. "Uh, yeah. It is."

We'd gotten really good at playing rooftop baseball, mostly because we'd given up on regular baseballs—after losing way too many over the side of the roof—and had switched to the much safer Wiffle ball.

"You playing again?" I asked, a teasing grin taking over my lips.

His gaze cut over to the door, where another bat was propped by the entry closet.

I covered my mouth with my hand. "Oh, Laurie. It's because of the threat, isn't it?" My heart hurt. "I'm so sorry. I didn't mean to make light of it. Seeing this just made me remember all those times we would practice on the roof, pretending we were starting for the Mariners."

Laurie dipped his chin. "It's okay, Meg. I wanted to have a little protection, just in case." He let out a low hum. "But remembering your powerful swing, what I *should* do is have you follow me around for protection."

I puffed out my chest, then said, "I was pretty good, wasn't I? I think I was mostly excited that I'd found something I could beat you at, since I hadn't won a stairwell race in years."

"Well, maybe we'll have to revive that competition too since I just got another win in the stairwell." Laurie shot me a smirk before returning to poring over the information on the screen.

"Okay, I found the assistant." But any tension that had been evident in Laurie's posture leaked out as his gaze caught on something on the page.

"What?" I tried to move off the couch, but Leo weighed too much and he pinned me to that spot.

"Kenny Knapp lives in Louisiana." The flatness to Laurie's voice made it sound like he was a balloon that had lost all its air.

"Oh." I adopted a similarly bleak tone.

Even Leo's cute, floppy ears drooped.

"So he couldn't have been the one to kill Mathias unless he flew here," I said.

"Right." Laurie pushed his chair back from his desk and ran a hand down his face.

I was about to set the bat down and peel Leo off my lap so I could head home, when there was a knock at the door, causing Leo to jump off me anyway while he let out his standard three warning barks.

Laurie and I froze. His surprised expression told me he hadn't been expecting anyone. Swallowing, I gripped the bat tighter. Laurie moved toward the door, grabbing the other bat. Leo barked again, making me feel safer. Even if he was the sweetest guy, those three warning barks sounded intimidating.

Holding the bat low, Laurie peered through the peephole. I waited behind him, holding on to Leo's collar with my free hand, fingers tightening around the leather with each passing second. Laurie exhaled, stepping back to open the door.

Ronny Arbury stood on the other side. "Evening, Laurence." He saluted him for some reason. "Oh, and Meg. Great. Just passing along word that Nancy is calling for an emergency building meeting. Downstairs, in the lobby." His attention settled on the bat in my hand, and his jaw jutted back in surprise.

Ronny was in his forties and, despite being the deli manager at a local grocery store, maintained he could "hit it big" in Hollywood at any moment. Because of that belief, he treated any encounter with people as an audition and strove to prove he could act his way out of "any type of bag." Sweet as the man was, reading a room wasn't on his list of positive attributes.

"We'll be right down, Ronny. Thank you." Laurie saluted back before closing the door.

It was that kind of thing that had made me truly fall for Laurie. Instead of teasing Ronny or making him feel awkward for the salute, he did it back, making Ronny feel like it had been the right thing to do.

"An emergency meeting? What do you think that's about?" Laurie asked as he deposited the bat back behind the door. He took Leo from me and settled him in his dog crate with a biscuit.

I returned the bat I was holding to its place next to the couch while he did so. "It has to be about Mr. Miller. Right?"

"There's only one way to find out." Laurie's eyes flashed with intrigue and we started for the door.

Ronny, Wendell, Paul, and Mrs. Porter joined us in the hallway. The door of 4E swung open with a flourish, and Winnie Wisteria swooped out of her apartment as if she were stepping foot onto a stage. None of us actually knew much about Winnie—if that even was her name. We all just assumed she had to be a local actress, but if you ever asked her anything concrete about her life, she made up an excuse and left immediately.

"I never realized it before, but your floor is very actor-heavy," I whispered to Laurie as he locked his door behind us.

He grinned. "It really is."

Wendell, not an actor but the owner of a disturbing number of snakes, held the stairwell door open for everyone, and we shuffled downstairs. In times like these, when we knew everyone would convene in the lobby, we tried to reserve the elevator for Mrs. Feldner on my floor and the Rosenblooms on the third floor. My floor mates, Quentin, Bailey, and Alyssa joined us in the stairwell, as they wound down the stairs from the floor above.

Everyone merged toward the bottom of the stairs, the chatter among the residents growing in volume. It sounded like everybody was in the dark about the topic of the meeting, though that didn't stop them from making loud conjectures, which only increased in volume as we all bottlenecked at the stairwell exit into the lobby.

The second-floor people were helping Nancy as we arrived. They'd already moved the big table out of the way, so the rest of us got to work putting out folding chairs. Together, we had everything settled in a few minutes. Nancy stood at the front of the group, forgoing her podium. Given that clue, and the fact that we were approaching her bedtime—she already had curlers in her hair—this had to be an emergency.

"Morrisey, Morrisey." She put her hands out and pumped them up and down.

People quieted down, ready to listen to what this was all about.

"I've just had a call from Detective Anthony," Nancy said.

A few gasps escaped the rows in front of me and Laurie.

Nodding along with their surprise, Nancy said, "She informed me that the body in apartment 3B was, in fact, Mathew Miller." Nancy flicked an index finger in the air amid the inhales and exclamations that followed, showing there was more. Once it had quieted significantly, she added, "Even more shocking was learning the reason his fingerprints were on file was because he got caught running a con as Mathias the Medium, back when he was younger, some kind of psychic persona he created. But apparently, that nonsense didn't stop. He's been running a phone psychic hotline out of that apartment for decades, right under our noses." She shot a meaningful glance at the people sitting in the front row.

"You're telling me I spent two hundred dollars calling that Phillip phone psychic when I had one in the building?" Shirl Rosenbloom asked with a frustrated sigh.

"The man in 3B was psychotic?" Edna Feldner yelled from the second row.

"Psychic," Art yelled from where he sat next to her.

Darius shrugged. "But we probably can't rule out psychotic too."

Nancy put a hand on her hip. "I will not have you talking about the dead like that. You know better, Edna."

Mrs. Feldner frowned and looked at Darius, who smiled sweetly in her direction.

"I have something to admit." Ronny Arbury stood.

We watched him with bated breath.

"Laurence isn't the only one who saw Mr. Miller." Ronny gestured toward Laurie. Everyone whispered and glanced toward us. Ronny steepled his fingers, bringing them up to his lips. "I saw him the day he died. He was taking his trash to the chute, and he told me his life was in danger."

"What?" someone yelled.

"I live on the third floor, and I've never seen him taking out his trash," Bethie scoffed.

"Why didn't you say something?" another person called out.

Laurie asked, "Did he say why he was in danger or how he knew?"

Ronny fidgeted for a moment, like what he was about to say was going to be very difficult. "Actually, I lied. I never saw him. Sorry, I'm preparing to play a character who stretches the truth, and I needed to practice it in a large group. Thank you." He bowed forward.

Angry exclamations flew toward Ronny, who pouted as if he was offended and sat down.

"This is why no one believes you about the rosemary," Julian called out once the rest of the insults had died down.

"We should be more alarmed that there's a killer among us rather than focusing on the dead psychic," Winnie Wisteria said.

"Winnie's right." Quentin stood. "Isn't it a bad idea for us to be all in one place like this? We're so easy to find."

"The killer can't take us all at once. We should *always* be together, I say. Safety in numbers," Hayden shouted. A smattering of applause followed his statement.

"This is a complete mess," Laurie whispered to me, his closeness sending a shiver up my spine. He stood. "Everyone, Detective Anthony seemed incredibly competent. I'm sure she will catch whoever did this to Mr. Miller, a murder which was most likely personal, so the rest of us don't need to worry. We're safe."

About half the crowd calmed at Laurie's words. The other half huffed in disagreement. I sat somewhere in between.

Had that speech been for the sake of the residents, or was that really how Laurie felt? He and I had *just* been researching the case before this. Did he want to stop? Had we hit a dead end in his mind?

Behind me, I heard Wendell whisper, "*We* might be safe, but I heard Laurence got a threatening note from the killer."

I swallowed the lump in my throat, wishing this hadn't just gotten so much more complicated.

FIFTEEN

After the emergency building meeting, I helped put away my fair share of chairs before sneaking off to the stairwell while someone chatted with Laurie. I needed some space to think about what had just happened.

When I entered my apartment, Ripley stood by the window, looking out over the late-night wanderers through the streets of Pioneer Square. It was our favorite time to people-watch.

"How was the date?" She raced over to me with a smile as wide and hopeful as mine had been earlier.

Plopping my purse on the table next to the door, I sighed. "It wasn't a date."

Ripley stopped short and checked the clock in the kitchen. "It sure seems like a date, if you've been gone this long."

"We've been at a building meeting for the past half hour." I heeled off my shoes and went to collapse on the couch, face-first.

"I missed a building meeting?" Ripley whined. "You should've called me."

I peeled my cheek from the couch cushion, shooting her a scowl. She knew as well as I did that there was no way to call her to me.

"Sorry," Ripley said. "You know, I honestly thought things were going well since you went to a second bar. Where did you go after Flatstick?"

"Huh?" I used my arm to prop myself up.

Ripley blinked. "You had to have gone to a second location farther north because Spencer and I went to see this great band playing at Neumos, and I've never been able to go that far before."

I shook my head, sitting up. "We were at Flatstick, and then we came back here."

"That means..." Ripley paced by the window.

She didn't need to finish the sentence. The tether was getting longer. And while that news usually made me happy—I wanted Ripley to have her freedom—tonight, it was just one more punch to the gut, one more reminder that I might be alone forever.

Ripley moved to sit next to me on the couch. "Hey, let's return to this not-date date you two had. What happened? Was he mean?"

I let out a dry laugh. "Not even close. He was perfect."

"So, what's the problem?" She leaned forward so she could see my expression better.

My hands lifted and fell into my lap in a gesture of defeat. "He's just nice. He's perfect without trying. When he says lovely things, it's because he's Laurie, not because he has feelings for me that extend beyond friendship."

"Hey, that's not necessarily—"

"It is. He complimented me a bunch tonight, and we even

worked on the case a little together once we figured out that Evan Grady couldn't have been the one to kill Mr. Miller. But then at the meeting, he said all these nice things about Detective Anthony too. Then he told the residents that she's smart and capable, and we should leave the case for her to solve. So ... message received."

Ripley chewed on her lip for a moment. "Jealousy really isn't a good look on you, babe."

"I'm not jealous." I shot up from the couch but turned back toward her. "Well, maybe a little. Mostly, I'm confused. Laurie's never been one to play games. I'm not sure what to think since he seemed totally into the investigating we did after we got back from the pub, only to say the exact opposite at the meeting." I pressed a thumb into my aching temple.

"Maybe he just said that for the sake of the Morrisey folks. He probably doesn't want them to think you two are working on figuring out who did this, especially since he got that threatening note." Ripley's voice held a hint of a pleading tone, telling me she really thought I should assume the best intentions of Laurie rather than jumping to the worst possible conclusion.

She had a point. I sank back onto the couch. "Yeah, maybe you're right. But it still doesn't change the fact that he's never going to see me as anything but Meg, his childhood friend."

"Or, and hear me out, have you possibly placed Laurie so high on that metaphorical pedestal, you don't think you'll ever compare?" Ripley cocked an eyebrow at me.

"What pedestal?" I snorted.

"I seem to remember you having Tucker Harrison on a very similar—"

I shot a glare in her direction.

She held up a hand. "*Non*-romantic, but you had him on a

similarly high pedestal. Is it possible that you're letting yourself believe nothing could ever happen with Laurie because you can't handle being rejected again by someone else you idolize?"

"Ouch." I winced.

"Laurie's a person, flawed just like all of us," Ripley said.

I plopped a pillow into my lap and punched my fists into it for a moment. "I wish it wasn't so late, or I would march down to the market and see if I could talk to Heather about this."

"Maybe you don't need to." Ripley settled next to me on the couch.

I gasped. "You're right." I stood and rushed over to my purse to grab my phone.

"Wait. I meant that you don't need to because you should trust yourself to solve these issues alone, without the help from a psychic." Ripley stood warily. "What are you doing with that phone?"

"I don't need Heather because there's someone else I can call. And I'd bet they don't care that it's so late." Pulling up a browser, I searched for *Phillip Phone Psychic*. "Downstairs, Shirley Rosenbloom made some offhanded comment about how she couldn't believe she'd called some guy named Phillip when there was a psychic in the building the whole time. Maybe Phillip can give me some answers."

Ripley made a throat-clearing noise. "Um ... Megs, I don't know how to put this, but I definitely don't think you should be making life choices based on a psychic's advice, especially not one you talk to on the phone."

"You were all for it when we talked to Heather." I clicked the link that came up: phonephortunesbyphillip.com. Twenty minutes was only twenty dollars. Shirl must've talked to the guy for a long time to rack up a bill of two hundred dollars.

"Yeah, but don't you remember Spencer's warning about his buddy's girlfriend, who broke up with the guy because he didn't have a tattoo?" Ripley groaned. "I was all for you listening to Heather when it was about checking Yelp reviews. I'm less excited about it now that you're looking for a yes or no answer about whether Laurence likes you. Are you ready to be the main character in a similar cautionary tale?"

"Asking doesn't mean I have to listen to the answer," I argued.

Ripley cocked her head in silent dispute, but she didn't leave. In fact, she came up behind me and read over my shoulder. "Ugh, he spells fortunes with a ph? Gross."

I moved across the room even though I knew it was just a temporary solution, and pressed on the link to pay for a twenty-minute phone call. Once I'd input my payment information—including an extra charge for an "after midnight" fee, which told me he was probably on the East Coast—the line rang. I put it on speakerphone.

"This is Phillip," a man answered the call. "What fortunes do you need told on this ... er ... day?" He stumbled over the last part, as if he'd rubbed at his eyes and looked out the window to see only darkness.

"Hi, there. My name is Meg, and I have a question about love." My voice shook with nerves as I spoke.

"You're not supposed to tell him that," Ripley hissed as she stormed over. "If he's a real psychic, he should know that stuff."

I stuck my tongue out at her like the mature woman I was.

"So, Meg," Phillip said, bringing my attention back to him. "You have a question about love. I must let you know that love is one of the more difficult emotions to read. I can attempt to answer your questions, but please know that my visions have limits in this area."

I swallowed. "That's okay. I understand." Pulling in a steadying breath, I said, "There's a guy I've liked forever. That's not even an exaggeration. I've loved him my whole life. We grew up together, which is part of the problem. I think he'll never see me as more than a friend."

"Okay," Phillip said contemplatively.

"And I've just moved back to the same building, so I'm seeing him again after five years apart. I thought it might be a new start for us, but something happened tonight that tells me he won't ever see me any differently."

"Can you tell me what happened?" Phillip asked.

Ripley glared at me, clearly unhappy with him asking for more information, but she didn't voice her concerns.

"We went out to a local pub. You see, there was a murder in our building yesterday, and we were investigating into someone we thought might've been the killer," I explained.

Ripley held her thumb and index finger up, closing the space in between them to show me I needed to shorten my story. I blabbed when I got nervous.

I continued. "We had a good time, and he seemed excited to look into the crime with me, but then we had a building meeting about the death, and he told everyone we should leave it to the police."

"Ah, would this be at the Morrisey? In Seattle? You're referring to Mathias the Medium's death?" Phillip asked, an edge to his tone.

I blinked. "How'd you—"

"I'm a psychic, remember?" he snapped harshly through the phone.

His words made goose bumps form on my arms.

Ripley threw her arms up in the air, then whispered, "Or he searched for your area code, and the death made its way into the papers already."

"I can answer your question, Meg." Phillip had returned to his calm demeanor. "I'm getting a powerful feeling that you should not investigate into this man's death in your building any more than you already have. Doing so would not only put your life in danger but would jeopardize Laurence's life as well. As for Laurence, I rarely get this strong of a reading when it comes to love, but the man is clearly only interested in friendship from you. He hasn't said anything to you about it because he values you as a companion and doesn't want to lose that aspect of your relationship. If you try to take things further, however, I believe he will completely shut himself off from you and you'll lose him forever."

His words were a punch to the gut, but one of them in particular made everything shift around me. "How'd you know his name was Laurence? I never told you that."

Phillip let out a tired exhale. "Meg, how many times do you need me to repeat it? I'm a psychic. Honestly, most people are happy to hear they're getting the *real deal* in exchange for their coin," he snapped. "Well, you still have time left. Is there anything else you'd like to ask me?"

If I'd thought hearing Laurie's name leave the man's lips was chilling, it was nothing compared to hearing him say the word *coin* instead of *money*.

Pulling in a shuddery breath, I said, "No, that was it. Thank you." I disconnected the call, dropping onto the couch before letting my phone slide through my fingers.

"Meg, that guy might've known a few names, but that

doesn't mean he knows anything about you and Laurie." Ripley raced over to sit next to me.

Gulping, I managed to nod. "Don't worry, I'm not going to trust anything he says."

Ripley frowned. "Because you finally believe you're good enough for Laurie?"

"No, because I recognized his voice. Not at first, but once he got angry and said that word, coin, I knew it. He was one of the men I heard fighting in the stairwell after the meeting yesterday. He knew so much about what had happened because he was there when Mr. Miller was killed, not because he was a psychic. And I think he knew Laurie's name because he's the one who threatened him."

Sixteen

Ripley was rarely speechless. One of her superpowers was always having something quippy to add in any situation. So the fact that she was silent for an entire minute following my statement about recognizing Phillip's voice told me she was genuinely shocked.

I wasn't handling it particularly well either. "He's the killer," I blurted even though I had almost no hard evidence proving that to be true.

"But didn't the recording say he was on East Coast time?" Ripley asked, finding her voice.

"He could've been traveling. He could've flown out here to take out his biggest rival." I knew I was stretching, but anything seemed possible because I *knew* in my gut he'd been here yesterday.

Ripley thought it through. "They're both phone psychics. We have no idea that they were rivals. Maybe Phillip is best friends with ... the-man-who-never-left-his-apartment." Ripley said the last few words slower as she comprehended how naïve that sounded. "Okay, let's at least look online and see if there's any proof of this rivalry."

Happily grabbing my laptop, I brought it over to the couch and searched for *Mathias the Medium rivalry with Phone Phortunes by Phillip*. I grimaced at having to misspell fortunes but hit the enter button and waited for the results to populate.

Ripley and I exhaled in tandem as we watched a whole host of links show up on the screen. Headings like, "The two most popular phone psychics battle it out" were joined by descriptions like, "Infamous rivals, Mathias and Phillip don't hold back as they criticize one another."

"Well, that's pretty clear." Ripley sat back. "But Mathias has been around for decades. It sounded like Phillip was a middle-aged man as well. If they've hated each other for so long, why would Phillip choose now to kill Mathias?"

I pointed at the screen. "This might have something to do with it."

I'd remembered something from my visit to Mathias the Medium's website the other day. Clicking through to it, we read the full-page script advertising an online seminar that had been scheduled to take place next week about "How to spot a fake psychic." Underneath the title text, a few bullets made the flyer, one of which was "Misspelling words in their title."

"Phortune," Ripley whispered.

I swallowed, then gasped. "Not just phortunes. Phone Phortunes by Phillip. PPP."

"What does that mean?" Ripley's question was flat; she hated being out of the loop.

"When Evan was telling Laurie and me about how he paid someone on a forum for Mathias the Medium's address, he said there was another user who was also interested. Their username was PPP1979." I turned to face Ripley. "What do you want to bet that Phillip was born in 1979?"

"Aw, man. That guy's giving my birth year a bad name." Ripley pouted.

I ignored her comment and said, "Mathias called Phillip out as being a fake, or was about to."

"And Phillip found him and took care of him before he could," Ripley said. "And you swear he was one of the people you heard in the stairwell that day."

I nodded. "The other person was telling Phillip he wouldn't go along with his plan, and Phillip asked him if he would do it for double the money."

"Could the other person have been Mathias?" Ripley asked.

Having never seen or heard the guy, I wasn't sure. But it checked out with the story. "Maybe he was trying to bribe Mathias to leave his name out of the seminar, and Mathias told him no?" I wrinkled my nose. That part wasn't really making sense at the moment. "Regardless, we need to tell the police." I stood.

Ripley held out a ghostly arm, creating a barrier neither of us wanted me to cross. "Hold on there, it's late. Detective Anthony isn't still at work. Why don't you sleep on it, and we can tell her in the morning?"

"Right." Though I doubted I'd be able to get any sleep with thoughts like these swimming in my mind.

Saying good night, Ripley went off, probably to hang out on the roof with Spencer, and I went to bed. I hated how much I wanted to tell Laurie about this break in the case, but he wanted us to leave the investigating to the police. The last thought I had before drifting off to sleep was how much I hoped Phillip's phortune was a lie.

BEING A NIGHT OWL, I wasn't an early riser most of the time. Which made the fact that I was up and ready to go by eight the next morning a big deal. Going to the police with the name of a person I was fairly sure killed my neighbor was good motivation, though.

"Heading out for the day, Nutmeg?" Art asked as I made my way through the lobby and toward the front doors.

He and Darius sat in their usual space to the left of the entrance. It looked like I wasn't the only night owl who was up early today. George occupied the long couch, laying down, arms folded behind his head.

Chewing on my lip in discomfort, I said, "Yep ... uh, just have some errands to run." I hoped that would get me out of a conversation about where I was actually going.

It wasn't that I didn't trust Art and Darius. But I didn't have experience going to the police with the name of a killer on my lips, held like a secret note in my pocket. The clandestine nature of it all had me acting a little cagey.

The sparkle that came over Darius's face at my mention of errands made me momentarily worried he was going to ask me to pick something up for him while I was out. Usually, I wouldn't mind such a request, but today I had a mission and wanted nothing to impede my important business at the police station.

"You know, you should try getting the things you need delivered. We've been doing that with our groceries and ... heck, what did you have delivered the other day, Art?" Darius snapped his fingers at his friend.

"Toothpaste," George answered.

"Toothpaste," Art supplied, a moment later.

George winked at me from the couch.

"You can get anything delivered these days." Darius sat back as if he never planned on leaving that chair.

"That does sound nice," I told him.

Just then Quentin walked out of the elevator and stopped in front of the mailboxes. My need to leave grew considerably. I wanted to talk about the weather even less than I wanted to hear what groceries Art and Darius had delivered. It was also a hot day, which only increased the likelihood that any conversation about weather would last longer than usual.

Seattleites were used to the rain and the cold, but it was the heat that really threw them for a loop. They could chat about hot weather exponentially longer than they could about the rain. Which meant talking to Quentin wouldn't simply be a conversation about temperatures, but heat records from the last century.

I turned back toward the Conversationalists. "I'm hoping to get some fresh air, though, so I don't mind going out today. Thanks for the tip." I waved and headed for the front door.

Outside, Ripley and Spencer were waiting for me on the sidewalk.

"Spencer's joining us?" I asked, turning to the right immediately in case any Morrisey people followed me out the doors to do more chatting.

"If I can," Spencer said, jogging to keep up.

"We'll see how far he can go." Ripley shrugged, smiling over at him.

I was happy to see her having fun with Spencer, but it did sting, especially after hearing about me and Laurie last night from Phillip. Since he was likely the killer, the things he'd said about me being in danger were meant to scare me away from investigating. But had the part about Laurie been made up as well? The sabotage-happy voice in the back of my mind wondered if there was some truth behind what he'd said. He'd obviously seen us together. Had he noticed something I'd failed to because I was too close to the situation?

For the next few minutes, we planned out what I was going to say to Detective Anthony as I walked the four blocks up to Fifth Avenue, where the Seattle police headquarters was located. Having seen the put-together detective in action, I could guess that she was a fan of precision and facts. I tried to keep my speech within both those parameters: precise and factual.

"Oh, Spencer remembered something last night," Ripley said when we were done planning and still had two blocks to walk.

"You did?" I looked over at him, only to see him drop his head to one side bashfully.

"It really isn't much, and we're not sure what it means." He kicked his toe against the streetlight we stopped at on the corner, only to watch his foot go right through it.

"There was a sun on someone's shirt, and he said he thinks that might be important, something to do with his life or his job." Ripley powered on with the explanation, obviously seeing it as more of a triumph than Spencer did.

"Well, that's something." Seeing we were still stuck at this light, I pulled out my phone and typed in *sun logo business Seattle 1990s*. "Did you happen to work for any solar companies?" I asked, noticing a large portion of businesses that used a sun as their logo were in the solar energy business.

Spencer scratched his temple. "I don't think so."

"Yeah, solar energy wasn't as prevalent back then, was it?" I checked with Ripley, who shook her head.

I returned to the search results. Other than the solar companies, a dentist from Nevada came up and a consulting firm from California. The light turned and I tucked my phone away.

I took a breath for all three of us as we stood in front of the station. We walked forward, and Ripley entered alongside me, but Spencer vanished, just as he had when trying to enter our apartment.

"At least we know he wasn't ever a criminal," Ripley said, entering alongside me.

Inside, I stopped by the officer sitting at the front desk.

"How can I help you this morning?" she asked brightly.

Just as with Heather from the market, this greeting was more along the lines of one I would expect to receive at a trendy coffeehouse, not a police station. But Officer Hart was obviously awake and chipper, and I was going to take her positivity.

"I need to speak with Detective Anthony. She's working on a homicide investigation at the Morrisey, down the street. I think I have very important information for her." I pushed my shoulders back and tried to appear as confident and reliable as possible.

The cheery Officer Hart's expression dropped, along with my hopes.

Oh no. Did I say the wrong thing?

"I'm sorry. Detective Anthony isn't in until lunch today." Officer Hart grimaced in a way that seemed like she was personally affected by this news. "You can leave a message for her. Or you can come back. I'm not sure how far you had to travel to get here, though."

"A note's good," I blurted, not wanting to see the pleasant officer disappointed any longer than I needed to. "I can leave a note."

Officer Hart handed over a blank piece of paper, a clipboard, and a pen, then directed me to sit in one of the chairs lined along the outer edge of the entryway. I sat and started to write what we'd planned on the way here. Ripley helped me out, saying it just how we'd practiced it so I could write it word for word.

Dear Detective Anthony,

This is Meg Dawson from apartment 5A at the Morrisey. Remember when I told you about the argument I heard between two men before we found Mr. Miller's door open, and subsequently his body? And remember that I didn't recognize either of the voices? Well, I heard one of them yesterday, and I think this person might have had a real motive to hurt Mr. Miller. This is silly to admit, but I was feeling lost, so I called a phone psychic, thinking they might help me with my issue. I guess all the talk about Mr. Miller being Mathias the Medium got me thinking about phone psychics. Anyway, Phillip of Phone Phortunes by Phillip was the person I called. As I talked *with him on the phone, I recognized his voice as one of the two I'd heard that day in the stairwell. Being that the two were rivals, and Mathias/Mr. Miller was about to run an online seminar about how to tell a phony psychic—one of his first points being misspellings in their titles (see above for the name of Phillip's business)—I think Phillip may have had cause to want to threaten Mr. Miller not to include him in the seminar. I'd be happy to answer more questions about this.*

I thought about letting her know about Evan and the other username interested in Mathias's address, but I decided not to bring that up unless it was necessary. I signed my name and left my phone number.

Ripley came with me to hand the note over to Officer Hart, but she stayed behind, making sure the officer really intended to get the note to Detective Anthony once I turned my back. Halfway through the lobby, she caught up with me.

"She wrote a note on the top that said *Attention: Det. Anthony,* so I think we're in good hands," Ripley reported.

I stopped short.

"Megs, I saw her do it. Don't worry. I think we're okay." Ripley walked ahead.

But that wasn't why I'd stopped. I jerked my head toward the big bulletin board next to the entrance. Ripley got my nonverbal message and whirled around to look at it too.

Even though I couldn't see her face, I could tell when she saw the flyer, by the way her shoulders tensed. She stalked forward. I followed on her heels.

There, on the bulletin board in the downtown branch of the Seattle Police Department, was a "Missing" poster. The picture on the flyer was of Spencer.

SEVENTEEN

I swallowed as I read the date on the missing person flyer. They'd posted it on Saturday, the day Mr. Miller was killed.

Ripley's expression was an unreadable medley of so many emotions.

"His name wasn't Spencer," she whispered as she stared at the paper. "It was Clark," she read off the flyer. "Clark Bowlen."

Reaching around Ripley, I pulled the flyer off the bulletin board.

"What are you doing?" she asked in a sharper tone than she normally used with me, which spoke to the intensity of what she was going through.

"I'm going to tell Officer Hart that he's dead," I said defensively. "Whoever put up this flyer deserves to know." I spun toward the desk and was about to walk forward when Ripley appeared in front of me.

She put a hand on her hip. "Oh? And how will you prove you know he's dead? Are you going to march over to that officer and let her know you've seen his ghost?"

"Good point." Pulling the flyer toward myself, I said, "Well, maybe I'll just ask if there's been any information about him."

"Better." Ripley stepped aside.

Officer Hart's face flashed with confusion as she noticed I was back. "Did you have something else to add to your note?"

I shook my head. "I saw this missing person flyer on my way out, and I think I might've seen this guy on the day he went missing, around Pioneer Square."

Holding out her hand for the flyer, Officer Hart studied the picture carefully, revealing the sad truth that there was more than one person missing in this part of the city. Her features lifted with recognition as she took in the photo. "You know what? I'm sorry. They should've taken this down." The way she shoved the piece of paper under her desk told me she was reluctant to break the sad news to me. But I could also tell she was a truthful person who didn't want to lie. "I'm so sorry, honey, but they found him ... dead. He was in an alley around Pioneer Square Park with a head injury. His roommate put up the flyer when he didn't come home. Unfortunately, a guy passed out in an alley isn't always cause for alarm, so they didn't find him until this morning."

"That's awful." I felt tears welling up in my eyes, despite the fact that I'd already known Clark had died. Having gotten to know him, though, made hearing the truth behind his final resting place even harder. "I'm sorry to hear that."

Officer Hart nodded. "Never take a single day for granted, that's what I say." She shot me her best smile before patting the note next to her on the counter. "I'll make sure Detective Anthony gets this when she comes in today."

I thanked her and started toward the door once more. Ripley walked next to me in a bit of a daze. The man we'd just seen on the flyer was waiting for us when we exited the building, having made the trip back from the Morrisey while we were inside.

"Oh, no. Did the detective not believe you?" His broad shoulders dropped, and a muscle in his ghostly jaw tensed. "That's the worst."

The pain evident in Ripley's features told me I needed to be the one to tell him.

"Spencer..." I stepped forward.

He took a step back as if I were scaring him.

"We know what happened to you," I finished before I lost my nerve.

"What? How?" His attention jumped from me, to Ripley, to the station we'd just exited, then back to Ripley.

"There was a missing person flyer with you on it," I explained.

"First of all, your name isn't Spencer. It's Clark Bowlen," Ripley took over. "And when we went to ask if they had any information about you, the officer told us they had found you."

"Dead." The word was a whisper.

Again, he'd known he was dead. It shouldn't have been such an emotional moment, but it was.

Squeezing his eyes shut, he said, "How'd it happen?" He wafted his hands toward his chest like he was daring us to punch him. "Come on. I can take it."

I cut my gaze over to Ripley. She nodded.

"The officer said they found you dead in an alley with a head injury, that you'd probably been there for a couple of days." I shifted my feet uncomfortably as I watched the words land on Clark.

He blinked his eyes open. "An alley?" His fingers raked

through his long hair as he paced. "Like, someone mugged me?" He shivered. "Okay, now I'm glad I don't remember any of it."

Ripley huffed. "Yeah, it's definitely better that way."

Her words felt like a second punch to my gut. It was yet another way Ripley differed from most spirits. The majority of ghosts we met couldn't recall the details surrounding their final moments. I'd always wondered if it was a coping mechanism, a way to protect them from the sometimes-awful end to their lives. I knew Ripley relived her car accident all the time. I'm sure she wished she didn't remember it.

As if this was all too uncomfortable for her, Ripley started walking back toward the Morrisey. Clark and I followed.

"So I wasn't the same guy that old lady Opal told you two about," Clark said as I jogged across the next street, taking advantage of the pedestrian walk sign.

"I guess not." I shrugged. "That story never really made sense when I thought about it, though. You can go up to the different floors of the building and the roof. That guy only stumbled into the lobby before he died."

"And I'm not from the nineties?" Clark puffed out his cheeks and put a fist next to his head, letting his fingers shoot out like an explosion. "Mind blown."

"Yeah," Ripley said, looking back at the two of us for the first time since she'd stormed off. "How do you know so much about the nineties if you were about the same age as Megs here?"

"Only one way to find out," I said as I pulled out my phone and searched for Clark Bowlen and '90s. The first result that popped up made me giggle. "You had a blog called *The 4-1-1 on the Best Decade,* and it was all about your love of the nineties." I clicked on one of the posts. "You go on and on, and on, about how much you wished you could've lived back then."

Ripley beamed. "I knew I liked you for a reason."

If Clark could've blushed, he would've been beet red at that point. As it was, he ran his fingers through his long hair and flipped it to the other side.

"There anything about a sun on there?" Ripley asked, peering at my phone screen.

I clicked back to the main page of his blog but couldn't find any sun logos.

"So are you still around because you need help figuring out who jumped you and left you in that alley?" Ripley asked as we walked.

Clark shrugged. "I guess."

"Maybe that's why you showed up at my door," I suggested. "Your spirit knew I'd help you figure out who killed you."

"Sure. That sounds right." Clark seemed overwhelmed.

We arrived back in Pioneer Square Park, but I didn't feel like going back inside the Morrisey, so I settled around one of the colorful bistro tables in the shady park. I just hoped that attack-happy pigeon the Squares were obsessed with wasn't anywhere close by. Clark wouldn't be able to follow us inside the apartment, and I didn't think he should be alone at that moment. He was zoned out where he sat across from me at the bistro table.

Pulling up a new search window on my phone, I typed in Phone Phortunes by Phillip and then clicked on images. I'd recognized Evan from his social media pictures, so maybe I could do the same with Phillip.

"Anything?" Ripley asked as she glanced over my shoulder.

"I don't know." I pressed my lips together. "A few guys

show up, but they all look like nondescript, middle-aged white guys. If one of these is actually him, I'm not sure even if I *had* seen him, I'd be able to pick him out of a crowd."

"And that's not even taking into account that he was probably trying to hide or had a murder weapon in his possession," Ripley said. "He was probably trying to get rid of it."

I sat up straight. "Omigosh, Ripley, you're a genius."

She lifted her chin with pride. "I know, right? But also ... why?" She squinted one eye.

"There was a guy on the third floor who I think might've tossed something down the trash chute. He held that bottle of liquor, and the bow was on the ground outside the trash chute later when I walked by. Maybe he dumped the murder weapon down there, and the bow came off the bottle while he did that."

"The bottle was a ruse," Ripley said as she understood. "He was pretending to deliver a gift to Mathias, but he killed him instead."

I got to my feet and paced. "We need to go check the dumpster."

Ripley adopted a sour expression.

"Oh, come on. You can't smell. We have to check to see if there's a murder weapon down there. Based on the way Mr. Miller bled, I'd say we're looking for something stabby." I gestured like I was ramming a knife straight ahead.

"Remind me to never get on your bad side," Ripley muttered.

I chuckled, and we headed for the building. A few feet away, we came to a stop and checked behind us.

"Clark, buddy? You coming with?" I asked as we crept back over to where he was still staring off at nothing in particular.

"We're going to dig around in the dumpster. Doesn't that sound fun?" Ripley gave him a thumbs-up.

"I think I might stay here, if that's okay." Clark looked up at us for just a moment before staring down the street again. "I'm just ... thinking." He wiggled his fingers near his temple.

"Okay. Sure." I took a step back.

Ripley followed me. "We'll come check on you in a bit."

We exchanged worried glances and resumed walking toward the Morrisey. Instead of going inside, however, we circled around the back to the alley where the big dumpster sat.

"You think he's going to be okay?" Ripley asked.

"I hope so." I tried to adopt my saddest expression, but at that moment, the overwhelming smell of the dumpster hit me, making me gag.

The metal trash chute clung to the backside of the building next to the elevator shaft, like a garbage slide feeding into an opening in the dumpster lid just big enough for the chute. Like most things in big cities, the top of the dumpster was locked with a dead bolt to prevent people from adding their trash to ours and hiking up our monthly fees with the city.

But locks and walls didn't matter when I had a ghostly best friend. I turned toward her, wearing my biggest smile. "Have I told you I love you, and you're the very best friend a girl could have?"

She waved a hand toward me. "Sure. Yeah. Gotcha." Pushing back her shoulders, she stretched her neck from side to side. "Okay, I'm looking for a stabbing implement."

With that, she disappeared into the side of the rusty metal contraption. I tapped my foot and studied the alley behind the building as I listened to a string of curses flow from the big dumpster.

"Oh, bleh." Ripley faked a gagging noise. "I just found a fish head in one of these bags."

Shivering, I said, "I don't think it'll be in a bag. He tossed it on its own. You're looking for sharp things. Knives or shards of glass ... I don't know. Anything that seems like it could stab and kill someone."

A man in a business suit walked by the alley just at that moment. I raised my hand in a hopefully friendly greeting, realizing how creepy my last statement was. He hurried away from me.

"I'm trying," Ripley said with a grunt from the dumpster. "I don't want to go all sketchy."

As was the case with most ghosts I'd encountered, when Ripley used her ghostly energy to manipulate objects, it drained her—making her more transparent and slow, like the ghosts from movies. She called it going "sketchy," and it was second on the list of things she hated just under having a living person walk through her.

"I appreciate you," I called out as I paced in front of the dumpster.

"Yeah, yeah, yeah," she muttered back.

Too much anticipation had built up around this moment, and I couldn't stop fidgeting. But as I paced, a small, high-pitched sound caught my ear, making me stop.

"Ripley, was that you?" I called out, wondering if that had been the squeak of someone who'd just encountered something really gross.

"You gonna let me search, or are you gonna keep talking to me?" she shot back from within the dumpster.

"Sorry. I thought I heard something." I returned to pacing.

The high-pitched sound came again. Stopping, I regarded

the dumpster where Ripley was still making all sorts of discontented sounds. I didn't want to call out and make her mad again, but there was definitely something in that dumpster with her, and it was calling out for help.

Careful not to touch anything in the alley that would ruin my clothing, I knelt down and checked underneath the large metal contraption. There were some undefinable, yet still disgusting, pieces of garbage underneath the container, but nothing moved. The sound shot out again, clearly coming from the dark abyss underneath the dumpster.

I grabbed my phone from my pocket and turned on the flashlight, shining it warily into the space. I wasn't sure I was ready to see some of the shapes under there in the light. The light landed on what was definitely a diaper sitting next to some kind of rotten piece of fruit. But then the beam of light reflected off two large circles near the far corner. I peered closer. A small black animal crouched next to a lump of wet toilet paper. The noise came again. This time, with the context of a visual clue, I identified it right away as the meow of a kitten.

I turned off the flashlight so I wouldn't blind it and scooted closer. "Hey, little kitty. What are you doing in there?"

"I'm looking for the murder weapon!" Ripley called out from the dumpster. "And did you just call me little kitty?"

Barking out a laugh, I accidentally scared the kitten, who cowered even farther back into the shadows. I held out a hand. "Oh, I'm sorry, little one." Before Ripley could accuse me of adding another cute nickname to the list, I added, "I'm not talking to you. I found a kitten under the dumpster. I'm trying to get it to come out."

"Oh..." was all the response I got from the dumpster.

Although I'd grown up primarily around dogs, our

neighbor Iris used to have a big orange tabby cat. Iris and Penny had been best friends, so I'd spent almost as much of my childhood in apartment 5B as I had in 5A. The cat had long since passed away, but I had fond memories of growing up around that fluffy guy. Remembering how Iris used to call him to her, I made kissing noises and wiggled my fingers in the kitten's direction.

"Come here, little one. I won't hurt you," I cooed.

The kitten blinked twice, but then it crept forward a few quick steps before stopping.

"That's it." More cooing noises. More finger twiddling.

It opened its mouth and let out a high-pitched meow of terror as it raced forward the rest of the way to me, stopping just short of me being able to touch it. Small, dirty, and matted as it was, it looked like it was 90 percent ears and big green eyes. I pulled my hand back, not wanting to scare the thing by reaching out too quickly.

"What happened to you?" I breathed out the question.

The kitten stared up at me, letting out one more meow before it took the last few steps. I scooped up the tiny thing, noting how its ribs showed through its short fur. I wasn't even sure it weighed a pound.

Wishing I had something better to wrap it in, I untucked my long T-shirt from my shorts and made a small hammock out of the extra material. My arm cradled underneath the little baby, and I grinned down at it as it immediately began to purr and knead at the shirt with its tiny needlelike claws.

"Ahem." Ripley's voice startled me. She floated above the dumpster, scowling down at me and the kitten.

"Look at it," I said in a high-pitched voice that could've

matched the tone of the screams the kitten had emitted not so long ago.

"Yes, very cute." Ripley's tone was deadpan. "I think I found something."

I gasped, startling the kitten. "Sorry," I said to it before checking with Ripley. "Was there a knife?"

Ripley shook her head. "There are a few broken bottles in here, but none of the pieces seem to be bloody in the least, and they don't look like they'd be the right size to stab anyone. But I did find the bottle of liquor you saw that man in the hat holding. There's blood on the corner and the label."

"You think he stabbed him with a bottle?" I asked, unsure how that would even work.

"I don't know, but I also found a baseball hat. The hat has a logo on it from a delivery company called Under the Sun Deliveries." Ripley turned to face toward where we'd left Clark. "The logo is a sun, just like Clark remembered last night."

EIGHTEEN

Ripley's expression darkened. "Do you think Clark..." Her question was small and unfinished, but I understood what she was asking.

As much as I wanted to reassure her, we knew nothing about Clark other than his love of the nineties and how he'd died. He seemed like a nice person, but I wasn't naïve enough to think people couldn't pretend to be something they weren't. Maybe the whole amnesia thing was part of a devious plan to distract us from finding out he was really the killer.

"No," I said in answer to Ripley's question. "The killer left Laurie that threatening note when Clark was already waiting for us in front of the apartment. He'd already died. Plus, the guy I saw holding the bottle had short hair," I said, almost to myself. "I would've recognized Clark's long, curly hair, even if he'd tried to hide it under a baseball cap."

"Unless he didn't work alone," Ripley suggested, proving I wasn't the only one who'd contemplated the option that Clark might've been hanging out with us to distract us from catching the actual murderer.

"Or"—I motioned to the dumpster—"the bloody items in there are completely unrelated to Mr. Miller's death." I shrugged.

Ripley pressed her lips together, unconvinced. "There's only one way to move forward. We have to ask Clark."

I met my friend's serious gaze and nodded. She vanished. Moments later, she returned, Clark appearing soon after.

"Did you find something?" His expression danced with excitement.

"We did, but it brings up more questions than answers," I said, unsure if Ripley was ready to talk.

Clark flinched as he noticed the ball of black, matted fur in my shirt. "What's that?" He moved back a few feet as if the thing could hurt him.

"It's a kitten. I found it in the garbage." Defensiveness edged my words, and I hugged the matted thing closer to me. "That's not the point. I need you to follow Ripley and look at something." When he balked, I added, "You're a spirit. You can't get dirty."

"Oh, right." He chuckled, then glanced at Ripley. "Lead the way."

She hesitated before saying, "It's a navy-blue baseball hat." She moved into the dumpster and Clark followed.

"Dude, I know that sun symbol," was all I heard.

Ripley reappeared moments later. If she could look pale, I think I would've been worried she was about to throw up. I shot her a frown that I hoped said, *don't jump to conclusions just yet.*

Clark stepped through the dumpster, smiling. "Under the Sun Deliveries. Did I work for them? I think I might've."

Awkwardly holding my phone and the kitten at the same

time, I typed the company's name into a browser. The information came up quickly.

"Well, it is a Seattle-based delivery company. The office is a short bus ride away. It's down past the stadiums," I said. "The garbage truck won't be here until Wednesday, so this isn't going anywhere. We can let Detective Anthony know when she calls." Which I hoped would be soon. "Shall we go check it out?"

"Sure, but"—Ripley pointed to my shirt—"what are you going to do about the kitten?"

"Oh, right." The little bundle was so light on my arm that I almost forgot it was there. "Yes and get this little one checked out as well." I searched for the closest veterinarian and put the directions into my phone. "We can do that on the way."

I didn't have my purse, so I needed to go back into the building. Not wanting to jostle the kitten too much, I took the elevator. After grabbing an old towel I used for cleaning paintbrushes, I wrapped the kitten in that, changed my shirt and headed out.

It wasn't as weird as I anticipated taking the kitten on the bus with me. I kept it hidden as much as possible, not sure if pets were allowed—though I'd once seen a man sitting with a chicken in his lap, so ... I got a few weird looks, but people's general acceptance of the matted black thing wrapped up in the towel told me I wasn't the only one who had weird bus experiences on the regular.

The veterinarian clinic was bustling when I got there, but the lady behind the counter took one glance at the tiny baby wrapped in the towel and melted.

"Omigosh, what happened?" She stood, her hand covering her mouth.

"I found it under a dumpster behind my building," I

explained. "It's really thin, but super sweet. I was hoping someone could check it out and see if it's got a microchip." I highly doubted it, given how small and gross the kitten was.

My concerns were mirrored in the skeptical once-over the woman gave the animal. Checking her computer, she said, "Our doctors are all with patients at the moment." She frowned as she clicked around. "And we're all booked up for the rest of the day."

The hope I'd momentarily experienced disappeared.

Until she said, "But, if you don't mind leaving the little one, I'll take it to the back and have the techs look it over. A doctor might have a minute or two in between patients to do an examination as well."

My heart hurt at the thought of leaving the kitten, but I knew it would be safe. "I actually have a few errands to run. I can come back in a bit to check on it."

The woman held out her hands to receive the towel-wrapped bundle. "We'll take good care of him or her." She sent me a reassuring smile.

I left my contact information and a card to keep on file for any expenses and treatments. That taken care of, I met up with Ripley and Clark on the sidewalk outside. An awkward, tense air sat between the two spirits. I recognized a fight when I saw one.

"You two okay?" I asked, shooting them both questioning glances.

"Great." Ripley folded her arms in front of her.

Clark ran a hand nervously through his long locks. "Super great."

Ripley raised her chin. "All of us are telling the truth."

"Yeah. We are." Clark narrowed his eyes at her.

"Okaaay." I walked forward, following the directions to the delivery company's headquarters.

A large orange-yellow-and-red sun loomed over us as we walked up to Under the Sun Deliveries in SoDo. The shop next door made killer sandwiches, and I noticed my stomach grumbling at the delicious smells emanating from the building. Maybe I could grab something to eat on my way back.

The inside reminded me of the waiting room of a tire store, but it smelled like a combination of coffee and perfume instead of rubber. It was compact, only holding a few chairs and a desk, proving most of the work this company did took place behind the scenes. Behind the doors, voices spilled out from the back room.

Clark's face lit up with recognition. "Okay, I definitely know this place." He didn't wait for me, but simply wafted straight through the wall into the back room.

Ripley and I shared an annoyed look. She couldn't follow him since neither of us had ever been here before.

"Can I help you?" The woman behind the desk smiled up at me with a grin that could give the sun logo a run for its money on the brightness scale.

Contemplating my options for a split second before I had to respond, I pretended I knew nothing about Clark's death. It had worked at the police department after all.

"Yes, I'm hoping to get in touch with someone who works for you. His name is Clark Bowlen," I said.

I immediately regretted my choice. The woman's cheery face crumpled into a red, puffy mess of tears in a matter of seconds. She held up a hand, using the other to grab a tissue to dab at her eyes and blow her nose. It took her the longest minute of my life to get herself under control enough to say,

"Clark"—she sniffed—"Clark doesn't work here anymore. He passed away." Three more big tears spilled down her cheeks.

"Oh, I'm ... I'm so very sorry." I stepped forward, not sure what to do next. "So, you knew him, then?" I asked.

Ripley scoffed from where she stood, arms crossed, in the corner. "No, duh, Megs."

Gritting my teeth at her bad mood, I focused on the woman behind the desk. She nodded, blowing her nose once more.

"He was one of our delivery guys. He's worked here for two years," she said with an air of awe that made me wonder if he'd been their employee with the most seniority.

Her face lit up as someone walked through from the back room. At first, possibly because of the long hair, I thought it was Clark, and I was dealing with another ghost seer like me. Then I remembered she hadn't noticed Clark when we first entered, nor had she reacted at all to Ripley.

"Everything okay, Ellie?" The man closed the folder in his hands and strode over to her, sporting a worried expression.

Now that he was closer, I could see marked differences between him and Clark. First of all, his hair was straighter, though just as long and a similar color brown. Next, he had a goatee, a contrast from Clark's clean-shaven face.

Ellie dabbed at her eyes again. "Yeah, sorry for breaking down. This woman just came in asking about Clark, and I—" Her chin crumpled, and she let out a squeak, cutting herself off from finishing that sentence.

The man regarded me, an accusatory scowl in place, as if I'd made Ellie cry on purpose. "What did you want with Clark?"

But before I could stutter out a response, Ellie said, "Spencer, don't snap at her. It's not her fault he's gone."

My eyes went wide. "Spencer?" I whispered before I could stop myself.

"Yeah, I was Clark's roommate." He swallowed, his features tight as if he might join Ellie in needing one of those tissues.

"Roommate, huh?" Ripley walked around the guy as she studied him. "That's why the name was important."

As Ripley talked, I ran through the options of what I could say to these people to move forward. None of them were good; all were downright awkward. Seeing my chance to escape before things got weird, I said, "I'm so sorry, but I have to leave." Then I rushed out of the office.

I didn't stop until I was around the corner of the building. My breath came in gasps.

"Meg, what gives?" Ripley asked as she caught sight of me. She followed me into the alley.

"I had no exit strategy. Next time, I need an exit strategy." I shook my head.

Ripley hunched in defeat. "Okay, but now we have no way of getting Clark to come out of there."

"Do you want him to?" I asked. "You seemed pretty mad at him at the vet."

She scratched at her neck. "I may have mentioned that I was worried he might have worked with someone else to kill Mr. Miller, and now he's mad at me."

"Riiipleey." I stretched her name out into a groan.

"What? Sometimes it's better to just come out and say it." She pursed her lips. "Except, I think this might *not* have been one of those times."

"There you are," Clark said, walking straight through the wall next to me.

I jumped. Ripley screamed.

"I thought you'd ditched me in there." He tucked his long hair behind his right ear.

"No," I crooned, immediately saddened by the hopelessness in his tone. "We just got caught up in a couple of people who were pretty sad to hear your name, and I didn't know what else to do, so I ran."

Clark nodded as if he would do the same. "I couldn't find anything in there with information about how I died."

"Well, we found something interesting," I said, noticing that Ripley was still a little standoffish with him. "We found Spencer."

At the name, Clark's face brightened. He stood up straighter.

"He was your roommate," Ripley said, her words like a peace offering.

"Okay, that's it. Who are you talking to?"

I jumped as Spencer came storming around the side of the building.

"And why are you talking about me?" Anger sizzled in his tone, and he stalked over to me.

NINETEEN

Heat rose in my chest and along my neck. I'd been caught talking to not just one ghost, but two. Flashbacks of elementary school, of being called a freak for talking to myself, jumped into my mind.

"I was ... I talk to myself sometimes," I started, wincing as I summoned the courage to look up at Spencer.

"Meg, maybe you should run. He looks pretty upset." Ripley's tone held a warning, and she wouldn't take her eyes off Spencer as he stopped a few feet in front of me.

But as I stared into Spencer's eyes, I felt déjà vu. I'd just seen a very similar emotion conveyed in Ripley's expression when I'd confronted her about Clark. Frustration was evident, sure, but there was also a fair bit of fear and sadness too. It was the face of someone who needed to know the truth but wasn't sure they could handle it.

"Tell him to take a chill bucket," Clark, stepping forward.

My eyes flicked to him in question. He nodded. Ripley shrugged.

"Spencer, I need you to take a ... chill bucket," I said carefully, observing Spencer's expression for signs that he might call the cops on me.

Spencer blinked, the anger in his eyes replaced with recognition and then confusion. "Wait. What did you just say?"

I glanced at Clark, not sure what it meant.

"It's what we say to each other when we need to cool down because one time, our friend Tony got really mad, and Spence dumped a bucket of ice on his head, telling him to take a chill bucket instead of a chill pill." Clark grinned. "Hey, that's a memory. I remembered something!" He pointed to his brain in celebration.

I, on the other hand, was feeling less celebratory. Because even though the chill bucket comment had, indeed, chilled out Spencer for a moment, it also left me with no reasonable explanation for how I knew that inside joke between Clark and his friends.

Spencer's eyebrows couldn't rise any higher on his forehead as he waited, and I could see the confusion turning back into frustration, by the second.

Finally, I blurted out, "I can communicate with ghosts. I've been talking with Clark ever since he died."

A nervous laugh spilled out of Spencer.

"I can see and speak with spirits who can't move on after they die," I explained, trying to sound as calm and rational as possible. "And Clark is one of those. He's here, right now. That's how I knew to say the thing about the ice bucket. He said you dumped one on your friend Tony's head when he was worked up about something."

Spencer stared at me, fear flashing behind his eyes. He raked a hand through his long hair. "I don't know. Ghosts?" He paced around and shot another accusatory glare in my direction. "But you knew about the chill bucket." He chewed on his lip. "Okay," he said. "If Clark's here, ask him what his employee number is." Spencer jabbed a thumb toward the delivery company office behind him.

I checked with Clark, who shook his head.

Clearing my throat, I said, "So ... he doesn't know that, but he also has amnesia and doesn't remember most things. I think the ice bucket thing just came to him, much like how he randomly remembered that a sun logo was important in his life."

Spencer's lips parted. "Because of the head injury that killed him?"

"That's my guess." I kicked at the sidewalk. "I've never encountered a ghost with amnesia before, so it's new for me too."

"He has no idea what happened?" Spencer asked. "The cops thought he'd been mugged and left in that alley to die."

"I'm trying to help him figure it out." I pulled in a deep breath before I said, "Look, I'm not sure *how*, just yet, but I think Clark was involved in a murder that happened in my building the same day he died. I live at the Morrisey over in Pioneer Square."

"You think I'm involved too?" Clark glared at Ripley.

"Clark would never hurt anyone," Spencer spat out the retort at the same time.

Clark's anger morphed into pride as he beamed at his friend. "I knew Spencer was a good guy."

Holding up both hands, I said, "I don't think he actually hurt anyone either. But a few things aren't adding up, and I think going back to his apartment might help jog his memory.

The only problem is that Clark doesn't remember where it is. Can you help us with that?"

Spencer sighed. "Um, okay. I guess. Let me just let Ellie know that I'm taking off for a bit." He disappeared around the corner, whispering, "This is so bizarre." And I wondered if he would return.

I waited out front with the ghosts. If I'd thought the air was awkward before, it was nothing compared to the angry silence that sat between the three of us now.

Thankfully, Spencer came back. He pointed me in the direction the apartment. "It's just a few blocks over. We can walk."

I followed him.

After a block, and about thirteen furtive glances over at me, Spencer coughed and asked, "Can I talk to him?"

A small smile pulled at my lips. "Yeah, he can hear anything you say."

Clark, already walking next to Spencer, gave him his full attention.

"He's next to you. To your left," I said, hoping that wouldn't freak him out to know.

Spencer gulped but looked straight at Clark. "Man, I really miss you. I know we were roommates, but you were also my best friend. And I want you to know that I won't replace you as our lead singer in Cover Love Bone." Spencer turned to me. "That's our Mother Love Bone cover band."

"I figured," I told him.

Turning back to his friend, Spencer said, "It just—I'm so sorry this happened to you. You are such a good dude and … yeah." He ran his fingers through his hair at the same time Clark nervously flipped his long locks to the other side.

It warmed my heart to see the two friends getting some sort of closure out of a tragic situation.

"Can you tell him that all feelings are totally mutual, and that he definitely has to replace me in the cover band because that's a sick name, and he *cannot* waste it." Clark's eyes shone with a mixture of pride and sadness.

I relayed the message to Spencer, who said, "Well, it's gonna be hard to fill your shoes, man. But we will, if it's what you want."

While she remained silent, I noticed Ripley inched closer to Clark as we walked, some of her icy attitude warming.

"So Clark was a delivery guy?" I asked Spencer as we walked.

He nodded. "Yeah, we both are." Coughing, he amended by saying, "*Were.*"

"That's why you can go in the halls but none of the apartments," I said, craning my neck so I could see Clark around Spencer. "What about the roof?"

Spencer must've been getting used to this whole me-talking-to-ghosts-in-front-of-him thing because he snapped his fingers and pointed at me. "I know this one. Clark told me about the first time he delivered to your building. He got turned around and thought there was one more floor than there actually was, so he went all the way up to the roof by accident. He said it was so cool and homey that he walked around for a while, taking it all in."

"That sounds right." Clark smiled gratefully at his friend.

As much as things were clicking together and questions were being answered, an uneasiness surrounded me like the summer heat. Most ghosts I'd met faded away and passed on once they figured out how they died. Not knowing how they'd died was the most common form of unfinished business. There were a few, like George, who had unfinished business not tied to who killed them or how.

We officially knew how Clark had died, yet he remained on this plane of existence. I had a bad feeling that the reason he was still around was connected with Mr. Miller's death, and that feeling settled like ice on the back of my neck.

Spencer came to a stop in front of an old warehouse building and unlocked the large metal door at the entrance. It wasn't a surprise since this part of the city was comprised of either former or current warehouse buildings, being more of the industrial section by the train tracks. And even though I'd seen a lot of stylish loft spaces created from similar Seattle warehouses, I could tell right away that this was not going to be one of them.

A few ratty rugs delineated different sections of the space. A drum set and guitars littered one area, probably the cover band's practice space. Sheets hung in the back corners of the sizable area next to mattresses that had only one sheet and one pillow each. There was a television zone, where a large flat-screen sat on milk crates in front of a grayish-brown couch, which looked like it definitely *hadn't* started out that color.

"Clark got that couch off a guy that said Eddie Vedder from Pearl Jam once crashed on it." Spencer puffed out his chest proudly as he caught me staring.

"Like, in the nineties?" Ripley asked, disgust in both her expression and her tone as she took in the piece of furniture.

"Cool." I gave him as much of a grin as I could muster.

The state of these twentysomethings' apartment made me realize how special Laurie was. His apartment wasn't only decorated, but it was clean and comfortable as well.

"Clark's bed is the one on the left over here," Spencer said, walking us over. "Watch the cords," he said as we passed through the music area and the myriad of amps and pedals that were gathered in the space.

Next to Clark's bed, a cardboard box held an old clock radio, which blinked twelve o'clock repeatedly. Two pieces of mail sat next to the clock. One was an unmarked envelope. The other was one of those generic credit card offers that most people automatically recycle, so it struck me as odd that he would keep it, let alone set it next to his nightstand. When I stepped closer to investigate, my vision went all wobbly for a second.

The name within both envelope windows was Mathew Miller. The address, his apartment at the Morrisey.

I swallowed, hard, as I remembered the mail that had been on the counter in Mr. Miller's kitchen before we'd found the body, but had been missing after.

"Clark, why do you have pieces of Mr. Miller's mail?" I snatched the things off the bedside table and held them toward him. But when I flipped the letters over so the address windows faced away from me, my blood turned cold.

Scrawled in all caps on the back of one was a message, written in red ink.

YOU MAY THINK YOU'RE SAFE, BUT I KNOW A WAY IN. YOU HAVE UNTIL 3 TOMORROW TO GIVE ME WHAT I ASKED FOR.

Fear prickled along the skin of my arms and torso, tingling down my legs as well. It was the same handwriting as the note that had been tucked under Laurie's door the day of the murder.

"What is it?" Ripley asked. She'd been fairly quiet since we arrived at the apartment, so the fact that she was speaking up meant my face must've looked pretty bleak.

I flipped the one letter over and waited as their eyes pored over the threatening text.

Clark held up his hands. "I didn't write that. I don't know who did ... or why I have it, but I know I didn't."

"If you don't know who wrote it or why you have it, how do you know it wasn't you?" Ripley cocked her hip with attitude.

Clark winced at Ripley's harsh tone. "It's not my handwriting." He jogged over to the music area where set lists had been scribbled on the backs of receipts. He gestured to one. "There. This is my handwriting. I know it."

Ignoring Clark, I turned to Spencer, realizing I needed to fill him in on what was happening. "Spencer, Clark swears this isn't his handwriting, and he's not sure why he has it. I need you to find a sample of Clark's handwriting for me."

Spencer walked over to the same receipt that had been tacked to the wall and motioned to the set list. "He wrote this."

Holding up the threatening note next to it, my eyes jumped from one sample to the other as I picked out the differences. The capital letters that made up the threatening note didn't match the capitals on the set list.

"What about you?" I asked Spencer. "Can you show me a sample of your writing?"

Spencer paused for a moment, fear in his expression as he took in my serious energy, but he moved over to the drum kit and fished a folded piece of paper out of a bag filled with drumsticks that sat next to the bass drum. He handed it over, and I went through the same analysis.

Handing the paper back, I said, "Neither is a match."

Ripley breathed a sigh of relief even though she didn't have lungs anymore.

"Mr. Miller was one of Clark's favorite customers, though," Spencer said. "He stopped by pretty much anytime he was working to make sure the guy didn't need anything. I mean, the man had a mannequin in his apartment as decoration, he was *that* lonely."

Clark seemed as confused as we were. He didn't remember.

Spencer, our only hope for memories, added, "He said Miller was a recluse who wouldn't open the door for anyone but him. He trusted Clark because he had a compassionate soul."

Clark flipped his hair to his other shoulder, fidgeting in his embarrassment, but worry engulfed me. Ripley's gaze darted over to meet mine. The way one of her eyes twitched a little told me she'd realized the same thing I had: if Clark was the only one Mathias the Medium would open the door for, he was the only person who would have the opportunity to kill him.

TWENTY

Fingers shaking with the weight of what we'd just learned, I held up the threatening piece of mail so I could snap a picture of the text. But as I was about to hand it back, I hesitated.

"Do you mind if I take this?" I looked from the letter to Spencer.

It wasn't as if he had any reason to keep it.

Spencer rocked back on his heels. "Nope. Go for it. One less thing for me to get rid of." He considered the space as if the decision about what to do with his deceased friend's stuff weighed heavily on his mind.

To me, it didn't really seem like Clark had much more than that bed, but I didn't have time to stick around. It was already after noon. Hopefully, I'd be getting a call from Detective Anthony soon, and I wanted to make sure I was ready for her. We had a new piece of evidence to add to the file. I tucked both letters in my purse.

Parting with Spencer outside the apartment, I started back toward the veterinary clinic, hoping I'd given them enough time with the kitten. Ripley joined me, causing Clark to trail behind us. She and I shared a few furtive, meaningful glances as we worked our way up north, but kept any thoughts about what it all meant to ourselves.

Because it was noon, the sun shone directly above me, beating down on me as I walked. Closer to the city, the high-rises provided more shade, along with the trees which were dotted along the sidewalks. Out here in the industrial section of town, the low warehouses did little to block anything, and I hadn't seen a tree for blocks.

So, by the time I reached the vet clinic, I was a little sweaty, medium grumpy, and a lot confused about what was going on with Mr. Miller's murder case. The lovely woman at the front desk immediately buoyed my spirits by holding up the tiny black kitten the moment she saw me.

It seemed she'd been cuddling with it behind the desk while she answered phone calls and emails and waited for me to return.

"We gave her a bath, so that's why she's still a little damp," the woman, Annette, explained after going over each of the treatments they'd done with the kitten. "You'll want to treat her for fleas first thing when you get home just in case any hung on, and I wouldn't let her around any soft furnishings for a few days because of that. She'll need to be on the special diet and the medications I mentioned for the next few days."

"She?" I held up the little kitten so I could get a better look at her.

Ripley stood off to the side, tapping the toe of her boot, but her face softened into a smile as she took in the tiny thing.

Annette nodded. "She's about eight weeks old, extremely malnourished, and definitely not microchipped. So ... she's all yours. I've already made you a follow-up appointment for next week, as well as the boosters she'll need for those kitten vaccines." Annette leaned closer to me. "As you saw today, things fill up fast around here."

"I can't thank you enough," I said, picking up the cardboard carrier they'd given me so I could transport the little jellybean back home safer than simply wrapped up in an old towel.

I walked out of the vet clinic a smidge dazed, but fully a cat owner.

It was a pleasant distraction for the next couple of hours to head back home and get the kitten settled. I made a makeshift litter box for her out of a tray and a bunch of shredded newspaper, and set her up in the bathtub with a nice, cozy blanket.

Once I was in front of my computer, I ordered a proper litter box, litter, kitten food, and a bed for her, along with a few other fun items, like toys and scratching posts. I smirked to myself as I noticed the items would be delivered by Under the Sun Deliveries by tomorrow evening, but the humor turned to concern once more as I was reminded of the letter tucked inside my purse.

I was just tossing the flea treatment wrappers in the trash when my phone rang. I didn't recognize the number, but my phone guessed it was coming from the Seattle Police Department.

Detective Anthony.

"Hello," I answered, hoping the desperation I felt to speak with her wasn't coming through in my voice as much as it buzzed through my body.

On the one hand, she was calling me back, which was a good sign, but it had also been hours since she was supposed to have arrived at work. Maybe she got busy, or maybe she wasn't inclined to take a handwritten note seriously.

"Meg, this is Detective Anthony. I received your note. I'm sorry I'm late returning your message. If you have a moment, I would love to talk with you more about what you wrote."

I nodded emphatically. "Of course." I thought about the threatening note in my purse. "Actually, there's been a development, and I have a new piece of evidence to bring to you. Should we talk in person? I can be there in ten."

It wasn't just the note from Clark's bedside table, which I needed to hand over. I wanted to be there, in person, when I explained to her how I knew everything I'd discovered surrounding this case. While I could explain away the reason behind my discovery that Phillip had been one of the people fighting in the stairwell that day, I hadn't been able to come up with anything that sounded remotely rational for how I knew about Clark, Spencer, or the note I was about to hand over.

Something told me that coming clean to a detective about my ability to talk to ghosts wouldn't be as easy as it had been with Spencer. Regardless, it was a conversation I needed to have in person, not one I felt comfortable having over the phone.

Detective Anthony paused. "Um, sure. I'll see you in a few."

After hanging up the call, I made sure the kitten was all set with food and water. She must've had a rough handful of weeks alive so far because once I'd placed the blanket in the bathtub, she'd fallen fast asleep.

"She looks like a little black jellybean, doesn't she?" I said to Ripley before stepping back and closing the bathroom door.

Ripley watched me with the intensity she reserved for when she was really worried about me.

"What? I thought you liked cats." I tensed.

She scoffed. "I do. It's not the kitten that concerns me, Meg. I'm nervous because I think you might be preparing to tell Detective Anthony about your ability." Her eyebrows lowered over her brown eyes.

"What if I am?" I asked. "What if it comes down to what I know, or the killer walks free? I couldn't handle that, Rip."

"I know. I wouldn't expect anything less. But I just want you to be prepared. It was easier with Spencer because you had Clark to feed you inside jokes, and I think Spencer is also incredibly trusting. Detective Anthony strikes me as much less so. And you won't have her best friend standing by to help."

Holding Ripley's gaze with mine, I said, "I will try everything I can to not tell her. I promise."

"Okay. Let's go." Ripley nodded.

She tensed considerably once we entered the hallway, but Clark wasn't waiting for us. Ripley didn't relax until we'd made it outside and down a block without seeing the other ghost. As much as I wanted to talk through what she was feeling about the object of her recent ghostly affections, I needed to stay focused on the impending conversation with Detective Anthony.

Entry into the headquarters building was much smoother the second time. Officer Hart recognized me and showed me back to the detective's desk right away. Detective Anthony rose as I approached, thanking the officer and gesturing for me to have a seat in one of the chairs set up across from her desk.

"Thank you for coming in, Ms. Dawson." Detective Anthony couldn't have been more than five years older than me. It might've sounded odd for her to address me in such a superior way, I would've much rather she just call me Meg, but the way she held herself reminded me that age was so much more than just a number.

The woman in front of me not only had an established career, while I'd just decided to throw the towel in on the one I'd been working toward thus far in my life, but she was also an obvious leader in her workplace. Coworkers greeted her as they passed by. She was probably the person who didn't always go out with the group for after-work drinks, but whom everyone would call if they had a problem they needed solved.

Ripley wandered around the desk. I almost wished she wouldn't. Her movement drew my focus away from the detective, and I didn't want to seem fidgety in front of the collected woman.

"I apologize that it's been a few hours. We wanted to bring Phillip Ellis in for questioning as soon as possible." She tapped her pen on the neat desk. Only a closed laptop, a single picture frame, a lamp, and a legal notepad took up the expansive space. "We hadn't even considered him a suspect until you brought him to our attention. Getting a confession out of someone who hadn't even been on our radar is a rare occurrence, I'll tell you." Her lips pulled into a tight smile, and her gaze flicked to the notepad next to her.

Ripley, having caught the motion, sidled over to stand next to the detective and peered down at the pad of paper. Her eyes went wide.

"Confession?" I blurted out. "So I was right? Phillip Ellis killed Mr. Miller?"

Detective Anthony pulled in a breath, causing her nostrils to flare.

"They're only charging him with manslaughter," Ripley read aloud, shaking her head in confusion.

I wasn't an expert in sentencing, but I'd seen enough television to know that the difference between homicide and manslaughter came down to the motivation behind the act of killing, whether it was planned out or not.

"It *had* to be premeditated." I fished the threatening piece of mail out of my bag and handed it over to the detective. "He left him this threatening note."

She pulled a piece of paper out of her drawer and held it up to the piece of mail. "No, this isn't a match for Phillip Ellis's writing, which makes sense, given that he did not kill Mr. Miller."

"What?" I spat out the question.

Ripley's eyes pored over the page of notes. "Phillip hit a delivery person from Under the Sun deliveries, over the head with that bottle of liquor and—" Ripley gasped, her hand flying up to cover her mouth.

My attention jumped from Ripley to the detective and back again.

"Mr. Ellis has an alibi for the time of Mr. Miller's death," Detective Anthony explained calmly.

"Yeah," Ripley scoffed. "He was at the liquor store around the corner buying a second bottle of whiskey to replace the first one, which he tossed down the trash chute when he realized it had blood on it. When he came back with the second bottle, Mr. Miller was already dead, and the police were there."

Tempted to ask Ripley questions, I had to weigh my words so that they were directed at the detective instead. "So what did Mr. Ellis confess to, then?" I asked, even though Ripley had already told me some of it.

Coughing in discomfort, Detective Anthony said, "His

charges are not something I can discuss with you, Ms. Dawson."

"He said the delivery guy was only out for a minute, and he immediately felt awful for hitting him on the skull," Ripley said, reading snippets from the notes. "He thought the guy was okay since he just seemed a little wobbly on his feet. Phillip didn't learn that the man he'd hit had collapsed in an alley and died from the head injury until he came in here for questioning." Her gaze shot up, and she locked eyes with me.

Clark.

Frustration filled me. Some of the anger was directed toward myself for ever questioning that Clark could've had anything to do with Mr. Miller's death. The rest of my exasperation was directed at Detective Anthony, and I let her know it with my next question. "Why did you call me, then, if you weren't going to tell me anything?"

She pushed back her shoulders in obvious discomfort. "I wanted to thank you and let you know that reporting Mr. Ellis was the right thing to do. You helped us bring justice to one case, if not the one you set out to solve." A muscle in Detective Anthony's jaw jumped as she said, "*You* were the one who wanted to meet in person."

"So much for thanks," I grumbled to myself. That was it. She had the letter with the threatening note on it, but that was all she was getting out of me. I wasn't about to spill my ghostly secret to her now.

I could see Ripley was still reading the notes, and I wanted to give her more time, so I pushed aside my annoyance with the detective and said, "I'm glad I helped. You know, I thought about not saying anything." I let my eyes flick to my lap nervously. "Calling a phone psychic wasn't exactly my proudest moment, and it was a little embarrassing to admit. But it makes it worth it if I helped catch Mr. Ellis in ... whatever it is he did." I opened my hands to show I didn't know because she wouldn't tell me.

Ripley's eyes tracked right and left faster now. She was doing one last pass through the information. She needed more time.

"You and your fellow Morrisey residents don't have to worry about Mr. Ellis anymore," Detective Anthony said. She pushed her chair back a few inches, preparing to stand.

"Oh." I held up my finger, pretending to remember something else. "I wanted to mention Mathias the Medium's assistant, Kenny Knapp," I blurted out before I could think of anything better.

Frustration rose inside me as I realized I couldn't tell her how I'd come to suspect Kenny. Then it came to me. I might not be able to tell the truth, but I could tell a convincing lie.

"A different psychic, one I talked to over in the market, told me I should look into the assistant when I mentioned the murder," I told her. "Might be worth investigating."

"Mr. Miller's assistant has an alibi that we've already confirmed," Detective Anthony said, but I didn't miss that she wrote herself a quick note before standing from her desk.

I got to my feet as well, watching Ripley in the hope that she got out of the way before—

The detective walked right through her on her way around the desk.

I tried to keep my grimace hidden as the detective said, "But if you see anything else you think might be helpful in the Miller case, let me know." She handed me her card, not looking the least bit chilled after walking through my best friend.

To my surprise, Ripley stayed put, forgoing the usual shiver-dance she did anytime a living person passed through her spirit. She kept reading. It must've been important.

I waited for Ripley on the street in front of police headquarters for a few minutes. She appeared next to me, muttering to herself as she closed her eyes, the same way I memorized anything. Recognizing the sign, I waited until she opened them.

We puffed out our cheeks and made explosion signs next to our temples at the same time to signify our minds being blown, just like Clark had earlier, then laughed at how in sync we were.

"I read it, like, ten times so I'd be able to remember everything it said." She jerked her thumb down the street, back toward home.

"Yeah, I need details. It still doesn't make sense. Like, why was Phillip in the building in the first place? And what was the whiskey for?" I asked as I followed her, putting in my earbuds and pretending I was on the phone so I didn't have to think twice. I wanted to give Ripley my full attention.

Ripley stopped at a street corner with a red light, waiting for me. "Okay, I'm just going to start from the beginning. Phillip *was* upset about the online seminar Mathias was going to give next week. But he didn't fly here with the intent of hurting him. He hoped to talk with Mathias, plead with him not to say anything. He thought if they could just sit down and have a drink together, Mathias would see that he was a good person, even though he did mostly fake the whole psychic thing."

Snapping my fingers, I said, "Ah ha! He's a fake!"

Ripley frowned at me.

I glanced down, sheepishly. "Which means his fortune about me and Laurie just being friends wasn't real."

"Which you should've known already, but yes," Ripley said.

"Phillip has been here for an entire week, renting apartment 3E."

Eyes wide, I crossed the street with the rest of the pedestrians as the walk sign lit up. "Of course. It wasn't Clark renting the apartment. It was Phillip." I thought back to when I'd asked Nancy about what the person renting the place looked like. Middle-aged man hadn't fit with Clark, but it sure did with Phillip.

"And since Phillip can operate his business anywhere," Ripley explained, "he's just been taking calls from his room. Like the call he had with you. He wasn't on the East Coast at all. He's been monitoring apartment 3B, looking for his chance to talk to Mathias. He tried knocking, but didn't realize that Mathias was such a shut-in. He watched the deliveries Mathias got, never able to catch him opening his door, except for one delivery guy."

"Clark." I filled in the blank.

"Yep," Ripley said. "So, on Saturday, he waited in the stairwell for Clark to show up between three and four, like he had been the days prior. The building meeting had just finished, and people were still milling about down in the lobby. Phillip tried to talk Clark into taking a bribe of one hundred dollars in order to stick his foot in the door and buy Phillip enough time to rush over and get inside so he could offer Mathias the whiskey and explain himself."

"Terrible plan." I snorted. "And that must've been what I heard going down in the stairwell: 'I won't do it,' and 'I don't want your money' was Clark telling him no." It was odd to think that I'd heard Clark when he'd still been alive.

Ripley touched the tip of her nose with her finger. "When

they heard you, Clark took the chance to get away, rushing toward the apartment to warn Mathias."

"Maybe Clark was picking up Mathias's mail for him too. It's possible he found the threatening letter and was going to tell Mathias, but this happened before he could. Clark probably assumed the threatening mail had been from Phillip, and he was worried about Mathias," I deduced.

"Probably." Ripley shrugged. "Anyway, when Clark took off into the hallway of the third floor, Phillip chased him, panicked, and hit him on the back of the head with the bottle of whiskey as the only way he could think to stop him from warning Mathias."

I stopped at the corner in front of Pioneer Square Park to wait for the light to turn.

"Phillip, reportedly, caught Clark as he fell, and spent the next minute or so reviving him. He was worried everyone would start coming upstairs, since the meeting had just ended. When Clark came to, Phillip apologized and told him he'd help him get home. He guided him to the elevator and went back for Clark's hat and the bottle. There was blood on the bottle, which freaked out Phillip. He tossed it into the garbage chute, tucking the hat in his back pocket. By the time he returned to the elevator, the doors had closed, and Clark was on his way downstairs."

The pedestrian light turned, letting us know it was okay to cross the street. Once we were in front of the Morrisey, I plopped into the same chair at the colorful bistro table in the park as I had earlier. This time, everything felt different. I listened as Ripley continued the story.

"Phillip took the stairs, but when he got downstairs, he couldn't find Clark. Assuming the guy was okay, and now in possession of his delivery hat, he thought he might get another bottle and try to fool Mathias into thinking he was from the same company. He rushed to the nearest liquor store, bought a new bottle, but by the time he returned, the place was crawling with police officers."

I narrowed my eyes. "And he came up to see what had happened?"

"He said he was worried the police presence was about him hitting the delivery guy. But then he saw that Mathias had been killed, and he freaked out even more. He threw away the hat and left, staying away for a few hours before returning to the rental."

"In the meantime, Clark stumbled into an alley and fell asleep, the thing they always tell you not to do when you have a head injury," I concluded.

Ripley nodded slowly.

I had to admit that it checked out. And if the police were sure he was in the liquor store during the time of the murder, I supposed I had to believe that too.

"You did good, Rip." I sent my friend a half smile.

She grinned proudly.

I wasn't sure how I felt about celebrating such a terrible story, but I was glad she'd been able to get us the information for Clark's sake. Speaking of the ghost, he waved at us from the lobby of the Morrisey before starting in our direction.

"Feel like telling that story one more time?" I asked.

Ripley turned to see Clark approaching.

"I can do it if you're drained," I offered.

"No. I should be the one to tell him," she said reluctantly.

I went inside to give them their privacy. As nice as it felt to know the truth behind what happened to Clark, I was back at square one. Phillip *had* killed someone, but it hadn't been Mr. Miller. Not only did I have no idea who could've killed the building recluse, but I still had no clue who had threatened Laurie or if they might still make good on their promise to hurt him.

TWENTY-ONE

As much as I wanted to go straight up to my apartment and check on the kitten, the pieces of mail Clark had of Mr. Miller's were still bothering me. How had he gotten them? And why had he kept them? They were obviously from a day prior to Saturday since they had been back at Clark's place.

I veered left before the stairwell and elevator, stopping in front of Nancy's door. I pressed her buzzer and waited.

She answered the door from behind a bundle of Fourth of July decorations. Peering over the top, she said, "Sorry, hon. I'm trying to untangle these, and I didn't want to set them down or else I'm afraid they'll take over my apartment."

With everything happening surrounding Mr. Miller's death, Clark's appearance, and now finding the kitten, I'd forgotten about the Fourth of July party tomorrow. I was immediately glad Nancy had given me and Laurie passes on contributing anything to the get-together, sure I would've let everyone down if I *had* been assigned a dish to bring.

"Here, let me help." I walked forward, hands outstretched

as I helped contain the paper flag bunting on string. I kicked Nancy's door shut behind me and almost coughed in surprise at the sheer number of decorations littering the space. The red, white, and blue clashed with the pink-and-green décor of her apartment.

She turned to the side so she could see me properly. Her cheeks turned pink. "We've gone a little bigger with the decorations since you've been gone," she explained.

"You have." I laughed. Bobbing my head to get a better view of the mess in her arms, I asked, "Are we looking for an end?"

"That would be helpful." Nancy shifted the bundle slightly. "I'm sure it's in here somewhere."

"Ah." I grabbed at an end piece, careful not to pull too hard. Threading it through another, I freed one end from the large bundle. Then I followed it, Nancy moving the bundle to help me.

After a few minutes of working like that, Nancy said, "Sorry, Nutmeg. You came to me with a question. What did you need, again? I got distracted."

"Oh, right." I had too. "I had a random question about the mail." I scrunched up my face. "You know the long-haired guy that delivers to Mr. Miller a lot?" I asked, pretending I'd seen him around before he'd died.

Nancy nodded. Of course she did.

"Does he also grab the mail for Mr. Miller?"

Frowning, Nancy said, "No, dear. He's never stopped to get Mr. Miller's mail. Julian picks it up for him."

Julian? The bachelor in 3A? I made a mental note to look into if he had any reason to want to hurt his neighbor.

"Okay, if that's the case..." Pressing my lips together, I said, "I have a follow-up question. Who has access to the mailroom?"

Instead of filling our mail slots from the front, and having to unlock each one as they did so, the mailroom had an open back so our mail could easily be sorted into the twenty-five different slots.

Nancy blinked. "Just the mailman." She balanced what was left of the bunting bundle as she scratched at her nose. "But this is such an old building. Who knows if there's a key floating around here somewhere that could open it?" Her expression turned serious. "Are you having a problem with your mail?" The defensive stance she took made me want to hug her.

"No," I answered quickly, not wanting to alarm her. "It's just ... Mr. Miller. I saw a piece of mail in his apartment when Laurie and I were searching for him, before we came to get you. It had a threatening note written on the back." It wasn't the full truth, but it would do.

Nancy gasped. "What did it say?"

I hesitated at first, not wanting to scare Nance. But she was tough; she could handle it. "I'm paraphrasing, but something about how Mr. Miller wasn't safe because they could get inside. Then they told him he had until three o'clock, on the day he died."

"The start time of our meeting." Nancy's eyes narrowed. "It has to be someone from the building, then, right?"

I bit my cheek in discomfort for a moment. "I didn't think so at first, but it seems more possible the more I learn."

"If it was, it must've been someone who didn't attend the meeting." She glanced down at the bunting in her arms and dropped it, rushing over to her office. "I took attendance. Hold on."

Disappearing into the space, the sounds of file cabinets opening and closing spilled out before she reappeared. Of course, Nancy would have the attendance sheet perfectly filed away already. Contrary to what it looked like with the decorations, she was usually in control.

She'd also found her glasses, and they were perched on the tip of her nose once more. "Let's see ... I mean, obviously Mr. Miller wasn't there. The McNairys weren't either. Also not a surprise." Nancy gave me a pointed look. "Julian said he had some work to catch up on, and Quentin was adjusting the water pressure for me in the mechanical room since it hiked up again." She tapped at her lips. "The Youngs are on vacation, of course." Her index finger jumped up and down the list as she counted.

But I didn't need her to find anyone else. "Julian wasn't there?" I asked, his name coming out with a croaky quality to it. "And he has access to Mr. Miller's mail?"

Nancy swallowed. "But why would he want to hurt Mr. Miller?"

Julian Creed was in his forties, had a successful career as an investment banker, and was a well-known serial dater in the Pioneer Square area. He'd only moved in a few years before I'd left for college, taking over the place when his mother passed away, but he'd always seemed nice enough.

"They were neighbors. Maybe they weren't on good terms," I suggested.

Iris was Penny's very best friend in the entire world *now*. But the two had started out as enemies when they were new neighbors, always fighting about Penny's late-night typing and Iris's early morning coffee grinding and music.

"If Mr. Miller was a phone psychic, maybe he was taking calls late into the night," I said, remembering the after-hours charge I'd paid Phillip to talk to him even though he hadn't really been out east.

Nancy shivered. "I would hate to think that man would do anything to hurt anyone. Plus, if they were fighting, how would he get Mr. Miller to open the door and let him in?"

Biting my lip for a moment, I said, "The threat mentioned that there was a way inside. Maybe he knew a secret entrance. Were their two apartments ever linked in any way?"

As someone who'd spent her childhood exploring the many nooks and crannies of the Morrisey, I knew the building was full of great hiding places. Laurie and I had used an old dumbwaiter to hide in until the adults worried it would break, and they boarded it up.

But Nancy shook her head. "Not that I know of."

And she'd been the manager for over twenty years. She knew this place like her favorite bread recipe.

"Well, I'll let Detective Anthony know about the mail situation and see if she can find out what Julian was doing during that window." I couldn't see much else we could do at the moment.

"I'll continue to get these decorations ready for tomorrow. Thanks for your help, dear." She patted my arm.

"Anytime." I crammed my hands in my pockets. "Oh, I wanted to let you know I found a kitten in the alley out back, so … I have a kitten now." I laughed.

Nancy beamed. "How sweet. What's their name?"

"I haven't named her yet, but she kind of looks like a black jellybean, so I'm leaning toward Licorice." Aunt Penny's writing snack of choice had always been black jellybeans. So much so that I associated the licorice smell with my aunt and the way she was always clicking away at her keyboard, penning another grand Scottish romance.

Nancy's face lit up. "My first cat was called Anise. I called her Ani for short."

Eyes wide, I said, "That's so cute. Do you mind if I borrow it?"

Nancy swatted a hand toward me. "Of course, honey. It'll be fun to keep her memory going." Her smile fell. "Watch out for her and that hole in the wall. Remember when that tiny dog Penny had went missing, and we found her a day later?"

"I'd totally forgotten about that." I immediately pictured the fist-sized hole in the corner of the room that seemed like part of the décor now. "I'll put a pillow over the hole, or roll up a towel and stick it in there."

"I'll add it to Quentin's list of repairs," Nancy said matter-of-factly. "He should have it patched up for you in no time. It's nice having someone in charge of keeping this place in good form for once."

Chuck, the maintenance man who'd worked for the building while I was growing up had been mostly useless, working harder to get *out* of fixing things for us than he had repairing anything. Nancy had tried to fire him multiple times, but he'd come up with a sob story about his chronically sick wife, so she never had the heart to go through with it. We either fixed things ourselves or learned to live with issues. I'd heard he finally retired a year after I left for college.

"I didn't realize Quentin was doing maintenance now," I said, though Laurie's mention of him, when he was talking about the locks on Mr. Miller's door, made more sense now.

Nancy shot me a sidelong glance. "Well, you didn't hear this from me, but the poor guy lost his job. He owns his apartment like you do, but he was worried he wouldn't be able to keep up with the monthly building fees. I told him he could trade fixing up things around here for the fees as long as he needed to."

"I'm sorry to hear that." It was nice of Nancy to support him like that and reminded me of yet another example of how people at the Morrisey looked out for one another. That was part of what made it so hard to believe Julian could've done anything to hurt Mr. Miller.

"Speaking of ..." Nancy said. "I should have him look at that kitchen sink of yours. I'll put that on his list too. Maybe we can finally get that fixed."

I thanked Nancy and said goodbye, promising to say hi to Quentin next time I saw him instead of avoiding him. I could talk about the weather for a few minutes. Steeling my resolve, I took the elevator up so I could use the time to call Detective Anthony. She wasn't in, so I left a message about Julian Creed, hoping Nancy and I were wrong about his involvement.

When I got up to the fifth floor, Ripley was waiting for me inside the apartment.

"Kitten's up," she reported.

"Anise," I said.

Ripley nodded in approval. "She ate some of that special food from the vet." Her eyes sparkled. "And guess what else happened?" She didn't even wait for me to guess. "Clark remembered almost everything once I told him the story from Phillip's point of view."

I blinked. "That's ... great." It took me a moment to process the news. "And he corroborated the story that Phillip couldn't have killed Mr. Miller?"

"Well, he'd just been hit on the head, so he said that part is still fuzzy," Ripley told me. "But he did say that Phillip approached him and said he just wanted to talk to Mathias, that they were old friends, and he'd traveled a long way to have a drink with him."

I mirrored her unease. I supposed that was as good as we were going to get.

"He *did* remember why he had the letters, though. That happened the day before." Ripley held up a finger. I listened with interest as she said, "Clark was late for the delivery after Mr. Miller's on Friday, so he burst into the stairwell a little too fast and collided with another guy from the building. He'd been holding a bunch of mail, and it went everywhere."

"Did he mention what the man looked like?" I asked, my whole body tensing as I waited.

Ripley's forehead creased. "He said the guy kinda looked like a silver fox."

"Julian," I whispered. Even though the man wasn't totally gray yet, I could definitely see someone describing him as a silver fox.

Unaware of my conversation with Nancy, or why Julian might be important, Ripley continued on with her story. "Clark helped Julian pick up the mail, and he apologized, but once he reached the bottom of the stairwell, he realized a couple of the letters had drifted all the way down there. He grabbed them, seeing they were both for Mr. Miller, and planned to bring them next time he did a delivery, on Monday. Clark didn't normally stop by on weekends," Ripley explained. "He didn't notice the threatening note written on the back until that night when he got home with the letters. He didn't take them with him on Saturday because he wasn't set to deliver to Mr. Miller that day, but as the hours passed by at work, the note bugged him enough that he decided to stop by the Morrisey and check on Mr. Miller around three o'clock." Ripley sighed. "And, as we know, he never even made it there because Phillip was waiting."

"So Mr. Miller didn't even get the threat?" I thought through the implications of that. "It really could've been Julian, since he dropped off Mr. Miller's mail."

When Ripley gave me a confused scowl, I filled her in on what Nancy had told me and how I'd called Detective Anthony to let her know she should look into Julian Creed.

Remembering one last thing from my conversation with Nancy, I added, "Oh, and Quentin's going to come and fix the sink. Isn't that cool? He's doing maintenance for the building."

"I'll believe it when I see it," Ripley said. "That thing's been broken your whole life." Pausing for a moment, Ripley said, "Wait. If Quentin is doing maintenance, do you think he has keys to all the apartments?"

"Probably." My eyebrows rose. "Oh! You think that was how he got inside, even though Mr. Miller wouldn't open the door?"

"It's worth it to double-check," Ripley said. "Though Quentin has about as much reason to want Mr. Miller dead as Julian."

"I'll ask him when he comes to fix the sink."

A small meow came from the bathroom, and I set my purse on the hook next to the door, excited to get to know my newest roommate.

Detective Anthony knew everything I did. It was clear the police had this case under control. I could let it go and focus on figuring out what I was going to do with my life. Easy, right?

TWENTY-TWO

The next morning, I got my chance to talk to Quentin when he came by the apartment, a toolbox in one hand and a leather tool belt strapped around his thin waist.

"Welcome," I said, stepping aside so he could enter.

I had Anise tucked under one arm. She was fast asleep again, going from manic zoom sessions around the bathroom one minute to sleeping like the dead the next. I'd run the flea comb over her a million times over the last twelve hours and had yet to find any more fleas, but I was still being cautious and didn't want to give her free rein of the apartment, especially not until Quentin patched up that hole in the wall. She was also still learning how to use the litter box, so it wasn't the worst thing for her to stay in the bathroom a little longer.

"Welcome back, Meg." Quentin nodded in greeting. "I don't think I've gotten a chance to talk to you since you moved back."

"Yeah, that's because you corner people and expect them to

talk about the weather," Ripley quipped from where she stood near the window.

Wincing as the guilt of avoiding him hit home, I said, "I know. We've been like ships passing."

If I were being honest, small talk was feeling less and less awful now that I was back with my Morrisey family. I wondered if maybe I'd just grown to dislike it so much over the course of moving from New York to Chicago and back to New York. When it was with people I loved and cared about, it felt easier.

"Supposed to be a hot one today," Quentin said, setting his toolbox down on the kitchen floor.

I avoided looking over at Ripley as she let out a wry laugh. "Perfect for a Fourth of July party," I said.

Rummaging around, he pulled out a headlamp and strapped it to his forehead. "I've got a lot on my list today, so I'm not sure if I'll get up there. I'll at least have to pop up and grab some of Nancy's brownies."

Each resident had at least one food they waited for all year. For me, it was the Rosenbloom sisters' Jell-O trifle: berry gelatin layered between fresh berries, homemade jam, buttery shortcake biscuits, and whipped cream. Growing up, it hadn't felt like summer had begun until I had a bowl—or three—of that during the annual rooftop picnic.

"Next year, once I'm more settled, I'll have to make Penny's famous red-white-and-blue rice crispy treats." I leaned back on the kitchen counter.

Quentin nodded. "I miss those." Crouching down, he opened the doors under the sink and moved onto his back as he clicked on the headlamp.

"Well, you let me know if you need any help," I said,

wandering away. I didn't want him to feel like he had an audience.

"Will do," he called from under the sink.

Ripley crossed her arms and said, "The keys."

"Oh." I stopped a few feet away. That was the problem with small talk; it distracted me. "I almost forgot to ask ... but when I was at Mr. Miller's apartment the other day, I noticed an extra dead bolt had been installed on the door. Is that something you installed for him? Like, could I get one for my door?" I asked.

Quentin huffed but kept working. "I didn't install that. He did it himself, and it's against the building agreement. The management has to be able to get inside in case one of us, you know, dies alone, and no one finds us."

I gulped, holding Anise closer.

"Once the police release the apartment, I'll have to go uninstall that." Quentin grunted as his forearms flexed through a particularly tight turn of whatever joint he was working on.

"Cool, okay. And Nance mentioned the hole in the wall too?"

"Yup," Quentin said. "I'll get to it right after this, which should be almost done." He tightened one last thing, then crawled out. Handing me the big bowl we kept underneath, he said, "You shouldn't need this anymore." Ripping a few sheets of blue paper towels off a roll he'd brought with him, Quentin placed them where the bowl used to be. "For the next few days, just open the sink doors and check to see that there's no moisture on these towels. They'll turn dark blue if there is. If it still leaks, call me, and I'll try something else." He swiped sweat from his forehead.

Holding the hand that wasn't cradling the kitten up, like I

was preparing to take the stand in a courtroom, I said, "I promise I will check it daily to see."

Quentin gave me a salute. "Okay, off to patch that hole. You said it's in the wall?"

"The left corner." I motioned to the place where the western wall of the apartment butted up to the brick exterior wall.

It only took him a few minutes to patch the hole, and then I was free to go up to the roof. Ripley and Clark joined me as I helped get the place decorated for the party. We were coming around to the understanding that Clark might just be around for a while, since his death was no longer a mystery and he was still here. Based on the way Ripley seemed lost in his eyes, she'd not only forgiven him for their fight yesterday, but she wasn't upset that Clark was staying.

The official start time of the party was around two when we would have a late lunch of barbecue, assorted salads, and red-white-and-blue desserts, but the party would go all evening, culminating in the Seattle fireworks tonight. From our rooftop, we could just see the top of the Space Needle, the setting of the pyrotechnic show the city put on each year.

After lunch, we packed the food in coolers that would remain on the roof so people could go back for seconds throughout the evening, and then the games began. There were always two sets of games going at once. Next to the greenhouse, there was either a game of bocce ball or Kubb happening. The standing and tossing games were easier on the older residents.

The other side of the roof became headquarters for active games like Scram Ball, a dodgeball adjacent game featuring multicolored wristbands, a foam ball, and hitting people with said ball. We'd experimented with a few Frisbee-based games over the years, but had lost too many over the side of the building.

It wasn't until I was taking a large bite out of my first hot dog that I spotted Laurie. I hadn't been avoiding him, but I'd been so caught up in the investigation that our paths hadn't crossed since that emergency building meeting Sunday night. He lifted his chin in greeting and made his way over to me, giving me just enough time to frantically chew the mouthful of food I'd just bitten off.

"Hey, stranger." He smiled at me, but I knew his expressions like I knew Ripley's. Even though his mouth was pulled into a grin, worry pinched at the skin around his dark-brown eyes.

Swallowing, I said, "Hey, back." I set the rest of the hot dog on my plate.

Laurie placed a hand on my arm, checked over his shoulder, and guided me over to the corner of the roof where we stepped behind one of the larger potted plants. "Meg, I owe you an apology." I didn't miss how he kept his hand cupped around my elbow.

"For what?" I asked, searching his face for clues.

He squeezed his eyes shut for a moment, as if trying to get rid of a memory. "I handled that conversation about your art the other night so poorly. I can see now that telling you I was frustrated with you for giving up was the wrong way to go about that. Instead of listening and being there as a friend, I tried to fix it." He scoffed as he let his hand fall away from where it had been touching my elbow. "I don't blame you for pulling away."

I couldn't think of what to say at first, mostly because it was too sweet. Laurie was outdoing himself on the thoughtfulness scale at that point. But I could see he was worried, and I needed to say something.

"Oh, Laurie. I wasn't upset about that." Pressing my lips together, I added, "I mean, I am bothered by the art stuff, but I wasn't offended by what you said. There are still a lot of things I have to figure out, and you're right, it's all stuff I have to work on, not something other people can solve for me." I stopped, unsure if I should say the next part. But he'd just been very honest with me, and he deserved to get that same respect back. "The reason I pulled away was because of what you said at that meeting about letting the detective handle the case. I wasn't ready to give it up, and I thought you were, so I tried not to pull you into it."

"That?" He looked over his shoulder once more to make sure there was no one within earshot. "I said that to keep all of them out of it. I didn't mean *you*. I was having fun investigating with you." His lips pulled into a half smile.

"Me too." I couldn't help the warm feeling that expanded through my chest at his words. "And, if we're being honest about what we should've done differently, I'm sorry I didn't just talk to you about it instead of assuming that's what you meant and pulling away."

He smoothed the sleeve of his T-shirt. "Meg, you never cease to be the easiest person to talk to. I thought I'd built you up over these years apart. My mom even complains about how I compare everyone to you. But I have to tell her it wasn't my imagination. You really *are* just this remarkable. I have no doubt in my mind that you'll figure out what to do next, and you'll be just as amazing at it as you were at your art."

Was I a person or had I just exploded into a million joyful

pieces of glass, sparkling in the summer sunshine? Laurie compared everyone to *me*?

"Penny would say the same thing about you to me," I blurted out before I could lose my nerve.

Was this about to be the moment in our lifelong friendship when we went from being friends to something more, like I'd always wanted? Would we tell our kids about the day everything changed, on the rooftop of the Morrisey at our favorite party of the year?

Laurie's phone rang, buzzing away in his pocket. "Sorry, I'm on call today, so I have to see what this is about." His hand grazed my elbow again before he stepped away to answer.

Based on the smoothness of his tone, and the way he kept telling the other person to take a breath and that he would help, I gleaned there was an issue at work. So I wasn't at all surprised when he turned around and said, "I've got to work, but I'll see you up here later for the fireworks, right?"

"I wouldn't miss it." The disappointment sitting heavy on my chest lifted a fraction. Maybe our moment could still happen, it might just be under the stars and colorful explosions instead of in the middle of the day.

Laurie raised a hand in a wave and veered toward the buffet, grabbing a few items to go before going back down to his apartment. I mingled for a while longer, but went to check on the kitten. Between lunch and the fireworks that evening, people flowed in and out of the party. The families with little ones usually took them down for some quiet time and maybe a nap so they could stay up later tonight. The older residents did the same, getting a laugh when they compared themselves to the toddlers.

After telling Ripley every detail from my conversation with

Laurie, Anise and I snuggled, napping together on the couch as the sun dipped lower in the summer sky. I woke just as Ripley was leaving. She and Clark were going to watch the fireworks from the top floor of the Columbia Tower. I didn't blame her. I'd want to see them from that vantage point as well, if I could.

When I reemerged onto the roof, dressed warmer, there was a fire going in the new firepit. The glow of the flames danced on the brick half wall that ran the perimeter of the building as my neighbors chatted, seated at the various table options around the roof. All the games had been packed away, and only the desserts were set out on the tables.

Everyone called out greetings as I moved through the different small conversational groups. But among the familiar faces, I saw one I hadn't expected.

"Opal?" I asked, confusion written in the lines I was sure were forming on my forehead.

The woman appeared to be in the process of being eaten alive by one of the outdoor chairs. The cushions probably weighed more than she did. She beamed up at me. "Ah, Megan. So good to see you again."

"What are you doing here? Visiting?" I asked, glancing over at Nancy, whom she'd been talking to. Maybe they were having a meeting of the building managers, past and present.

Opal's eyes lit up. "Actually..."

Nancy stood and reached forward for my hand. Patting it, she led me to her now open seat and directed me to take her place. "I'm going to make sure the desserts are all covered for the fireworks. You two have a nice chat."

Once we were alone, I turned to Opal, hoping she might finish her sentence.

She didn't disappoint. "I'm going to be moving back into the Morrisey."

"That's amazing. How?" But just as the question left my lips, I knew the answer. "Mr. Miller's apartment."

She touched her nose. "After speaking with you the other day, I called Nancy and told her I wanted to move back. I asked her to keep me in mind if you all ever had a unit open up. Imagine my surprise when she said something just had. She told me she'd keep me apprised of the situation with his estate. At that point, she wasn't sure if he had any living relatives he'd left the place to, as is so often the case with this building." She crossed one black-legging-clad leg over the other. "But as of today, she says it's going to be for sale, and I want to buy it."

"I'm so happy you'll be back." A feeling of warmth enveloped me that had nothing to do with the nearby firepit. My excitement waned for a moment. "And you don't mind living where a man ... died?" I whispered.

Opal blew a raspberry. "Oh, please. During the twenty-nine years I was the building manager here, with the number of people who stay in their apartments until they die at the Morrisey, you'd be hard-pressed to live in a place where someone hasn't died. And with the building's history, I'm sure there have been just as many murders. I'll just make sure I smudge the place before moving in."

Nancy bustled over with two servings of trifle. Opal and I thanked her, digging in and eating contentedly for a few seconds.

Her mention of smudging made me wonder about the local ghosts' inability to enter. Was that what Mathias had done to keep them away, or did he know a different method? Whatever he'd done had lasted even after he'd died. How long would such a block hold? Now that Opal mentioned it, Mr. Miller's apartment might actually be the *least* haunted of the rooms in the building. I smiled to myself at the inside joke.

As Opal and I ate our dessert, Julian came up onto the roof, leading a pretty woman in a sparkling dress. He wore a dark suit, and they looked like they'd just come from a fancy dinner. Picking at a pill on my sweatshirt, I realized with Quentin's confirmation that Mr. Miller was the only one who could've unlocked that dead bolt. Someone getting in through an adjoining room was the most likely option left. Opal's statement about how long she'd lived in the Morrisey got me thinking.

"Hey, Opal. Do you know if there are any secret passages between any of the apartments? Like, were any of them ever connected in a way that might make it easy to go from one to the other?" I fiddled with my now-empty trifle cup.

Nancy's answer yesterday echoed in my mind. It was a silly question. The Morrisey was an old building, but that didn't mean it had secret passages.

"Never mind. Sorry, that was a ridiculous question." I shook my head.

Opal studied me. After a moment, she said, "Well, now I'm not sure if you want to know about the passages or not."

"Wait. There are?" I sat forward.

Opal's eyes lit with the flames of the fire, dancing in the darkness. "I've never found them myself, but there are stories—so many they have to be real."

TWENTY-THREE

Scooting my chair closer, I checked around to make sure no one was listening and whispered, "What are the stories?"

Opal's mischievous grin was back as she moved a little closer and whispered, "Back when I was the building manager, a reporter came to do a story on the Morrisey's history. While he was writing, I gave him access to the building and any documents I could find to do with its construction. After he was done, he sent me a copy. It was fascinating." Her eyes glowed in the fire's light. "William H. Morrisey, the man who owned this building in the late eighteen hundreds, was a complete crook of a man." Opal exhaled a wry laugh. "He bought the place for close to nothing in the wake of the fire that took out the commercial district in 1889 and rebuilt. Like many others in Seattle at the time, he capitalized on the fact that the gold rushers were using our city as an outfitting location to gather supplies before they headed up to Alaska."

I listened like I had when I was a little girl, and Aunt Penny would make up bedtime stories for me about dragons and girls who went on adventures to solve centuries-old mysteries in far away kingdoms.

Opal took a sip of the punch sitting on the table next to her. "The reporter found tons of stories from the time that said Morrisey had ordered the builders to include secret passages into each of the rooms. His supposition was that if they stayed in Seattle on their way to Alaska, they would stop here on their way back. He hoped to sneak in and steal the gold from the boarders while they were asleep." Opal chuckled. "Of course, the average person hoping to 'strike it rich' didn't bring back half as much gold as they expected, if they found any. And once he'd robbed a few travelers, the building got a reputation for being dangerous. He lost all the money he put into it because no one would stay here. Morrisey's passageways were a bust, and they were eventually all boarded up." She shrugged.

I pulled a deep breath into my lungs, as if I'd been waiting to inhale until I knew how the story ended.

"And you've never found them?" I asked. "You have no idea where they are?"

"Well, they're in the walls, of course." Opal's eyes narrowed in a way that told me she thought I might be daft. "I can tell you they're not connected to the manager's apartment. I've searched every inch of that place and never found anything. Other people aren't as keen on letting me do a detailed examination of their apartments without knowing why. And it's very important no one finds out about them."

"Why?" I asked.

"Because if the residents knew there were secret ways to get into their apartments, no one would ever feel safe. It would be pandemonium," she scoffed.

My gaze caught on Julian across the roof with his date.

"Right, and it's safer if no one knows. There's just one problem with that. I think one of us *does know* about the passages, and he used them to kill Mr. Miller."

Opal raised her brows. "Oh. Yes, that *would* be a problem. You think the killer is someone in the building?"

Swallowing, I nodded.

Opal and I sat in silence for a few moments while the fire crackled next to us, and the small groups of residents chattered away.

"I have the key for the apartment," Opal said, breaking the quiet that had expanded between us. When I glanced over at her in confusion, she amended, "Three B. Nancy said that the detective cleared the apartment. I can't move in yet because a cleaning crew needs to go through the place, and they have to figure out what to do with Mr. Miller's belongings, but she gave me the key in return for my down payment."

I wasn't sure what she wanted me to say.

She huffed. "If you wanted to go in there and search for that passageway, I have the key." She continued to whisper, but it was much more forceful this time as she willed me to understand what she was alluding to.

"Oh!" I said louder than I should've. Smiling at the few residents who looked my way, hoping to show them that everything was okay, and there was nothing to see here. I turned back to Opal. "Actually, I would really appreciate that. Are you sure?"

She clicked her tongue. "Sure. In exchange, when you find that secret passage, tell me where it is, so I can put my heaviest piece of furniture in front of it when I move in." Her tiny body moved in a theatrical shiver.

Rummaging around in her purse, she pulled out the key and slid it into my palm, winking like we were spies. I nodded once, as covertly as I could, before standing, wandering over to the dessert table to grab a brownie. While I ate, I made sure Julian was still over by the greenhouse, chatting with his date. This was the perfect time.

Seeing my opening, I slipped toward the stairwell. It was late, and the fireworks would start anytime now. Usually, I was loathe to miss the show, but tonight the promise of answers about the death in our building was more enticing.

I slunk down the stairwell, hesitating twice when I thought I heard someone coming. Because of my slow progress, it took me an unnervingly long time to reach the third floor. Once I did, I found the hallway empty. I raced for 3B, fingers shaking as I inserted the key and turned until I heard the lock click.

The apartment door opened, moving in just a few inches, like it had that day Laurie had knocked. And just like that day, I stood at the threshold, frozen for a moment. The feeling of stepping forward was wrapped up in so many other decisions. It felt like something I couldn't take back.

I pushed open the door and stepped inside. Closing it as quietly as I could behind myself, I debated locking it once more. On one hand, I didn't want anyone coming in through the door to find me snooping around. On the other, the person I was most worried about knew a different way inside, and the door might be my only escape.

A flash of Mr. Miller racing for the front door, unlocking that dead bolt, turning the knob, and almost pulling it open before being jumped by the murderer flashed through my mind as I closed my eyes. Maybe that was why the door had been open. It wasn't how the killer had gotten inside, it was how Mr. Miller had tried to escape. It just hadn't quite worked out for him.

Gulping, I searched for the light switch. My fingers found it, but again, I froze. I wasn't sure what was worse, someone from the outside seeing a beam of light flash around the dark apartment, or someone from my building, who knew this apartment should be empty, seeing the lights on inside. I went with the latter option, partly because they might think the police left the lights on by accident and partly because the hairs on my arm were standing on end, and I could use as much light as possible.

But as light illuminated the apartment, a figure in the room made me bite back a scream. My heart slammed against my chest, and I backed up until I hit the door.

The mannequin. I'd forgotten about the creepy woman standing next to Miller's kitchen.

I considered turning around. Maybe I should wait until I had Ripley or even Laurie here with me. I gulped as I eyed the mannequin. Then again, I was already inside. I could do this. Right?

"You just stay over there," I ordered the mannequin, feeling better hearing my voice in the silent space.

Opal had been sure the passages were inside the walls. I turned to the wall to my left and then to the right. The wall to my right, where Mr. Miller's kitchen was situated, was closest to Julian's apartment. But the left wall held a built-in wardrobe, the bathroom, and bedroom in this unit. It seemed easier to hide a secret passage in something like a closet than it did in a kitchen. And that way, I could stay as far as possible from the mannequin.

Maybe I'd just read too many stories about secret worlds hidden within wardrobes as a kid, but I started there. All the closets in the Morrisey were built in. That, in and of itself, had never seemed suspicious to me before. But now that I knew of

William H. Morrisey's plan, it seemed like the perfect place to easily slip in and out of a room if you wanted to go unnoticed.

Opening the wooden door to the wardrobe, I pushed the few jackets Mr. Miller still had hanging there, to the right, away from the wall. Studying the leftmost wall and running my fingers along the edges, it didn't take me long to realize the whole panel moved. It was minute, only a millimeter or two, but it was enough for me to see that the side was not attached to the rest of the wardrobe.

If I were going all in on Opal's story about William H. Morrisey and his thief-ready passages, that meant they wouldn't need to be accessible from inside the apartments. Any handles or latches would likely be on the other side.

I leaned my weight into the panel, laying my palms flat against it as I felt it move, then I moved it to the left and right. It didn't budge on the left, but it slid to the right. Pushing it all the way open, I stared at an interior wall of the building. It was unfinished and only a few feet away from me, but big enough for a person to fit inside.

With one last inhale, I stepped forward.

Now I needed my flashlight. Actually, what I really needed was one of those headlamps Quentin had on while he was fixing my sink today, so I could keep my hands free. Oh well. I held my phone in front of me as I slid the door closed behind me. The passageway smelled like damp newspapers. Cobwebs and dust clung to almost every surface.

Just as I suspected, the entrance into the apartment held a lock on this side. They wanted to get in; it wasn't about other people getting out. Remembering the mannequin, I locked the panel to 3B, then used my flashlight to inspect the passageway.

To my right, toward the exterior wall, I couldn't see a thing.

The passage hit a dead end at the brick wall. The opening was tall, mirroring the fifteen-foot ceilings we had in our apartments. But as I swung the light to the left, I was confronted with something I didn't expect.

To the left of me, where the third-floor hallway would be, stood a partial wall. A brick and plaster surface rose in front of me for about eight or nine feet. Rungs from a vertical ladder stuck out of the wall, showing me exactly how the thieves would've made their way from one floor to the next. But even though the apartment walls continued higher on either side, there was about a five-foot gap at the top. The passage was dark.

Turning my focus to my feet, I noticed a hole in the floor just before the ladder and a similar crawl space below that. I got onto my stomach, shining my flashlight into that space. The dusty crawl space spanned the hallway area, the light illuminating other passages across the building.

I gasped. That was why the ceilings in the hallways were so much lower than those in our apartments. They had to leave space so they could access the passages between each apartment all at once.

Spinning around so I was on my bottom, which I was sure was now completely covered in dust, I tucked my phone under my chin, held on to the lowest rung of the ladder on the wall, and dropped into the crawl space just below the third floor. On my hands and knees to distribute my weight—the building was old, and I didn't want to come busting through the ceiling if I could help it—I crawled toward 3A, Julian's place.

I stopped at the opening of another passage to my left. Slithering like a dusty creature out of the hallway crawl space, I found myself in a similar passage in between the right wall of Mr. Miller's old apartment and the left wall of Julian's.

And directly in front of me was a panel. Living in an A unit myself, I knew this also led into the built-in wardrobe next to the front door.

But unlike the entrance to 3B, a large board had been placed diagonally over the door and nailed in place. From the dust and old nails, I could tell it had been there for decades.

Julian Creed couldn't have been the one to sneak out of his apartment and into Mr. Miller's.

TWENTY-FOUR

Any relief surrounding my realization that Julian probably wasn't the killer was put on hold as I took a few moments to scour the whole passage in between 3A and 3B to make sure that was the only way in or out of the apartment.

The moment I thought I was feeling more comfortable in the crawl spaces, I would hear a distant screech or the scuffling of small feet. I made a note to talk to Nancy about getting someone to look into pest control for the building.

Satisfied that Julian couldn't have traveled between his apartment and Mr. Miller's, I decided to move on.

The only problem was that I was stuck. Not physically. I could technically turn around and go back to where I'd come from. I could climb one of these ladders to the fourth floor or go down to the second.

But what would I be searching for?

I was at a suspect dead end. Julian had been my last guess, an admittedly weak one at that. Sure, the discovery of the passages answered the question of how the killer had gotten into 3B, but that didn't help me much if I didn't have an inkling of a clue who in the building wanted him dead.

Chewing on my lip, I decided it was best to turn back. An uneasy feeling in my stomach stopped me, and I peered up toward the fourth and fifth floors. I wished I had tools with me to block the entrances into mine and Laurie's apartments, just like someone had done with Julian's.

I pursed my lips. Who was to say someone hadn't? Maybe Mr. Miller's was one of the few still open. Knowing it would give me peace of mind, I decided it was worth the climb.

By the time I reached the crawl space just below the fourth floor, my fingers ached from clinging to the small vertical ladder rungs. Scooting toward 4B, I let out a frustrated sigh as I saw the entrance to Laurie's apartment was not blocked off.

Exhaling my frustration, I climbed up one more flight to find mine similarly unhindered. Great. I was about to head back down to the third floor—it was time to rejoin the party; I was sure the fireworks would happen any minute now—when the light of my flashlight landed on something caught on one of the exposed beams in the crawl space. It was the corner of a blue material. It was soft, almost quilted between my fingers as I picked it up.

I sucked in a quick breath. It wasn't fabric, but paper towel. My mind replayed Quentin laying a few sheets of the stuff under the sink earlier when he'd fixed the leak. Something told me they didn't have the special color-changing paper towels back in the gold rush days when William H. Morrisey's guys were moving through here.

Which meant this had to be from a recent passage-goer. And no one else in the building had cause to carry around maintenance-type items like this. It also didn't help that it was here, in the crawl space of the fifth floor, Quentin's floor.

A shiver raced down my back as I pointed my flashlight across the crawl space toward apartment 5E. Could Quentin have something to do with Mr. Miller's death? He had about as much motive to kill the guy as Julian had, but my gut told me I needed to check. His entrance could very well be blocked off, too, helping me rule him out as easily as I had with Julian.

Sticking to the beams, I eased across the ceiling of the fourth floor. As I crawled, my conversation with Nancy yesterday replayed in my mind. Quentin had lost his job, so he was doing maintenance around the building to pay for his monthly building fees. It was hard to picture my neighbor, who constantly talked about the weather, hurting anyone, but I also knew that money issues made people do things they wouldn't normally do. Had he figured out that Mathew Miller was actually Mathias the Medium and asked him for money? Was that what the threatening note had been about?

There was only one way to find out. I moved down until I could slip into the passage between 5E and 5D. My heart rate rose as I stood in front of the entrance into apartment 5E. Not only was Quentin's entrance not blocked with anything, but the latch was undone, proving he'd recently used it—possibly very recently.

A terrible chill moved over me as I wondered if he was here, in the passages with me right now. If he was, he might already know someone had figured out his secret. I needed to hurry. My fingers hovered over my phone screen. I wanted to call Detective Anthony, but I knew the detail-oriented detective would need more proof than the corner of a blue paper towel I'd found in the crawl space.

I pressed my ear up to the panel, listening to Quentin's apartment. Hearing nothing inside, I slid the panel open as quietly as I could. Just as with Mr. Miller's, the passage led me into Quentin's built-in wardrobe. Although it was dark inside, I could see light spilling in through the cracks.

I waited for a full minute, breathing as evenly and soundlessly as I could, just in case he was inside. Once I was sure I was alone, I slipped out, peeking around what I could see of the apartment.

His place was a mess. I'd never seen inside in all the years I'd grown up here, so I couldn't speak to whether this was a normal state for him or if he was in a spiral of depression, but he sure wasn't using his time between handyman jobs to clean. Dirty dishes piled in the sink. Take-out containers littered the counters and the coffee table next to a dusty couch. The bedroom door was open, showing off an even messier bedroom.

My footsteps were as light as possible as I crept over to the bedroom and peered inside. He wasn't here. I edged over to the desk, which was covered with piles of papers and scribbled handwritten notes. None of the numbers made sense to me, but I recognized the name of a few major league sports teams.

Had Quentin gotten into gambling? Recognizing the writing, I pulled out my phone and located the picture I'd taken of the threatening note written on the back of Mr. Miller's mail.

Swallowing, I held it up to one of the notes on Quentin's desk. Other than being written in different-colored ink, it was an exact match. The letters were all capitalized in the gambling notes just as they had been on the threat.

A pile of mail sat to my right on the desk. I didn't need to open any of them to know they were past-due notices for bills. The red stamp on the front was clear enough. Seeing the mail reminded me of what Nancy had said about the mailroom. If an old key to the mailroom had been floating around the mechanical room downstairs, Quentin could've gained access to the mail, not only to write that threat to Mr. Miller, but possibly that had been how he'd figured out Mr. Miller was, in fact, Mathias the Medium, in the first place.

And although I was sure Mathias had racked up quite a bit of money over the years running a successful phone-in psychic operation, the reason Quentin targeted Mr. Miller became clear as my gaze caught on one note that had been pinned to the wall behind the desk.

It was a betting slip from Emerald Downs, the local racetrack, and the word *WIN* had been scrawled along the top. Then, along the bottom, another note read *TIP FROM 3B*.

So it hadn't been money he wanted from Mathias the Medium; it was psychic tips about which way to bet. And it had obviously paid off once. Had he threatened Mathias to make him help again?

Because I'd broken into his apartment to find this evidence, I was pretty sure none of it would stand up in court, but at least I knew. I pulled up my recent calls and clicked on the one I'd received from Detective Anthony. It was probably the phone on her desk, but it was worth a try. I clicked on the line and waited as it rang.

"Detective Anthony," I said as loudly as I dared. "This is Meg Dawson from the Morrisey. I believe the killer was Quentin Maples of apartment 5E. He lost his job, has a gambling addiction, and has access to each of the apartments since he's the maintenance person for the building. Please let me know if you get this."

Not mentioning the secret passageways had been a last-minute decision, but I felt good about the omission. I'd already admitted to the woman that I'd called a phone psychic. If I started rambling about passageways between apartments, Detective Anthony might think I was losing it. It would be much easier to tell her about the spaces when I could show her in person. But at least she had the information about Quentin for now.

Crawling back through the space above the hallway, I heard a dog barking.

"Leo?" I whispered, recognizing his bark and that it was coming from the direction of 4B.

At first I thought he might've heard me in the passageway, a creak he wasn't used to or a board groaning, but the barking continued. It wasn't the three alert barks Laurie had taught him. These barks were low, with a growling quality to them. That was the sound of a dog in distress.

Was something bad happening in Laurie's apartment? My heartbeat ratcheted up. He'd left the party to take care of that work emergency. Had he gone back up, or was he still inside?

Suddenly, the barking stopped. The abruptness felt eerie, making me shiver even though the passage was stuffy and hot.

Scooting over to the northern passages, I crept down the ladder and stood in front of the sliding door into Laurie's apartment. It was open an inch. Someone had entered, but not from the door. Quentin was inside, with Leo and possibly Laurie. Now the silence worried me even more.

Had he done something to hurt Laurie? Though, even if Laurie *was* up on the roof, Leo was still inside. If he'd killed a man over money, would he hurt a dog to keep his secret? I decided I couldn't take the chance. I had to check on Leo.

Sliding the panel open, it deposited me into Laurie's front

wardrobe. The door was open a few inches, like Quentin hadn't completely shut it in his haste. I ducked behind a jacket that smelled like Laurie and listened.

It was deathly quiet.

Being that the wardrobe faced the apartment door, I couldn't see anything from inside. I was going to have to leave the cover of the wardrobe if I wanted to check on Leo.

Slowly pushing the door open, I crept out into the entryway. I craned my neck around the bathroom and scanned the space. I couldn't see the bedroom from here, but Laurie wasn't in the living room or kitchen. Leo was still in his crate. He was lying down, licking a wooden spoon that Quentin had stuck into his crate. The thing was covered in peanut butter. But was it just peanut butter or had Quentin added something else—something harmful—to the treat? Before I could think more about that, I caught a movement by Laurie's desk.

Quentin was rummaging through the drawers. Keeping my eye on him, I crept over to the front door and unlocked it, giving myself another option in case I needed to get out quickly. Now that Leo was in the picture, the passage wasn't an escape option. I could barely navigate those vertical ladders by myself, let alone carrying a large dog.

The lock snicked open quietly as I solidified my escape route. Heart pounding, I studied Quentin's back as I moved closer to Leo, unsure what my plan was but knowing I needed to get between him and the dog.

Despite the lure of peanut butter, Leo noticed me walking toward him. His floppy ears perked up, and he stood, wagging his tail. I winced as Leo's tail hit the crate over and over again, the sound reverberating through the room.

Spinning around, Quentin glowered at Leo. Anger crumpled his features as he followed the dog's excited gaze, and he registered my presence. I was still feet away from the crate when I stopped, hand outstretched.

"Meg." Quentin took a step forward, then stopped. "What are you doing here?" He eyed the closed apartment door, then my dusty clothing. His gaze flicked over to the wardrobe I'd left open when I'd snuck out of it.

It wasn't any use lying.

"I'm here to stop you from making a mistake, Quentin," I said carefully as I moved closer to Leo.

"Freeze, young lady." He was probably only twenty years my senior, but when people had known you since you were a child, it seemed they forever had the right to call you a young lady.

Leo was still panting and wagging his tail, none the wiser.

"Did you give him something harmful?" I asked, emotion straining my voice and causing it to shake.

Quentin scoffed. "It's just peanut butter. I needed him to shut up so I could search the place."

"For what?" I pleaded.

His expression darkened. "I know he has that letter with my note to Miller on it. It wasn't in the apartment after Laurence searched the place." He spat the sentence out like an accusation.

"*You* took the mail." Understanding encompassed me.

Quentin was right that it was missing from apartment 3B, and that someone else had it. He just had the wrong person. Nancy's guess about a mailroom key floating around the place had been correct. And Quentin, now spending a lot of time in the mechanical room, had found it.

"Wait. How'd you know it was just Laurie who went inside the apartment?" I asked.

235

The assumption that my thoughtless comment about Laurie having seen *the guy* only made sense if the killer was an outsider. Quentin knew about Laurie's 'sighting,' so why had he targeted Laurie instead of both of us?

"I was in the secret passage with Miller, waiting for the two of you to leave." He cleared his throat. "I heard you stay in the hall, and I know Laurie went through the mail."

"You killed him in the passageway?" I hadn't seen any blood in the space just outside of Mr. Miller's apartment.

"No, I just kept him quiet. I wanted to give him another chance to reconsider my offer," Quentin explained. "He tried to escape out into the hall the first time. But when you and Laurence left, and we came out of the passageway, Miller saw you two had left the door open and he ran for it." Quentin coughed. "Well, he tried to. It was never my plan to hurt him. I was even going to give him a cut of my earnings!" He raked a hand through his hair as he scanned the apartment. "I just have to find that letter, and everything will be okay."

"What makes you think Laurie took it?" I asked.

"At first, I thought he showed it to the cops. I'd left a note for him about the times I could come by to fix a cabinet door, and I figured he recognized my handwriting." Quentin's eyes flicked around the room in paranoia. "But I was in the passages while he talked to the police. He didn't tell on me. Which means he wants something from me, and he's going to leverage that note for money."

"Has he?" I frowned.

"Not *yet*, but he keeps dropping hints. He's asked me to come to his apartment and fix small things every day since, and each time he mentions the murder and asks if I have any ideas about leads. It's all part of his tactic, to make me nervous. Well,

I decided to take things into my own hands and steal the letter back before he could use it against me."

The man had pieced together half truths and worries until he found an enemy he could focus his guilty attention on.

"Laurie doesn't have that letter," I said, sliding my back foot closer to the dog crate.

Quentin's eyes settled on me, inching away from him. "So it was you who took it? But you didn't go inside. It sounds like we have more to discuss." He growled and pointed to the couch. "Sit." When I didn't move at first, he walked over to the kitchen and grabbed a knife from Laurie's knife block.

I gulped and did as he said. "What's your plan here, Quentin?" I asked. "Are you going to kill me too?"

"I don't know. Okay? I'm not sure!" His face turned a purple red. "Just give me a moment."

The sight of him losing his temper was too terrifying. I had to glance away. I tried to calm my hammering heart by looking at Leo, remembering the last time I'd sat on this couch. That night had been so lovely. Leo had been draped over my lap, not in his crate looking forlorn.

My brain pinged something else from that night. The bat Laurie had next to the couch, the one he'd kept there ever since receiving the threat. Then I noticed the windows behind Leo were open, letting the stuffy apartment cool down after the hot day. A plan formed in my mind.

I didn't think as I reached for the bat. Hopping to my feet, I got into my best batting stance and started yelling, "Warning bark!" over and over, hoping Leo didn't just follow the command when it came from Laurie.

"Shhh. Stop it!" Quentin raced toward me, startled as Leo let out three deep, growling barks and then three more.

I kept repeating the phrase, and Leo kept barking. I could only hope the racket was reaching the rooftop and that the fireworks hadn't started yet, or they weren't going to hear a thing.

Quentin quickly got his bearings, pointing the knife toward me. I gripped the bat and held it high like I was waiting for a pitch from Laurie on the roof.

He came at me with the knife. I let the bat fly.

Even though I had a powerful swing, it was harder than I realized to hit a person I'd known my whole life in the head with a bat. At the last moment, I angled the swing down, catching him in the arm instead.

The knife he'd been holding in that hand clattered to the floor. Quentin's face crumpled in pain, and anger seared his gaze into mine, but then he wrenched his arm around and grabbed the bat with his other hand, attempting to wrestle it from my grasp. Leo's barking became louder and more desperate as I struggled. He knew I wasn't okay. He pawed at the crate and whined in between barks.

Quentin finally pulled the bat free from my grasp, the motion causing me to fall to the floor. My heart sank as he adjusted his grip.

The door to the apartment burst open, and in spilled what seemed like the entire population of the Morrisey, led by Laurie. His eyes flashed from Quentin, to me, to the weapon in Quentin's grasp. With a quick side movement, he grabbed the bat he kept by the door, swinging faster than Quentin could and knocking the other one out of his hands.

Nancy's voice rang through the mess as she talked to a 9-1-1 dispatcher: "There's a man attacking someone in our apartment building..."

Paul Kelley and Julian Creed grabbed Quentin, pulling his hands down by his sides.

"It's Quentin," Paul yelled back at Nancy, as if to stop her from calling the police. "What's the meaning of this? Why are you attacking Meg?" he demanded.

Laurie held out a hand, helping me up. He gave Leo the quiet command as he eyed the kitchen knife in the middle of his living room.

"Quentin murdered Mr. Miller," I croaked out the words.

Everyone in the room stared, silence encompassing the space.

"Quentin, I—" Nancy's voice cut out, and she readjusted the phone to her ear as if someone had started talking to her again. "Yes, I'm afraid we do still need the police. We have a murderer restrained, but please hurry."

TWENTY-FIVE

The fireworks started just as the police filed into the Morrisey. This time, Detective Anthony wasn't with the uniformed officers. The scene was surreal: the police arresting Quentin while the Seattle skyline illuminated with fireworks out the windows of Laurie's apartment.

I sat in a heap next to Laurie, who leaned against Leo's crate as he comforted the dog amid the myriad of new people flooding into his apartment.

"Is he okay?" I glanced over my shoulder.

Laurie nodded. "He seems to be settling down."

"I'm sorry I got him all riled up. It was the only thing I could think of at the moment."

The dog's chest rose and fell in a big exhale as he settled his head down for the first time since everyone had arrived.

"I'm glad you did," Laurie said. "It was the barking that got my attention on the roof. I'm just glad you're okay." He reached out and grabbed my hand. "So ... secret passages in the Morrisey?" He made the same explosion gesture next to his temple that Ripley and I had recently used to show our minds were blown.

I nodded as the police attempted to corral the surprised, chattering Morrisey residents, still agitated after they'd learned about the secret passages. Apparently, the dog wasn't the only one I was riling up tonight. Opal had been right. It was pandemonium. But I'd had to tell them. I was covered in dust, and Laurie had noticed that his front closet was open. Everyone had looked to me for answers.

And I'd had them.

"If I hadn't found the passageways in search of a murderer, I think they would feel a lot cooler," I said. "But now I can't help but consider them ..." I wrinkled my nose as I thought of the way Mrs. Feldner had described them. "Creepy as all get-out."

Laurie and I chuckled at the memory of the older woman's loud exclamation, but I knew it was a coping mechanism to help us get through the spine-tingling realization that there were secret ways for people to sneak into our apartments.

"How'd you figure out it was Quentin?" Laurie asked.

I told him about the piece of blue paper towel and the snooping I did in his apartment. "I was heading back to 3B when I heard Leo barking. Between that threat you got and the distressed sound of his bark, I had to check if he was okay. Once I got here, though, Quentin was just going through your stuff."

Laurie's eyebrows lifted. "What was he looking for?"

"He'd written a threatening note to Mr. Miller on the back of one of his pieces of mail, and he thought you took it from 3B when you were in there."

Snapping his fingers, Laurie said, "That's why the mail was missing."

I nodded. "When you didn't turn it over to the cops, he thought you were going to hold it over him and ask for money in return for your silence," I explained, having a hard time making Quentin's reasoning make sense.

"That's why he kept getting more and more anxious every time I asked him to fix something in the apartment." Laurie scratched Leo's head through the crate as the pieces clicked in his mind. "Yesterday, I went down to get my mail while he was working on the light in the bathroom, and I found him snooping in my bedroom when I came back. He said he'd left a tool in there the day before, but it gave me the creeps."

"Yeah, he was desperate. And terribly wrong." I let out a thin laugh.

Laurie wet his lips. "Meg, I still can't—" He stopped himself and shook his head. "I was just about to say that I can't believe you risked your life to come make sure Leo was okay, but I can. You're just that kind of person."

Unable to handle the compliment without turning beet red, I focused on Leo. "I couldn't let anything happen to my favorite guy." I smiled at the now-contented dog.

Laurie's face pulled into a mock frown, and I could tell he was about to pretend I'd offended him by implying *he* wasn't my favorite guy. I'd set myself up for it, and I could see it all play out in front of me like a terrible slow-motion fall. Even though it would be a joke to him, there would be too much truth behind the statement for me to lie and say he wasn't.

Things felt like they'd changed between us since the roof. But was I ready to tell Laurie the truth about my feelings for him?

Detective Anthony swept into the room at that very moment, saving me from having to make that decision. Instead of her usual suit, the detective wore jeans and a sweatshirt. Her hair was braided in a thick plait that whipped around as she searched the apartment for the officer in charge.

"She looks like she came straight from a barbecue," Laurie commented as Detective Anthony approached a uniformed officer. "I wonder if they called her or if she came in on her own."

"Knowing Detective Anthony, probably the latter." I watched the woman with admiration as she listened attentively to the officer. "It's just what happens when you love what you do."

Laurie ran his shoulder into mine. "You'll find your thing too. Don't worry."

"Thanks." I was about to admit that ever since I'd been back at the Morrisey, I'd felt more like myself again, which made me realize maybe I wasn't in the best state of mind when I'd quit art back in New York, but Detective Anthony strode over and crooked her finger at me.

"Can I talk to you, Meg?" she asked, flashing a smile at Laurie while she waited for me to stand up. The excitement I felt at her use of my first name, instead of the more formal Ms. Dawson, was clouded by that brief but telling interaction.

I followed the detective over to the side of the room until she spun around and pushed her shoulders back. "I owe you a big thank-you, and also an apology. First of all, thank you for the call." She pulled out her phone. "My family had been giving me a hard time all night about being on my phone, so I put it away. But I was able to make them all see why I forward my office phone to my personal cell when I got your message. Sorry I'm a little late. As for the apology..." She winced. "I'm sorry for being so short with you yesterday when you stopped by headquarters. You've helped solve more than a couple of cases and I shouldn't have treated you like a common nosy neighbor."

Her wording gave me pause. "More than a couple?"

"Well, there's this one." She gestured around us. "Then there's Phillip Ellis, who we've got in custody for killing Clark Bowlen. And the third is Mathias's assistant. I looked into him after you mentioned his possible involvement. He was stealing people's bank account numbers and wiping out their accounts. He confessed that he'd been planning on quitting anyway and wanted to tank Mathias's business. We were able to give the FBI all the information they'll need to charge him and prosecute."

I bit back a grin. Evan Grady had been right.

The detective let out a wry laugh. "I don't know how you did it, but every person you accused was actually guilty of something."

Not *everyone*. She was probably being kind not bringing up the message I'd left her about Julian, and she had no idea about my doubts surrounding Clark's involvement.

She took out her phone to record and said, "Do you want to tell me how you figured it all out?"

I told her everything about tonight. I explained about the passageways William H. Morrisey had built on purpose to steal from the boarders in his building and how Quentin had used them to access the one man in the building he hadn't been able to get to with his maintenance key.

THE PLACE HAD CLEARED out except for me, Laurie, Nancy, and a few police officers a short while later, after I was done explaining my story to the detective. Nancy and Laurie stood next to the passages as the police came back from sweeping them for any evidence that might help with their case against Quentin. Though, judging from the way he'd spilled everything to me, the man knew he'd been caught, and there was no point in lying.

Detective Anthony and I walked over to join Nancy and Laurie as the last police officer came back through the passage. He slid the panel shut and nodded at the detective.

"We'll let you know if we need anything else from you in the coming days, but it looks like we can get out of your hair for tonight." Detective Anthony directed that statement at Laurie, then Nancy.

"What do we do about the passages?" Laurie asked. It was a blanket question to both Nancy and the law enforcement officers present.

Nancy was ragged. It was way past her normal bedtime. She sighed. "That's something we'll have to tackle as a building." She patted Laurie's hand and added, "Don't worry, dear. We'll figure it out. Just not tonight." She yawned.

With that, we left Laurie's apartment, and I dragged myself up to the fifth floor. When I walked into the apartment, Ripley was curled into a ball on the couch. Her ghostly shoulders shook, and tears streamed down her face when she glanced up.

"How were the fireworks?" she croaked.

"What's wrong?" I raced forward, sitting next to her.

Face crumpling in on itself a little, she pressed her lips together. "Clark moved on about an hour ago."

It all clicked into place. The police had arrived at about that same time. That was too coincidental to look past. "So *that* was his unfinished business," I whispered, almost more to myself.

"What?" Ripley sniffed.

"Quentin killed Mr. Miller." I gave her a sad smile. "Clark's unfinished business must've been helping us get justice for Mr. Miller. One last errand for his favorite customer."

More tears streamed down Ripley's face at the realization.

"Oh, Rip. I'm so sorry." I wished I could wrap an arm around her in a supportive hug. Instead, I could only be there for her if she wanted to talk.

"How'd you figure it out?" she asked after a few moments.

"It's a long story." I grimaced. "Maybe we should save it for another night."

Ripley nodded. "If you need to sleep, I totally understand."

I was tired, but at the moment, there was nothing more important to me than making sure my friend got through these hard feelings. And maybe hearing about the case Clark had helped us solve would help.

So I told her everything. After I'd reached the end, Ripley sniffed and cocked a mischievous eyebrow in my direction.

"You really think Laurie was upset he wasn't your favorite guy?" she asked.

I beamed. "I kind of think he was." I'd been uncertain when it had happened, but there was something about Detective Anthony telling me that almost all my hunches had been correct that gave me a boost of confidence.

"Well, on that lovely note, I'll let you get some sleep." Ripley stood. "I think I might go gather my thoughts."

"Okay. I love you." I held her gaze.

She smiled, her eyes glassy from residual tears. "I love you, too, Megatron."

And with that, she disappeared.

If I were a gambler, I would've bet all my money that she went up to sit on the tower where they'd spent their last hours together. But I'd seen, firsthand, what gambling could do to someone. I didn't want to end up like Quentin.

Checking on Ani before I went to bed, I took a moment to be thankful for how tonight had turned out, knowing it could've been so much worse.

TWENTY-SIX

The next morning, Ripley was still out when I woke up. But even though she was gone, I wasn't alone. Not only did I have Ani, but my buzzer rang every five minutes as every single Morrisey resident came to check on me, bring me food, and ask if I was okay. Well, *practically* every resident.

I still hadn't seen Laurie.

Considering my best friend had just lost the guy she was falling for, I figured I owed it to her to buck up and go see Laurie myself. But before I could leave, my phone rang. Penny's name flashed onto the screen.

"Hi, Penny." I grinned, excited to hear my aunt's voice.

"Hey, kid. How are you?" I knew there was no way to tell from her voice, but she sounded windswept and happy, like she was getting a lot of fresh air as she walked along the beautiful Scottish landscape. "Sorry I didn't call yesterday. Believe it or not, America's Independence Day isn't a holiday over here and we completely forgot." She laughed, the airy sound of it making me smile.

We. Right. Iris was still visiting for another few days. As glad as I was that she was there for my aunt, I was looking forward to having her back next door.

"How's everything going? You settling in okay?" I scooped up Ani and curled up on the couch, placing her in my lap. After another morning of finding zero fleas, I figured I could finally give her the run of the place. She'd been exploring all morning.

"Oh, it's beautiful." Penny sighed. Her tone told me she was smiling.

"That's great," I said. "And the house is everything you thought it would be?"

Penny had been more than a little worried about picking out her house from online pictures alone. But it had been "too perfect to pass up" and she hadn't wanted to wait for it to get snatched up by anyone else.

"Oh, even more. I can't wait for you to come visit, Megs." She cleared her throat. "So, tell me. How are things with you? Is the Morrisey everything you remembered?"

"Even more," I said, copying her words. Smiling down at the little black bundle curled in my lap, I added, "I have a kitten."

Penny gasped. "Tell me everything."

I laughed. "Okay, but it's a long story that involves a murder."

"Spill."

I did. Penny didn't worry about my safety or fuss over the part about me being trapped in Laurie's apartment with Quentin like Nancy or the rest of the building had. Penny was a highly independent person who'd taught me that I could take care of myself.

After her sister had died, she'd taken me in without hesitation, knowing my father would not be in the picture, at my mother's request. And while Penny had created a wonderful life for me, she also had her career which she loved. Once I was old enough, she would leave me alone to go write in a local coffee shop. It didn't hurt that I had Ripley or that when Penny came back, done with her words for the day, she would give me her undivided attention.

She also held me to high standards, something that hadn't changed over time, as was made evident when she asked, "Have you figured out a plan yet?" toward the end of our phone call.

I stood and paced around the apartment, staring out the windows. The truth was, I'd stayed up late last night, lying awake in bed thinking about that very question. There was something about facing a killer that acted like a metaphorical slap to the face.

"I have," I answered confidently. "I spent the last couple of months thinking that you and everyone who loves me were misguided in your support of my art. How could you possibly be objective about the level of talent I had? You were right, though. Being back here at the Morrisey reminded me a lot about the girl I used to be. For example, I don't think I hate small talk. I think I just got conditioned to hate it with people I had no investment in."

Penny clicked her tongue. "I told you. You turned into a grump once you moved to the Big Apple."

"Well, I don't want to go backward." I cut the air with my hand. "I know I'm not the kid I was when I lived here before, but I think I can take the best parts of her and move forward."

"Which means?" Penny asked.

"I'm going to try painting again. I want to see if I can rediscover the joy I felt when I first started." As I talked to my aunt about the decision, I felt even better about it.

Proving she hadn't grown any more sentimental since she left, Penny said, "Good. I'm glad you finally figured it out."

We chatted a little more about what Penny and Iris had planned for their last few days together, and then I ended the call.

"Okay, Ani. Wish me luck. I'm going to go talk to Laurie." I lifted the kitten off my lap and set her on the couch.

She stretched, making the cutest little squeak, and then settled back into a ball, purring away.

I had no idea what I was going to say to him, but I needed to see his face, to figure out if what he'd said to me last night was still true. At the very least, I was excited to share with him the decision I'd made about painting again. I could already picture the way his eyes would sparkle and a smile would take over his entire face. Beyond that? I was going to leave it up to what my gut told me to do. I couldn't feel my fingers as I pressed his buzzer.

Laurie opened the door after the first ring, his expression a mix of surprise, followed by happiness. "Hey, how are you doing today?"

But I couldn't quite concentrate on him because I was too focused on what wasn't there. There had been no warning barks from Leo, and there was no dog being held back at his heel.

"Where's Leo?" My voice shook with the question. "There wasn't anything other than peanut butter on that spoon, was there?" I locked eyes with Laurie and saw his filled with sadness. "Omigosh, is Nancy making you get rid of him for some reason? I'll tell her the barking was my fault." I turned toward the door, ready to march down to the first floor.

Laurie reached out and grabbed my hand, stopping me. "He's fine, Meg. Nancy told me he's a hero and is welcome here whenever." Laurie dropped my hand and ran his over the back of his neck. "He's staying with my friend for a bit."

"Because you don't trust it here?" I had to admit, I still felt a little shaky about the passages too.

He shook his head. "I'm leaving town for a while." He exhaled what sounded like pent-up frustration. "That phone call I got yesterday while we were talking on the roof, it was my coworker telling me one of our projects hit a major roadblock. After I got back to my apartment, my boss called me and told me I'm flying over to Japan to figure it out. He wants me there in person to check on the hardware."

"Japan?" I breathed out the word. "For how long?"

"That's the thing; I don't know. It might be a month. It could be a year. They want me to leave tonight. That's why I took Leo to my friend's place. He has two other dogs and a fenced yard. Leo's in heaven." He looked around the apartment. "And just when I got myself all moved back in." He let out a dry laugh.

I wasn't sure what to say. There was a momentary relief from knowing Leo was okay, but it was short lived as my brain processed Laurie leaving. "Do you want me to water your plants?" I asked numbly, but as I scanned the room, I realized he didn't have any.

"Haven't even gotten around to getting any for the space yet, so I guess it works in my favor." He shrugged, but then he met my eyes and reached forward again, holding on to my hand. "I'm most sad about leaving you, Meg. I think you're the part of the Morrisey I'll miss the most." He leaned down and placed a kiss on my forehead.

My eyes slid shut, acting as a guillotine for the few tears that had been hanging at the bottoms of my eyelids. They fell, rolling down my cheeks. I sniffed and wiped them away as he pulled back.

"Will you keep in touch?" I said, instead of, "I love you and I have loved you forever. Please don't fall for anyone while you're gone."

He grinned, but there was a sadness behind it. "You're not getting rid of me that easily."

Saying one last goodbye, I backed away from the apartment. Once I returned to my place, I found Ripley on the couch, sitting next to Ani. It was my turn to devolve into a crying mess as I told her about Laurie leaving. We spent the next few hours wallowing together and commiserating about having our perfect guys slip through our fingertips.

But later that evening, I was done feeling miserable. I wanted to smile again.

The first thing that came to my mind was painting.

Without overthinking the impulse, I went over to the box of art supplies I'd packed away before leaving New York. One by one, I unpacked them onto the desk by the window, the place where Aunt Penny used to write.

Ripley didn't say a word as I worked, but I could see the grin that pulled across her face.

I liked the idea that the act of painting might heal us both a little that day. And for the first time in months, I listened to the familiar sound as the paintbrush swept across the rough canvas. A spark of joy lit in my chest.

It was good to be home.

THE MORRISEY WILL
RETURN ...

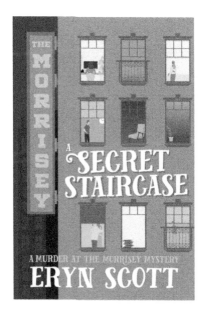

Meg Dawson and the rest of the Morrisey residents can't handle anymore surprises in their beloved downtown Seattle apartment building. So, when Meg finds a secret staircase leading down to the famous Seattle Underground, she's tempted to turn back.

The area was supposed to be closed off long ago. But turning back isn't so easy when she stumbles on not one, but two bodies in the hidden space. And even though the two deaths are separated by a century, the victims have more in common than Meg first realizes.

Meg must sort through the Underground's storied past to find the truth about who or what took the two lives if she has any hope of stopping it from happening once more. This time, the next body might not take a hundred years to show up.

Get your copy!

Join Eryn Scott's mailing list to learn about new releases and sales!

Also by Eryn Scott

STONEYBROOK MYSTERIES

Ongoing series * Farmers market * Recipes * Crime solving twins * Cats!

A Murder at the Morrisey Mystery Series

Ongoing series * Friendly ghosts * Quirky downtown Seattle building

Pebble Cove Teahouse Mysteries

Completed series * Friendly ghosts * Oregon Coast * Cat mayors

Whiskers and Words Mysteries

Ongoing series * Best friends *
Bookshop full of cats

PEPPER BROOKS
COZY MYSTERY SERIES

Completed series * Literary mysteries * Sweet romance * Cute dog

About the Author

Eryn Scott lives in the Pacific Northwest with her husband and their quirky animals. She loves classic literature, musicals, knitting, and hiking. She writes cozy mysteries and women's fiction. Join her mailing list to learn about new releases and sales!

www.erynscott.com

Printed in Great Britain
by Amazon

37821200R10152